PRAISE FOR JON TALTON

The Gene Hammons Novels
City of Dark Corners

★ "Talton shines in weaving together the mystery elements of the plots with historical events from the Prohibition period. Fast-paced, gritty, and exciting, this one will have fans of both Depression-era and southwestern-set crime fiction begging for more!"

—*Booklist*, Starred Review

"Talton continues his project of embroidering Arizona's criminal history by digging into the depths of 1933... Authentic Depression-era atmosphere...and real-life walk-ons."

—*Kirkus Reviews*

★ "This gritty stand-alone deals with Phoenix's rough-and-tumble past and its questionable police force in the 1930s. Talton excels at creating the ambience of historic Phoenix. [Suggested] for fans of realistic historical mysteries or Phoenix Noir."

—*Library Journal*, Starred Review

"References to movie actors and other celebrities of the day, as well as speakeasies and bootleggers, lend atmosphere to this well-crafted tale involving desperate people who could easily disappear."

—*Publishers Weekly*

"Succinct, wry descriptions run alongside the fast-paced plot… The journey is thoroughly satisfying."

—*Publishers Weekly*

High Country Nocturne
Winner of the 2016 Spotted Owl Award

"Talton keeps the reader guessing throughout, but Mapstone's learned, insightful first-person commentary is what really stands out; his comments about the decline of the Phoenix he's always called home are particularly revealing and believable."

—*Publishers Weekly*

The Bomb Shelter

"Clear writing, an intricate plot, and credible characters make this entry a winner."

—*Publishers Weekly*

Also by Jon Talton

The Gene Hammons Novels
City of Dark Corners

The David Mapstone Mysteries
Concrete Desert
Cactus Heart
Camelback Falls
Dry Heat
Arizona Dreams
South Phoenix Rules
The Night Detectives
High Country Nocturne
The Bomb Shelter

The Cincinnati Casebooks
The Pain Nurse
Powers of Arrest

Other Books
Deadline Man: A Thriller
A Brief History of Phoenix

THE
NURSE
MURDERS

JON TALTON

Poisoned Pen
PRESS

Published by Poisoned Pen Press, an imprint of Sourcebooks
P.O. Box 4410, Naperville, Illinois 60567-4410
(630) 961-3900
sourcebooks.com

Cataloging-in-Publication Data is on file with the Library of Congress.

Printed and bound in the United States of America.
WOZ 10 9 8 7 6 5 4 3 2 1

For Susan

A NOTE ON LANGUAGE

This novel is set in America of nearly a century ago. I generally use the vernacular of that era. But readers should be aware that this included commonly employed racial epithets that would be highly offensive today. Even polite references to ethnicity or gender in this era would sound hurtful or disrespectful to contemporary ears and sensibilities.

—Jon Talton

PART ONE

No Flesh Has Peace

One

Whoever designed the new gas chamber at the Arizona State Prison had a sense of humor. The prisoner, wearing only shorts and shoes, ascended thirteen steps into the airtight execution room. There he would be strapped into a straight-backed chair, sealed inside, and wait for the pellets of potassium cyanide to drop into the bath of sulfuric acid, releasing their poison. Thirteen steps, a tip of the hat to the thirteen loops on the hangman's noose.

Arizona only recently stopped hanging. This was after Eva Dugan's execution in 1930, when the rope decapitated her. My brother, Don, and I were Phoenix Police detectives, assigned to witness the event. Her head rolled within six feet of me while the body spurted arterial blood. Five people fainted. Don, as was his way, chortled. So, the gas chamber was ushered in, the most modern and humane, or so they said, form of execution. The Hernandez brothers had been the first to use it, two years earlier.

Today's dawn star was Jack Sullivan, twenty-three years old

with wavy sandy hair, so scrawny that his ribs pressed against his skin. He never learned to read or write. But he knew how to use a gun. I was at least partly responsible for him being here.

His mother, Mrs. Ella Hansen of Houston, hired me after her son was accused of shooting a railroad policeman at Bowie, east of Tucson. The bull was frisking hobos taken off a boxcar in the Southern Pacific Railroad freight yard. I was good at finding people, and there was no shortage of missing people during the Depression. She said he'd come to Phoenix, and she wired me fifty dollars to locate Jack before the police did. She feared they'd shoot him on sight as a cop killer. As a former policeman myself, I considered it a rational worry.

Finding him wasn't hard. I knew he'd end up on Red Light Row. He used money stolen from the railroad bull to pay for a dapper wardrobe and the company of a pro skirt. She worked in one of the houses of ill repute secretly owned by Kemper Marley. Hidden hallways allowed someone to peep inside the bedrooms, and Kemper allowed me to use them. Marley wasn't a voyeur. He used the peepholes for leverage, to take photographs of local bigwigs cheating on their wives. It took two days before Jack arrived.

After he enjoyed himself, he found me waiting in the large front sitting area, where johns chose their girls and went to the bedrooms. I made him put on his coat, handcuffed him, and marched him safely to police headquarters. I could tell the cops on duty wished they could have found him first, to shoot and ask no questions. But now that I witnessed the prisoner hand-off, all they could do is book him and take him up the elevator to the cells. That didn't mean they wouldn't give him a good beating on the way.

Mrs. Hansen had arrived by train for the short trial in Cochise County, where I had put her up at a Bisbee hotel on my tab. The verdict had never been in doubt. Neither was the appeal. When clemency had been denied, she had collapsed, screaming, "Oh, God! Forgive them, God!" I had to comfort her as best I could and had escorted her to the penitentiary to visit Jack one last time.

She couldn't bear to watch the execution. They had said goodbye, and I had driven her to the little town of Coolidge, where she had entrained for Texas. She had even thanked the prison officials for their kindness, but beneath her forced composure she had been in a terrible state. It had been the day the German zeppelin *Hindenburg* reached the United States after a record sixty-two-hour flight.

Now, wearing my best suit, I stood among the dozens of official witnesses watching through a wide window into the boxlike chamber painted institutional green. All were friends of the bull, who had once been a Cochise County deputy. They were there for revenge. Only I came as a representative of his mother.

The few seats were already taken as Jack was marched in and tied down. He was smoking a cigar and grinning at us. No resistance. The warden, an owlish man, occasionally glanced at a telephone, in case a stay was ordered by the governor. The phone remained silent.

"Want a hood?" This from the burly guard captain.

Jack shook his head.

"Is there anything you want to say to Warden Walker?"

"Yes," Jack said. "I want to thank all of you fellows. You have certainly been fine to me. I want to thank my lawyer. If I had paid a million dollars, he couldn't have done more for me."

I looked around for his lawyer and seeing none wondered about that part. Money could buy plenty of reasonable doubt in this state. And there was reasonable doubt. The murder weapon was taken from the railroad bull and used against him. The three other hobos who were caught all testified against Jack. I wondered if they had conspired to frame the young man, but it was too late for such doubts.

The warden shook his hand and turned to leave.

"And I want to thank Gene Hammons," he said. My head snapped forward at the mention of my name. "I know you did your best to protect me and turn me in safe, look after my dear mother. Maybe in another life I'd be a private detective, too. I know my brother holds a grudge, but that's not Christian."

It was an interesting statement because neither a priest nor a minister was present.

"Anything else?" the captain asked.

Jack nodded. "I didn't have a fair trial."

With that, the officials stepped out one at a time. The chamber was sealed, and the pellets dropped into the two vats beneath his seat. He sniffed and coughed, his smile gradually melted away and the stogie fell from his mouth. He peered down beneath his knees into his personal abyss.

For just a few seconds I was back on the Western Front when the Germans lobbed mustard gas shells toward our trenches. I got on my M2 gas mask securely as the cloud enveloped us. My buddy a few feet away bungled his and fell, suffocating. I had no time to help him because we fixed bayonets to meet the stormtroopers coming our way, and come they did, shadows in the eyeholes of my mask. Don still suffered from being gassed and hit by shrapnel.

I rarely thought of the Great War now, except when the nightmares came. My emotions had rebuilt. That's what I told myself.

In combat, you get numb very quickly. Almost anything becomes routine, however horrific. Fear is another matter. Combat soldiers never get over their fear, even if they refuse to admit it. The waiting, waiting, waiting before battle makes the fear worse. Then, the intimacy of battle. Sometimes we fought to the death at handshake distance. Other times we huddled in trenches and foxholes, helpless as artillery rained down. Later, the fear caught up with me. And yet...at nineteen I had seen things, experienced thrills, that no civilian ever would. Belleau Wood and Château-Thierry and Saint-Quentin Canal...just place-names for young people now.

A hard shake of my head pushed the memories away.

Jack began to struggle against his restraints. Hands turned to fists, but escape was impossible. First, he tried holding his breath, but it was hopeless. Panic flooded his eyes. He inhaled and exhaled the colorless gas several times. His head snapped back. After about thirty seconds it came forward, then slowly dropped to his chest, eyes still wide open. Eight-and-a-half minutes later, the gas chamber was pumped out with an eerie wheezing noise and two doctors stepped inside, pronouncing him dead. The witnesses were silent, the room smelling of sweat and satisfaction.

Afterward, I leaned against my car smoking a Lucky Strike, letting the tobacco fill lungs that still operated. I was happy to let the other witnesses leave first, whether taking a bus to the train or driving, most back to southern Arizona. Good Christian people. Pillars of their community. They strode across the parking lot with no second thoughts, some conversing among themselves. They paid me no mind.

Then I was alone. I tossed the coffin nail to the ground, got in the car, and drove back to Phoenix, brooding. A dust devil paced me for a mile, judging me. How was this execution Christian? Who were we to throw the first stone? If I even muttered such misgivings to Don, he would have laughed at me or tried to punch me in the face. He was definitely Old Testament eye for an eye, especially with a cop killer, even if he'd lost his faith.

The new Supreme Court building was completed in Washington, D.C., last year. I saw photos of it. Carved above the marble temple were the words: EQUAL JUSTICE UNDER LAW.

I didn't have a fair trial.

I'd already sent the fifty bucks back to his mother. That didn't stop Jack Sullivan's brother from promising to kill me.

"Maybe I deserve it," I said to the empty landscape. The desert doesn't sleep. Yet history presses long and hard on this place, especially on Phoenix. It rose from the ashes of the Hohokam civilization, ancient irrigators who disappeared. Maybe we would, too.

———

Back in Phoenix, I was slowed by paving work under way on Van Buren Street. The federal government was the now biggest employer here, directly or indirectly, with New Deal projects.

Otherwise, it had been an unsettling spring. Germany, under Adolf Hitler and the Nazis, remilitarized the Rhineland. I was stationed there with American occupation troops after the Great War. France, with the largest army in western Europe, did nothing to stop it, even though the move was a violation of the Treaty of Versailles. Headlines about a "war scare" lasted a few days, but Germany got what it wanted.

In a "gesture of friendship," Hitler signed the Anglo-German naval treaty. I didn't trust him. Don was even more vehement that a new world war was coming. President Roosevelt signed a bill expanding the U.S. Army. As if to underscore Germany's growing power, the *Hindenburg* cruised to the United States, a swastika on its tail fin. Mussolini invaded Ethiopia and the League of Nations did nothing. The *Arizona Republic* carried a headline from the South, "Mob Lynches Colored Man," as if it was an everyday occurrence, which it seemed to be there. In Phoenix, an infestation threatened the precious citrus crop. Farmers frantically gassed and tented the trees. To be sure, we enjoyed the Masque of the Yellow Moon, our annual harvest celebration, and the Philadelphia Orchestra played at Phoenix Union High School's auditorium. I went stag, my longtime girlfriend gone a long time. My ticket was free as part of my compensation for guarding some priceless instruments at the Hotel Westward Ho while the musicians were out for dinner. I was tempted to open the case holding a Stradivarius violin, just to touch this treasure. But I didn't. Some six thousand people attended the Easter service nestled in the buttes at Papago Park.

Now, I ate lunch at the Saratoga and walked to my office on the third story of the Monihon Building at First Avenue and Washington, on top of Boehmer Drugs and young Doc Mapstone's dentistry practice, next door to Newberry's. For a moment, I was certain that a man was tailing me and not trying to hide it. I paused in front of store windows, using them to help reflect the sidewalk behind me. He stopped, too. This wasn't Jack Sullivan's brother. The man was well dressed, with handsome features and wearing an expensive suit and straw boater. When I looked again, he was gone. I set aside my jitters and mounted the steps to my office.

The economy was better, so the accountant who shared the suite with me had left for better accommodations in the new Professional Building. The secretary we shared went with him for better wages. Now the outer office, behind the door with GENE HAMMONS, PRIVATE INVESTIGATOR etched in the glass, was left unlocked for waiting clients. My inner office was secured when I was gone. Today someone was waiting for me, unusual for a Saturday.

He was dressed in an ordinary business suit, starched shirt, and necktie. His dark hair was thinning, more visible because he was shorter than me and he had his hat off. His unhealthy pallor and the worry lines etched across his forehead were also memorable. He introduced himself as William Jordan, and I led him to the inner office, taking his straw Panama and placing it alongside my fedora on the hat rack. The inside band was stained with sweat. I showed him to one of the client chairs and took my own seat behind the desk with a legal pad for notes.

A good five minutes passed before he spoke. I wasn't going anywhere.

"I represent a victim of a kidnapping." He hunched his shoulders forward. "His fifteen-year-old nephew was taken two days ago."

After a long pause: "That night we received a phone call demanding ten thousand dollars for his release. We need a trustworthy man to deliver the money. It's to be done tomorrow night, one a.m. They said you should park across from Riverside Park, walk to the middle of the Central Avenue Bridge, then leave the bag on the west-facing sidewalk and walk back. If all is in order, they'll release him and send him to walk to meet you at the north end of the bridge."

I asked if they had contacted the police or FBI, and of course they hadn't. The kidnappers said if the cops got involved the boy would be killed. "Send him to you in pieces," they said.

"We're willing to pay you five hundred dollars to deliver the money and wait for the boy," he said.

The Lindbergh baby kidnapping was only six years ago. That turned out badly. Bruno Richard Hauptmann, convicted of kidnapping and murder, died in the New Jersey electric chair in April. Last year, up in Tacoma, the nine-year-old son of wealthy timber magnate J.P. Weyerhaeuser was snatched and only released after a $200,000 ransom had been paid. The kidnapper was caught by the FBI after trying to pass off one of the bills to buy a railroad ticket.

The crime came closer to home two years ago when a six-year-old girl, June Robles, was abducted from outside her school in Tucson. It was the same year John Dillinger and his gang were captured there at the Hotel Congress. The little girl was the granddaughter of a wealthy cattleman. Nineteen days later she was found buried in the desert, in a wooden cage. The crime was still unsolved.

"I need to know who I'm working for," I said.

He nervously knotted his tie. That was when I noticed his big hands and the scars on his knuckles. "It's enough to know my name. You come highly recommended as a man who can handle himself."

"Highly recommended by who?"

He turned murky. "I asked around."

"Is this your nephew?"

"No," William Jordan said, "he's the nephew of my employer. His anonymity is important. He's a well-known citizen who values his privacy."

I lit a cigarette and took a long drag, assessing what I'd heard. "You understand that the boy could already be dead, right? And the money will be wasted." Better to get the worst case out of the way first. "I'm also not comfortable having so little information."

He dropped more bread crumbs, but only that. The boy didn't make it home from school. When his chauffeur arrived to pick him up, he was already gone. No threats had been made before his disappearance. Yes, the chauffeur and other help were trustworthy and had been with the family for years. The kidnapper was specific over the phone: The ransom was to be paid in used, unmarked, randomly numbered twenties, none of them issued by national banks.

I watched the circular fan spin overhead and gamed it out in my mind. For the kidnappers, the plan had advantages. Riverside Park would be closed and dark by one a.m. Monday morning. Anyone coming and going could be easily observed. They could drive, headlights off, to the middle of the bridge from the south and snatch the money. Then they could release the nephew and turn around, leaving the way they came into the darkness of the citrus groves and farms of south Phoenix. It seemed well-planned. Their insistence on no currency from national banks—more easily traced—showed a level of sophistication. Maybe they had done this before. I'd never handled a kidnapping as a private eye and only assisted in a couple of such investigations as a young police detective, none as slick as this caper.

But it wasn't without risks for them. The bridge had almost as many disadvantages as advantages. It was three thousand feet long. When it was completed as the Center Street Bridge in 1911, local boosters claimed it was the longest in the world. They could be blocked off with cops waiting on the south end. Below was a dark, dry riverbed from which they could be observed. The bridge had streetlights that made this more possible. And all this was based on the kidnappers being on the level, that they'd actually fulfill their end of the bargain, release the boy, that he wasn't buried in the desert like June Robles.

He interrupted my thoughts.

"So will you do it, Hammons?"

I slid across a business card. "Tell your employer that I need his name and the name of the nephew. If I get those, I'll consider it."

"I just don't think he'll comply." He nervously rubbed the big hands together. "That's why he used me as an intermediary."

"So why not use you to deliver the ransom?"

He hunched forward. "I'm too old."

"You expect trouble?"

"I don't know. These people sound like they mean business."

"The scars on your hands tell me you've been in fights."

He told me that was long ago.

"And who are you?" I studied him. The crevasses on his fore-head deepened.

"Friend of the family." And that's all he said. But earlier he told me he was an employee.

I said, "Give it a try. Those are my requirements if I'm going to accept the case."

He left reluctantly. I heard the Monihon stairs creak as he walked down, wondering how much longer the 1889 building would survive. Standing at the window, I watched him pause at the sidewalk newsstand, then cross the street and go into the red sandstone Fleming Building. He was out again in ten minutes and walked north on First Avenue, quickly out of my sight. Maybe he made a phone call while he was inside. I tamped down any temptation to follow him. This case didn't feel right. Business was good, happy days were here again, at least in my professional life. But this wasn't worth it even if I had been desperate for cash. I regretted giving him my card.

I went back to my desk and called the detective bureau at police headquarters. Fortunately, Frenchy Navarre picked up. In a situation like this he was ideal.

"Geno!" he said in his thick Cajun accent. "Long time, no drink you under the table."

"I know. I've been busy. Sorry about that."

"What can I do you for?"

I told him I was curious if any missing person report had been filed for a fifteen-year-old boy in the past two weeks. He put down the receiver and went to check. In the background, I heard phones ringing, civilians filing crime reports, snippets of conversation in a world that once was mine.

He was back in five minutes. "Sorry, Geno. Not one report."

I thanked him and rung off. It didn't mean anything. Jordan's employer had been warned in the grisliest terms about going to the police. But the school might have reported it. Instead, the strange request sat in a gray zone of possibilities.

Two

I filed papers, trying to take my mind off the morning's execution and the afternoon's odd visitor. A tap on the door and I let in a messenger who handed me a note:

Please come to Pullman 4001 at Union Station.

No signature, no clue to who was summoning me. But I welcomed the walk. It was growing warmer as June approached. I needed to change to a straw hat myself. Getting rid of the suit coat was more problematic because it concealed my M1911 .45 caliber semiautomatic pistol in a shoulder holster.

I crossed Washington Street, busy with traffic and streetcars, then headed south four blocks to the depot. The harvest was in, and workers were busy in the produce sheds loading colorful boxes of oranges, grapefruits, and lettuce into refrigerated boxcars, the melting ice pooling beneath them. A small steam switch engine chuffed along Jackson Street collecting loaded "reefers" on the way to the yards, to be made up in freight trains speeding to the east.

The coupling of the railroad cars still sent me back to the

Great War. Certain sounds did that, made me flinch, and I fought off the urge to hit the ground.

I came down Third Avenue to the east side of the Mission-style building with its distinctive arches. Santa Fe's fancy new Super Chief had recently detoured off the main line through northern Arizona to give Phoenicians a look at this diesel-powered train of the future.

A Pullman car sat on a stub-end track. It wasn't unusual to see the sleepers sitting here, waiting to be attached to a passenger train. But that was in winter.

Many Pullman cars had names, but this one had only a number, 4001. I knew from my father, a Southern Pacific conductor, that numbered Pullmans were called "tourist sleepers," older, spartan, for tourist season. But 4001's dark Pullman green looked new. A generator was running. It was air-conditioned. I tapped on the door, and a Negro porter opened it, asked my name, then put down a step and beckoned me inside. I was met by a man with nearly black hair and wearing a new white suit.

"Mr. Hammons, thanks for coming." He gave me a firm handshake. "I'm Clyde Tolson, associate director of the FBI."

My years as a policeman taught me to conceal surprise, so I merely told him I was happy to come. Could he be investigating the kidnapping? But this was no ordinary G-man. And it wasn't an ordinary Pullman, either. We stood in a waiting area with an upholstered bench.

He said, "The director would like to talk to you."

That took extra effort to keep my facial muscles neutral. J. Edgar Hoover was famous. Earlier that month, he'd personally led the arrest of Alvin "Creepy" Karpis—Public Enemy No. One—in New Orleans. Now the Southern Pacific Railroad had brought him to Phoenix...for what?

Tolson moved with a feline grace, opening a door into a

spacious office, with a desk, chairs, and sofa. On the far wall was a Justice Department seal. But dominating the room was J. Edgar Hoover.

He was unmistakable from his newspaper photographs. He was finishing a phone call—I'd never seen a telephone in a Pullman car before—and he was smiling. I'd never seen him smile in those news pictures, either.

He replaced the receiver and strode forward, shaking my hand. He was several inches shorter than me and wearing a suit nearly identical to Tolson's only with a different tie and pocket square. Despite my best suit, I felt underdressed. Hoover wore a Masonic ring on his left hand and his porcine eyes looked me over.

"Thanks for coming on short notice, Hammons," he said. He invited me to one of the upholstered chairs in front of his desk. On top were neat stacks of files, a gooseneck lamp, a tallboy lighter, and a spotless ashtray. On closer inspection, the bottom of the ashtray was engraved with a fingerprint identification card. He offered me a Lucky from a polished cherrywood box, and I lit it with the tallboy. He lit one, too, passing it to Tolson, then fired one up for himself.

The director said, "You come highly recommended, a man who can handle himself." That was the second time I'd heard that today. He looked me over. "The star detective who caught the University Park Strangler."

Yes, that accomplishment when I worked at the Phoenix Police Department continued to follow me.

He talked fast as he sat behind the desk. "I'm surprised the police let you go, but I understand it was a budget issue, or bureaucracy—I hate it—and you've been quite successful as a private investigator. I'd wanted to meet you."

"The FBI is only a year old, you know. Before that it was only the Bureau of Investigation. President Roosevelt has been very good to the bureau. I'd say we deserve it, wouldn't you, Clyde?" Tolson leaned on the edge of the desk. "Definitely, sir. Last year, Senator McKellar was criticizing us, even claiming the director had never made an arrest."

"You got Karpis," I said, reaching to tap my Lucky into the large ashtray.

"Indeed," Hoover said. "I dare say that puts the bookend to the infamous criminals of our time. Bonnie and Clyde, Machine Gun Kelly, John Dillinger, Pretty Boy Floyd, Baby Face Nelson, Dutch Schultz, Ma Barker…" He counted them on his fingers. "Dead or in prison. Capone is in Alcatraz, going insane from syphilis."

He took a dainty puff of his cigarette. "We're not out of the woods yet. I estimate 150,000 murderers roaming the United States. Political grifters, disrupting police departments, are the brains behind the Dillingers of the land. In my speeches, I'm calling for a continuation of a war on crime. It's a national priority.

"You see, Hammons, someone like Senator McKellar doesn't understand what we're trying to accomplish." The rat-a-tat cadence continued. "It's not about Tommy guns and shootouts." He paused and leaned toward me. "Scientific law enforcement. Our laboratory is second to none and is pioneering the field. Fingerprinting. Professionalizing law enforcement. It's meant firing a lot of pinheads. We want agents with law degrees or who are accountants."

That let me off. Don went to the University of Arizona in Tucson. I never made it. The war intervened, and back home I followed him into the police department.

"But equally important is combating communist subversion," Hoover said. "That's where someone like yourself could be valuable. Someone who works hard and runs fast. That was how I succeeded in my first job as a delivery boy for the Eastern Market in Washington. Are you that kind of man, Hammons?"

"I'd like to think so, sir," I said. Still, I was surprised by the sudden shift from murderers to commies. "I don't think this is a hotbed of reds, Mr. Hoover."

"Not so fast, Hammons," he raised a finger. "Two years ago, the FERA strike led to a riot, and communist agitators were involved."

He was right about that. The Federal Emergency Relief Administration was intended to create jobs for unskilled laborers. Some went on strike in September 1934 and clashed with an angry crowd. The local newspapers didn't report it, but it was hard to avoid the smell of tear gas near the county welfare building, where the trouble started. Governor Moeur mobilized the National Guard, and plenty of people were injured in the melee. People talked about communist involvement, but I never put much stock in that. The issue was higher wages, and things got out of hand. Still, Don told me that some known reds from out of town were among those arrested.

The porter swept past and replaced the ashtray with a clean one.

"My point," Hoover said, "is that while many New Deal programs are doing good, they are tempting targets for communist infiltration and subversion. In addition, we're concerned about infiltration from Nazi Germany. God forbid, we have another war. But I don't trust Hitler and, while the FBI is committed to protecting the civil liberties of all, including German Americans, the Nazis are another threat we face. In every town without an FBI field office, we're looking for patriotic men with law enforcement experience, men like yourself Hammons, who can keep an eye on things. We can offer you fifty dollars a month to keep us informed."

It wasn't as if I needed the money. My business had been brisk. In addition to looking out for the Philadelphia Symphony, I was engaged to keep shady characters away from the Rexall Train, a rolling convention and display of the company's products that stopped at Union Station a few days ago. It was pulled by a sparkling blue streamlined New York Central 4-8-2 Mohawk steam locomotive. Some cars were open to the public—and a large crowd toured them—but others were reserved for druggists and contained products that criminals would have loved to filch. Rexall paid me more for this than I made in my first year as a private eye.

But now, sitting before Hoover, I felt put on the spot. Still, I said, "I don't need the money, sir."

He stiffened in his chair. "And why is that?"

"Because I'm a patriotic American, and I'll be happy to send the bureau any information I come across."

Seemingly satisfied, he was about to stand when I said, "One more thing, sir. We may have a kidnapping here."

———

Afterward, I stood in the sun beside the depot's carefully tended flower beds that greeted travelers, looking back at the anonymous Pullman car. I exited without portfolio: I wasn't a G-man. I wasn't anything but an informant—I had plenty of them when I was a cop—or worse, a spy, even if I turned down their money. The federal government was the largest employer in Phoenix now, and I didn't want to be on the payroll, too. The idea made me uncomfortable.

Hoover and Tolson discussed my visitor William Jordan but vetoed sending in an FBI "flying squad" to investigate until I knew more about the supposed kidnapping. It would have to be an interstate crime to fall under the jurisdiction of the FBI as a federal felony, a law passed after the Lindbergh kidnapping. That didn't jibe with the June Robles kidnapping in 1934, which the FBI did investigate. But I didn't have enough information to push it.

I wasn't going to tell Hoover about Kemper Marley's latest cruelty. Being the largest landowner in the Salt River Valley and having the post-Prohibition hold on liquor licenses and distributorship wasn't enough. Nothing was ever enough for Kemper. It's why he kept trying to muscle in on the gambling wire of Gus Greenbaum and the Chicago Outfit.

Kemper organized the Associated Farmers of Arizona, a group that effectively stomped out the CIO's attempt to unionize farmworkers. The pickers lived in horrendous conditions and worked without even a place to use toilets. "Communism" was how Kemper galvanized his landowner friends to beat and intimidate the CIO organizers until they left town.

Communism could be a powerful totem. I was still in the Army overseas in 1919, but we were well supplied with American newspapers and conversations with correspondents. I read about President Wilson's attorney general, A. Mitchell Palmer, who organized the Palmer Raids against radicals and suspected communists.

It was a time of fear—the Red Scare—soon after the Bolshevik revolution in Russia and when attempted revolutions struck defeated Germany. Those were put down violently by the *Freikorps* of demobilized German officers and soldiers. They were still stunned that the German Empire had lost the war, ended up as a republic, and were determined to get revenge. This was the seed that led to Hitler.

Back in the states, labor unrest spread. Letter bombs were sent to prominent officials and businessmen. Communist agitators were behind some of this. But plenty of innocent people were arrested, too. Some weren't released until Warren Harding became president. And the man in charge of carrying out the Palmer Raids was a young John Edgar Hoover.

———

With that thought, I turned away and started toward downtown. That was when I saw William Jordan watching me from the arched open-air waiting room on the east end of Union Station. Had he followed me? Suddenly he saw me and strode quickly toward the main waiting room, moving surprisingly fast for someone his age and seeming level of fitness.

But I was faster. I caught him as he opened the waiting-room door, holding it shut with my hand. Those scarred knuckles on his big hand caught my attention again.

"What's going on?" I said. "Why are you following me?"

"I'm not. Let me alone."

"Try again," I said, patting him down and finding a Walther PP, a semiautomatic pistol made in Germany, tucked in the small of his back. I'd seen only one other, when I was a policeman. The gun was introduced in 1929.

"What's this? Why are you following me with a gun?"

He stammered. "It's protection."

"From…?"

He started sweating. "The kidnappers."

I slipped out the magazine and slid back the action, a bullet popping out. It was ready to shoot. I dropped them on the floor.

"Don't bring an empty gun to a gunfight, Jordan." I opened my suit coat to show my shoulder holster. "You're a man of mystery, and I don't like mysteries."

"I don't want you going to the FBI. We were warned."

Now my warning bells were ringing. He pulled on the door, but I held it in place.

"What would make you think I'd go to the FBI?" Could he have known Hoover's Pullman was sitting behind us on the stub track?

"Call it instinct."

I studied his eyes, looking for tells, finding none. I let my hand drop.

"If you want me to consider taking on your case, this is the wrong way to do it. Tell your employer I need his name and the name of the boy."

I picked up his pistol and ammo and handed them back to Jordan.

"I'll do my best." He walked quickly through the hall, not looking back.

I'd never had a prospective client follow me, much less one packing heat. It was one more reason to avoid this case.

Three

The next day, Sunday, I sang in the choir at Central Methodist Church, as I had for several years. Our anthem was a choral arrangement of "Take My Hand, Precious Lord," a spiritual by Thomas Dorsey. He was a Negro gospel and blues composer, not to be confused with the big band leader Tommy Dorsey. I was a baritone with a wide range. The all-White singers did pretty well. As always, the music allowed me to lose myself in a better place. This time, a better one without the gas chamber, the FBI's strange request of me, and the mysterious Mr. Jordan. I knew the women in the chancel choir gossiped about me: Why wasn't a thirty-six-year-old man married and with children? It was none of their business, but what was church without gossip? It was none of their business that Victoria left me. Life doesn't turn out the way we hope.

That night found me at my apartment, the La Paloma, on Portland, overlooking the shady parkway that was encircled by the street. I poured myself a glass of scotch and put on a Duke Ellington record until it was lights out. But sleep didn't come, and by midnight my curiosity got the better of me. I went out to my nearly new Ford Cabriolet convertible, put the top down, and drove south through downtown. The days were growing warmer, but the night cooled down to the sixties, sometimes the fifties. I made my fedora snug against the breeze. I never heard again from William Jordan and wondered if the kidnapping story had been a hoax. But the handoff was scheduled for an hour from now. Maybe he'd found a more credulous or reckless courier. Maybe he'd decided to do it himself.

On Central Avenue, I waited at the railroad tracks for a passenger train rolling into Union Station. Most of the windows were dark, the passengers asleep on their way to Los Angeles. I heard the New Deal's Works Progress Administration was going to build an underpass here, but no construction was in sight.

Out of curiosity, I drove west along Jackson Street to Third Avenue, pacing the train. J. Edgar Hoover's Pullman car was gone. After the crossing cleared, I headed south, driving through the neighborhoods of Grant Park, Central Park, and Harmon Park. It was south of the tracks and most White Phoenicians simply called it Niggertown. It was a word my parents taught us never to use.

Some of the houses were simple wooden or adobe homes that dated back to territorial days. Others were substantial, where many of the city's Negro professionals lived. Deed covenants prevented Negros and Mexican Americans from owning property north of Van Buren Street. I edged along one of the barrios. Black and brown faces stared suspiciously at me. Music was blaring from one juke joint, Cab Calloway's "The Reefer Man." It was heading on to half past midnight.

Riverside Park, on the north side of the Salt River, was closed and dark. The sight made me sad. Beside a large swimming pool under shade trees, Riverside Park offered a large dance hall and entertainment space.

Victoria Vasquez and I went dancing there almost once

a week, jitterbugging until we were sweaty. We took part in a twenty-four-hour dance marathon. It was a happy place in hard times, where a cigarette girl was never far away. But that was before Victoria moved to Los Angeles, and we fell apart. At first, I blamed myself. I was obsessed with solving the University Park Strangler case, then, as a private eye, with catching Carrie Dell's killer. The cases took over an investigator's life.

But that wasn't the truth. She was chasing a dream that had no room for Phoenix, where she took photographs for the police, the McCulloch Brothers, and the newspapers—or for me. We were all too small-time, same with the idea of marriage and children, with me at least.

At drug stores and newsstands, I paged through magazines such as *Fortune* and *Life*, looking for her photographs, occasionally finding one. She took one of the new Supreme Court building. I didn't have the heart to buy a copy. I wondered what her life was like now or if she ever thought about me. I pulled into the empty parking lot and shut off the car. It was a moonless night. I took off my hat and set it on the empty passenger seat, crown down. That was the position a well-dressed man learned to use in order to keep the hat's shape.

Not a single car drove past.

But a few minutes later, I saw one creeping south on Central. I was afraid it might park here, and I'd be found out. But it came to a stop in the dirt on the other side of the street, shut off its lights, and a dark-clad figure emerged, silently closing the door.

The night was so quiet I could hear the door latch.

He walked quickly to the bridge and stepped south along the sidewalk across the meandering riverbed. I was an adult on my way to war before I realized rivers were supposed to have water in them. The Salt River was dammed to the northeast, providing the year-round water that irrigated our groves and fields. At the first streetlight on the bridge, I saw he was wearing some kind of cloak and carrying a soft-sided suitcase. I heard my voice. "Hell." William Jordan had found a courier for the ransom money. Or maybe this was Jordan himself, but, no, this figure was shorter. Phoenix had four private investigators I knew of, and none would touch the offer Jordan presented without more information.

But someone had.

He proceeded south into the darkness out of the streetlight toward the middle of the bridge. I squinted south, seeing nothing. Temptation made me want to get out of the car. But do what? I couldn't catch the figure on the bridge, and if I did, it could only add to the danger, the kidnappers seeing someone else, perhaps assuming he was a policeman—I still carried myself like one. I forced myself back in the driver's seat and checked my watch.

Ten minutes later, he came back. No bag. No kidnapped boy. Looking over his shoulder. He sat on the fender of his car and waited.

Finally, I quietly got out of my Ford and walked his way. I felt the weight of my shoulder holster and its M1911 pistol.

"The boy's not coming," I said in a conversational voice. "You've been had."

The figure swung my way as I was halfway across the two lanes of Central and pointed a gun at me. It was easily identifiable as a Colt Detective Special, .38 caliber, because I owned one myself.

"Stop where you are," came a woman's voice. "I will shoot."

Then, five beats later: "Eugene Hammons! Tall, blond, and handsome. Imagine seeing you here." She tried to sound casual, but I could hear the anxiety in her words.

The gun went away, and I tried to remember the voice. Only when she took down the hood on her cloak and shook loose her red hair did I recognize her.

"Pamela. What the hell are you doing? You're supposed to be a schoolteacher."

Pamela Bradbury. I met her three years ago when she was a student at Arizona State College in Tempe, and I was working on a complicated murder investigation. It was soon after I was booted from the police department, but Pamela's classmate was found dead by the railroad tracks. Someone had placed my business card in her purse, trying to frame me. Fortunately, Don retrieved it and saved me from being a suspect. It was all the more reason to find the real killer, which I eventually did—to my shock. Which brought me to Pamela as I was questioning the victim's classmates.

The girl I remembered was smart, sassy, teasy, and moderately helpful. She told me her unusual name meant honey and gave me the flirty benediction, "All honey, honey."

Now she shrugged. "Teaching didn't take. Spend my life teaching English to seventh graders? Even high school. Have a bunch of pubescent boys coming on to me? I wasn't going to swim in that sea of testosterone. No thank you. I didn't know what to do with a teaching certificate. I thought about leaving town, but I like Phoenix. So, I became a private detective."

"What?"

"You have something against women shamuses, Eugene?" I saw the anger in her green eyes. "Or don't you want the competition? You didn't strike me as that kind of man. You'd be surprised by how many women are more comfortable trusting a female private eye. They'll tell me things they wouldn't feel comfortable telling you. Anyway, you inspired me."

"I'm happy for you, Pamela. I'm unhappy you got messed up

in this. Now your client is ten thousand dollars poorer and short of the missing nephew. I warned him about that happening."

She glared at me. "Don't look so damned superior, Eugene."

Only Victoria had used my full given name. But she was gone. Also, Eugene the Magical Jeep had recently become a character with Popeye and Olive Oyl on the Thimble Theater comic strip. But I tried to push past my annoyance, for now at least.

We sat in her car, and I tried to unpack this mess. Sure enough, William Jordan had come to her, offering money to deliver the ransom. She took the job without knowing who the wealthy client was or the name of the kidnapped boy.

I said, "You took a hell of a chance for five hundred bucks. You might have been killed."

"He offered you that much? Damn. He only paid me one hundred. Another example of women being underpaid. But as you saw, I came armed."

Now it was my turn to shrug. "I hope you know how to use that revolver. Did you at least count the ransom money?" I asked.

"He wouldn't let me," she said.

"And you didn't look?"

She shook her head, brushed away rich red tendrils parted in the middle and reaching just past her shoulders. "I couldn't. The suitcase had a zipper with a lock on the end. It was very heavy."

All sorts of questions fired in my head.

"So it was heavy. Did you feel around the edges to get a sense what was inside? Maybe it wasn't even money. If it was locked, that means the kidnapper had a key. Might not even been a kidnapper. You might have been roped into carrying something else. Contraband. Narcotics. Stolen goods to be fenced…" My frustration made me light a nail. She took it from me and inhaled deeply, blowing smoke rings, like the first time I met her. I fired up another for myself.

"Now you're making me feel stupid," she said.

I told her she wasn't stupid.

"Does it help that I read mystery novels?" She smiled. "*The Maltese Falcon*, Erle Stanley Gardner's Perry Mason, Dorothy Sayers, Rex Stout, and Nero Wolfe. Archie is Nero's 'leg man.' I like leg men."

She did have nice gams, as I recalled. I said, "It doesn't hurt, but not every real crime is neatly tied up in the end."

What I didn't say was that, so far, she lacked the street smarts that would keep a private eye alive: Curiosity, attention to details, constant suspicion.

"So, what now?" Pamela folded her arms, and we looked south beyond the bridge, where, aside from a few farmers' lights and the Civilian Conservation Corps camp at South Mountain Park, only darkness looked back.

Four

We could have driven south across the bridge, but that seemed to be inviting more trouble. Instead, we returned downtown and parked in front of the all-night Busy Bee Café with its neon pollinator inviting us in.

Being near police headquarters, I faced the risk of running into old colleagues, but I was with a pretty girl late at night, so I was insulated from nosy questions. Ones like, "A kid's been found dead on the Central Avenue Bridge. What do you know about it, Hammons?"

As it turned out, at half past one in the morning, we had the place to ourselves. John Pappas, the owner and one of many Greeks who were Phoenix restaurateurs, was gone, leaving a skeletal night shift of a counterman and a Negro short-order cook to feed cops, railroad workers, printers and pressmen from the newspaper, and other denizens of the night. Unlike some places in Phoenix, the Busy Bee was not segregated.

We took a booth in the back, me facing the door. Over coffee, I made Pamela run through her encounter with William Jordan again. It sounded identical to his come-on with me, except for the money he offered her.

I asked her what she was to do with the boy if he had been released.

"Bring him to Jordan, who said he'd take him home. It sounded on the level. Rich man, chauffeur, a chance to save the boy."

Pamela sighed and ordered a slice of cherry pie for each of us. They were the last two slices left under the glass dome on the pie plate.

"Pie makes everything better, Eugene. Stimulates the brain cells."

"If you say so, Pam."

"Pamela. I'm not a Pam."

"Then let's make a deal. You call me Gene, and I'll call you Pamela."

She took my handshake with a smile.

We ate our pie in silence. My brain cells indeed gave me an idea, but it was risky. I tried to disentangle her from me, but she wasn't easy to shake.

"You want me to go home. Where are you going?" she said.

I looked around. "To find Jordan."

"It's the middle of the night."

"That's the best time. I learned that as a police detective."

"Then how will you find him?"

I told her I'd use the phone directory at the Busy Bee. Before she could respond, I was at the counter paging through it. But no William Jordan. Out of curiosity, I looked in the Yellow Pages, and sure enough under private investigators was "P. Bradbury" and in the Heard Building, fancier digs than mine.

When I got back, her arms were folded. "I know where he lives. I had to get the money, remember? It's an apartment just south of Roosevelt on Second Avenue. See, you do need me, Gene."

We left her car at the restaurant and she climbed in mine, handing me my fedora. It took us five minutes to find the place. It was a two-story stucco building, with a door that opened into a small lobby and a light in a wrought-iron fixture overhead. She pointed to a unit on the second floor.

The building was quiet.

It wasn't unusual for apartment lobbies to be kept unlocked. Some people even kept their doors at home unlocked, especially after the University Park Strangler scare faded. Except for the gangsters and kidnappings, ordinary crime was fairly low in the Great Depression, certainly lower than during the Roaring Twenties and Prohibition.

I led us up the stairs, which fortunately were more substantial than the creaky ones in my office building. The second floor held four apartments. Pamela pointed to Jordan's, which faced the street.

The door was cracked open. The smell of cordite was in the air. A gun had been fired.

I pulled out my gun, flipped off the safety, and thumbed back the hammer. The M1911 held eight .45 caliber rounds. Pamela's eyes widened.

"Wait here," I whispered.

She whispered back. "No way, Gene." She produced her revolver.

"Try not to shoot me."

She stuck out her tongue.

I tapped on the door, three knocks.

"Mr. Jordan? It's Gene Hammons and Pamela Bradbury."

Nothing. I slowly pushed the door open and leveled my M1911 into the room. A lamp was on, and William Jordan was facedown on the hardwood floor, his face partly visible. Those big hands with the scarred knuckles were splayed out in front, He was wearing a blue robe over pajamas. A pool of blood was spread out from where a bullet had been fired into his brain from behind. The blood mingled with brain matter.

Maybe Pamela made a sound, but I was moving into one bedroom, then the second one, both clear. I pulled out a handkerchief and opened closet doors. The killer was gone.

I holstered the gat and told her not to touch anything. Next, I made a quick inventory of the apartment. It was minimally furnished with a fireplace in the living room. No books or photos, nothing personal. The closets were empty except for one suit, one shirt, a tie, and a pair of shoes. I slipped my hand in the clothes pockets. No identification, nothing.

A suitcase was sitting beside the bed, packed. The same Panama hat with the stained inner band that he removed in my office sat beside it on the floor. The luggage tag said George Parris. It made me wonder if William Jordan was an alias and he was preparing to leave town.

And he was. Using my handkerchief, I unzipped the pocket of the suitcase's inner liner. Sure enough, he had a ticket on the Southern Pacific's premier train, the Sunset Limited, departing later that day for Los Angeles and San Francisco.

Digging into the suitcase itself, I felt paper. I carefully lifted the folded clothes and saw stacks of bills, randomly numbered twenties, wrapped in one-inch bundles. Beneath that I felt metal. It was the Walther. Nowhere did I find my business card. Either he discarded it or, a more troubling thought, the killer took it.

"The money is here," I said, showing Pamela the cash. "So, I have no idea what he gave you."

She looked at it a long time before I repacked the suitcase.

"One more thing. He might have known his killer."

"How can you tell?" Pamela asked, still a whisper.

"I'm guessing he opened the door, let the killer in, turned his back, and he came behind him and shot him. Looks like a .22 caliber from the entry wound. That's a weapon mobsters use for hits." I took her in my arms, spun her around, and showed how it might have been done. She shivered.

"It's not a sure thing," I said. "The killer might have ordered him to turn away and then shot him from behind. It's hard to tell. Still, he has a pistol in the suitcase." I told her about him following me to the train station, where I found it in the small of his back. "If he were worried, he would have armed himself before opening the door."

"That all makes sense."

"Is this place different from when you stopped by?"

"I can't say," she said. "He opened the door and handed me the case. I never came in. He seemed nervous."

I could understand why.

She brushed back her hair. "What are we going to do now?"

I said, "Get our stories straight."

———

We could have left the apartment as we found it and disappeared into the night. Made up a story about seeing movies and going to the Busy Bee before I took her home.

But the risks were substantial. What if a neighbor saw us, or a passing car—such as a police car—got curious. We could alibi up with the Busy Bee workers remembering us. But we couldn't produce ticket stubs from the theater.

I persuaded her to stick to a story that was close enough to the truth that if the cops separated us, each would stick to the same tale.

First a patrol car responded to my call from Jordan/Parris's telephone. It had been three years since I was on the force, but the older cop knew me. He was about my age, and we'd been friendly back in the day. His partner was a rookie, sandy-haired and with a face that looked as if it had never seen a razor. He certainly hadn't seen a murder like this, so when he turned pale and started coughing, the older cop spun him around and told him to go outside and wait for the night detectives to arrive.

"Meet Officer Earl O'Clair," the older cop said. "He's a good kid but this was his first dead body."

Fortunately, the night detectives were my brother and Frenchy Navarre. He was not to be confused with Phoenix's other Frenchy, Vieux—given name Marcellin—who became a rich man laying sidewalks across the city that bore his stamp in the concrete. He lived in a handsome Italianate mansion in the new Kenilworth district.

This Frenchy—given name Leonce—wore an expensive tailored blue suit from Goldwater's and a gold bow tie. He once told me shamelessly that he never had to pay for his fancy duds. If he flirted with waitresses, he called them "cher." Interestingly, he didn't drink or smoke. I'd never seen him lose his temper. He liked me.

Don, of course, was spiffy in a lightweight tan Prince of Wales plaid sports coat, tan slacks, blue silk tie, and perfectly shined shoes. Impeccably dressed, both effortlessly projecting the presence of homicide detectives—the adults were here. It was something I tried to emulate but never quite matched, especially my older brother. Both had their Hat Squad fedoras tilted just so.

Pamela and I waited outside, leaning against the fender of my car, with the young patrolman hovering nearby. He acted as if we were going to make an escape, but I knew the reality: he didn't want to go back upstairs where the dead man lay surrounded by his blood and brain matter. The only sound was the whistle of a freight train coming into the Santa Fe yard from the main line in northern Arizona. In half an hour, maybe a little less, Don and Frenchy came back down.

"I bet you it was a jig out to rob him, Geno," Frenchy

pronounced, brushing a piece of imaginary dust off his sleeve. "They always use razors, y'know. But sometimes a stolen gun. He was probably interrupted and ran away before he got the cash in the suitcase."

Don rolled his eyes. Any crime in Frenchy Navarre's mind inevitably led south of the tracks.

The art of the lie was to make it as close to the truth as possible. That was difficult with the tangle of both Pamela and me being approached by the dead man with the kidnap story. I tried to keep it simple.

"He came to my office saying the fifteen-year-old nephew of an important man had been kidnapped. They wanted someone to deliver the ransom, ten thousand dollars. I took a pass when he wouldn't give the name of the uncle or the boy. He called me at home…" I looked at my watch. "…maybe a couple of hours ago now, saying he wanted to meet me here. This is how I found him. The apartment door was partly open."

While Frenchy took down the basics in his notebook, my brother appreciatively looked over Pamela. "And where do you come in?"

"I'm Gene's girlfriend, Pamela." She gave a demure smile and slid her hand through my arm. "He brought me along. But he made me stay outside." Pamela gave her full name and address. Don looked at me with a raised eyebrow and a half smile.

"Well," he said, "you're way too pretty to be spending time with the likes of him."

Frenchy took her hand and inevitably called her "cher."

Aside from Don's curiosity about my love life, the girl seemed out of his suspicion.

Thank goodness they didn't search her and find the handgun. Nor did they separate us to interrogate us separately, as I would have done in my time on the force.

Frenchy looked crestfallen that it wasn't a simple robbery.

"Well, Geno, the ransom money is in the vic's suitcase," Frenchy said. "You were lucky to refuse the offer. You would have been played big-time. But I guess we'd better have Sheriff McFadden send men to the bridge and search the area. Be a damned shame if the boy was dead in the riverbed."

The Central Avenue Bridge was outside the city limits, and Frenchy was always happy to kick the can into another jurisdiction.

"Why did he call you at home, especially at this time of night?" Don asked.

I shrugged, using all my discipline to lean into the lie. "He didn't say. Just that he needed to see me now and it wouldn't wait. After I found him, I called you."

"He knew his killer," Don said.

"Or his killer forced him to turn around and shot him. A .22 has mob hit all over it."

Don shook his head. "It's too bad you're not on the force to show us how to do our jobs. As it is, you're just a civilian." He laughed. "Don't leave town."

I took Pamela by the hand and led her away. "Let's go before they start to get more curious."

Five

I slept late and didn't make it to the office until nearly noon. Before that, I stopped at Otis Kenilworth's barbershop for a haircut and a shave. The overhead fans were spinning to fight the morning heat. They also dissipated the cigarette and cigar smoke. Waiting my turn, I paged through the *Arizona Republic*. The international news was depressing. A potential Russo-Japanese war, Italy cleaning up its invasion of Ethiopia with the League of Nations useless, a military coup in Bolivia, and a looming Mexican railroad strike. Nationally, Alf Landon was looking to become the Republican presidential nominee, but he didn't stand a chance against FDR. Arizona was a staunchly Democratic state, and with so much New Deal money flowing our way, he was sure to win a second term if our state's sentiment was any indication. I skimmed Reg Manning's front-page cartoon, which again I failed to see the humor in.

The flag of the paper was unrelentingly boosterish: "How Phoenix Grows" it proclaimed in a box beside the newspaper's name. "Population! 1900: 8,344. 1910: 11,134. 1920: 29,053. 1930: 44,118. 1935: 109,912." That last number was the "metropolitan area." The city itself was around half that. Victoria taught me that the "masthead" was the box in a newspaper with the names of the publisher and top editors, while the "flag" was the paper's name on page one.

The "Little Stories of Phoenix Daily Life" on an inside page was more useful to me. With its briefs of comings and goings and even minor crimes, the feature was sometimes helpful to peruse for some business. Someone looking for a missing relative. Or a court case where I might offer my services to a defense attorney. It had been more than three years since I was fired from the police department, and although I missed the job, I enjoyed the freedom of being a "private dick," as Pamela put it with a lascivious smile.

"Come here often?" The question came from a man about my age with thick brown hair, thin lips, and a prominent chin. He had a German accent.

"All the time."

The customers were White, while Otis was a Negro, but he was the best barber in town. The men talked about Mussolini and Hitler and the boy executed in the gas chamber. I wondered if the overnight murder, which happened only two blocks away, would make it to the afternoon *Phoenix Gazette*. It was too much to hope that one of them knew anything about William Jordan or George Parris, or whether he had been a customer here. I wished I had a photo of the man to show around.

"I hate to hear Hitler's name." My German-accented companion gave a noticeable shiver. "He's going to kill all the Jews of Europe."

I knew how the Nazis kicked Jews out of the civil service after they came to power. Then, the Nuremberg Laws passed last year stripping Jews of their German citizenship, forbade Jews from marrying non-Jews, and other proscriptions. It was monstrous, but still...

I said, "You think it will get that bad?" Even my friend Harry Rosenzweig, who was a leader in Temple Beth Israel didn't worry about such an extreme outcome, despite the anti-Semitism of the Nazis.

"They blame the Jews for the defeat in the Great War," the man said. "It's one of Hitler's many lies, but a very dangerous one. I fought in the war as a German officer. A hundred thousand of us did. We were Germans, fully a part of German society. Until Hitler. But he's very popular. He's credited with pulling Germany out of the Depression, even though he's done it by building armaments, expanding the army and air force beyond what the Treaty of Versailles allowed."

Another man joined the conversation. "You know about the 'Radio Priest,' Father Coughlin?"

I said I knew about him but never listened.

"He has millions of American listeners," he said. "He says democracy is dead and the only choices are between communism and fascism. He says this is our last election, and he chooses fascism."

"That's absurd," I said.

"That's what many Germans thought in the last days of the Weimar Republic," the German said. "The military and the Prussian elite thought they could control Hitler and the Nazis when President Hindenburg named him chancellor. But he controlled them. The plan is all there in his book, *Mein Kampf*. But hardly any Americans or British have read it. Coughlin is viciously antisemitic, blaming the Depression on Jewish 'international bankers' and urging boycotts of Jewish businesses and having shops place 'Buy Christian' in their windows."

I was relieved I hadn't seen any such signs in Phoenix. Rosenzweig Jewelers was the most popular jewelry shop in Phoenix. The Diamond family's Boston Store was a prosperous department store. Jews played an important part in the city's life. Even Barry Goldwater had Jewish roots, although he was an Episcopalian.

"You're safe here," I said.

He sighed and extended a hand. I took it, two veterans of formerly opposite sides. "Samuel Herzfeld. Thank God, I got out in time. But my relatives are still in Germany, in Hanover."

I introduced myself, then Otis motioned me to the barber chair.

———

Shorn and shaved, wearing a lightweight Palm Beach suit from Vic Hanny's and a new Panama hat, I stopped off for a shoeshine at the stand run by "Mechudo" Torrez across from the courthouse and police headquarters. The nickname came from his rough appearance and long unkempt hair, but he always treated me well.

As a teenager, Torrez worked for the Negro who owned the stand while cleaning a nearby pool hall and sleeping on the tables overnight. The Negro passed the stand along to him a few years back and "Mechudo," whose real first name was Adolfo, was always tuned in, shining the shoes of cops, lawyers, judges, and gangsters such as Gus Greenbaum.

"Have a seat, Detective Hammons." The rough-looking man readied his supplies.

I stepped up and sat, watching the people walk by. "I'm a private cop now."

"I know, but you'll always be Detective to me, like your brother."

"Has he been by today?"

"Half an hour ago. Told me he and Frenchy were called out

to a murder last night. Man shot in the back of the head but no suspects. Awful way to die."

I agreed and let him work his magic on my shoes. He didn't mention a kidnap victim, and I didn't ask.

Finally, I climbed the stairs to my office. My first sign of trouble was that the inner door was unlocked, open one inch. I never left it unlocked. My second was being bashed from behind when I stepped inside. I imagined myself reaching for my gun or sap to fight back. But it was too late. The floor came up hard, and I blacked out.

When I woke up, Pamela was gently stroking my face and saying my name. The back of my head felt as if it had been in a collision with an anvil. I tried to sit up, went dizzy, and lay back down.

"What…?"

"I found you on the floor," she said. "You've got a nasty knot on the back of your head, and you're going to have a shiner from where you hit the floor. He must have ambushed you from behind when you walked in. You could have taken him in a fair fight."

My platoon commander in the Army said, "If you get in a fair fight, you did a Brodie." In other words, you messed up. I never planned for fair fights, whether as a cop or private investigator.

"I think you should go to the hospital, Gene. You probably have a concussion."

She was probably right. I felt the spot on the back of my head. Another inch higher and the blow might have killed me. Still, I felt well enough to say no.

The office was a mess. Desk drawers pulled out. File cabinets standing open. Even my framed commendations from the Phoenix Police and the photo of me with Amelia Earhart on her visit here were knocked sideways. The black-and-white photo didn't show the red of her shaggy hair cut short or her piercing blue eyes. She wore a tie that day. I smiled like a smitten idiot. Occasionally, she sent me a postcard from faraway places. She was married but didn't consider herself bound to her husband. That left inviting possibilities but wasn't a marriage I would want.

"You met Amelia Earhart?" Pamela asked, straightening the photo.

I nodded uneasily. "She took me up in her airplane."

"I'm impressed."

The intruder couldn't do much with the office safe, but it had scrape marks on the edges, nonetheless. If it was someone connected to the late Jordan/Parris looking for his cabbage, the money was safely locked in the evidence room at police headquarters. That made sense if he found my business card among Jordan's things. On the other hand, my assailant might have been the brother of Jack Sullivan, who promised to kill me. But that second guess made no sense. Even if he was interrupted before he could finish me off, why would he rifle through my office? I took a deep breath and sat up. Fortunately, my straw Panama was unharmed.

Again, she asked, "Do you want to go to the hospital?"

I shook my head and nearly passed out again from the pain.

"Then let's go to work. We have a case."

"Who's 'we'?" I asked.

"You and me. Pamela and Gene. We make a great team, don't you think? Anyway, do you know Helen Lincoln?"

The name rang a bell.

"The wife of John C. Lincoln?"

"Exactly. She contacted me—remember how I told you women private eyes had an advantage with women clients?—and we have an appointment with her in an hour. Let's get you presentable."

I stood and she straightened my suit coat and tie. She was wearing a blue dress with short sleeves and a hem just below the knees, showing shapely legs. Definitely easy on the eyes. I didn't want to admit it. I sure didn't want to admit a "we." I swallowed three aspirins without water.

"What's the caper?" I asked.

"Blackmail."

Six

We drove north of town, beyond where Central narrowed into two lanes lined by palm trees and handsome mansions on shady acreages. "Laterals"—irrigation ditches—ran along both sides, with culverts covered with dirt, allowing cars to enter the properties.

Pamela filled me in more as we drove in her car, a 1932 Desoto two-seater with a rumble seat. She drove, which was a good thing, considering the anvil strike on the back of my head. I gingerly touched my left cheek, which was painful and swollen. I'd make a great first impression on Mrs. Lincoln.

It was growing hotter, especially in town. The temperature dropped ten degrees once we were surrounded by the citrus groves. But by July, the Phoenicians with means would be sending their families to the coast on the Southern Pacific or at least to Iron Springs on the Santa Fe Railway to Prescott. "Summer wives" would fill the role of the men's mistresses. Three years before, I unraveled the murder of Carrie Dell, finding she ran a high-end call girl service for husbands who could pay. The girls were college coeds, although Pamela was not among them. Such was summer in Phoenix. The rest of us would be spending the night on sleeping porches and wrapped in wet sheets to battle the heat, going to more movies in air-conditioned theaters. "What do you know about John C. Lincoln?" she asked after we turned east on two-lane Camelback Road and passed the Shell station and Toy's Grocery, then plunged again into the cottonwood trees and thick rows of orange and grapefruit trees. The road's namesake mountain loomed ahead.

"Only what I've read in the papers."

He was from Cleveland, Ohio, where he started with $250 and built the Lincoln Electric Company, leveraging his own patents for electric motors and a revolutionary electric welding device. It made him a rich man, now aged seventy. He spent winters in Phoenix and was financing construction of a hotel in the empty desert between Camelback and Mummy mountains, set to open in December.

"I wish they'd leave the desert alone," I grumped.

"You can't stand in the way of progress, Gene."

"Doesn't mean I have to like it."

Between the economy picking up, New Deal money, and the chamber of commerce's "Valley of the Sun" marketing campaign, tourism was becoming big business. "Wintering" here had become an expression for those escaping the winter cold of the Midwest. Among the newcomer celebrities doing so was the architect Frank Lloyd Wright. He was a difficult man, but he'd paid me a hundred dollars to do a background check on a potential employee. He talked about building a home and architecture school far north of Scottsdale in the empty desert. It pleased him that at night he couldn't see any lights from the place.

It made me think again about Jordan/Parris. What was he doing here? Plenty of people were passing through in the Depression. Some stayed here for a fresh start. Phoenix was easy that way. I wondered how the murder investigation was going. If the dead man's story was true, his employer would come looking for him, the boy would be found dead or alive, and some of the mysteries of this case would be tied up. But something told me it was lies hidden in lies. Jordan/Parris was nothing he claimed to be, and he'd brought trouble to our doorstep.

"We're going to meet Lincoln's wife, Helen," Pamela said. "She's his third one. Considerably younger. His first two wives died. Anyway, Helen Lincoln was diagnosed with tuberculosis, so he brought her here, and within two years she was much better. The dry, clean desert air. They've given money to the Desert Mission in Sunnyslope, the one set up by Elizabeth Beatty and Marguerite Colley to help the sick and the poor."

Sunnyslope, in the desert north of Phoenix and across the Arizona Canal, hard against the North Mountains, had been a Hooverville early in the Depression. It was attracting better off "health seekers" now, or, in Lincoln's case, at least their money.

"But what about the blackmail?"

"She wanted to talk in person. That's why we're meeting her at their home." Pamela turned right onto a dirt lane in the groves which opened onto a two-story stucco hacienda with a red-tile roof. It was surrounded by orange trees, cottonwoods, a shaggy desert willow, and immaculate flower beds. It was two months past the fragrance of the orange blossoms, but I inhaled the many wonderful remaining scents.

Pamela took off her scarf and shook loose her hair. I appreciated how she wore it long and natural, as opposed to the fashionable wave look. I didn't appreciate how I was appreciating her. But there it was. I'd been attracted to her three years ago, when she was a student flirting with me, but I was true-blue loyal to Victoria then.

I could hear piano music before we reached the front door.

It was beautiful, Chopin I thought, and played with great expertise. Our parents had made Don and me take lessons as boys, and at moments like this I wished I had stuck with it.

A Mexican maid met us at the door. She wore a black uniform with a white apron and ushered us past the living room, kept cool by its high ceilings with dark timbers running across the expanse. A stairway with wrought-iron railings led to a second floor. A woman was playing a gleaming black Steinway grand piano, facing away from us, her back regally straight.

But she wasn't the client. The maid led us outside to a shady patio with expensive outdoor furniture where a woman stood to greet us. Introductions were made. Helen Lincoln was an average-looking brunette, midforties, who carried herself with confidence but was obviously surprised to see me.

Pamela gently took charge. "Mrs. Lincoln, this is my partner, Gene Hammons. He's a former policeman. And everything you tell us will be held in strictest confidence."

This seemed to relax her, and she invited us to sit. Lemonade was served. It was the best lemonade I'd ever tasted.

"What happened to your face?" she asked.

I was about to give a smart-ass response like, "you should see the knot on the back of my head," when Pamela again intervened. "He tripped on a rickety staircase." And that settled the matter.

"You'll have to pardon my stepdaughter, Louise," she said. The two women seemed about the same age, but I reminded myself that Lincoln himself was much older. "She's blowing off steam on the piano."

"That's beautiful steam." I smiled.

"She's really a violinist," Helen Lincoln said. "And a composer. Completely immersed in her music. So very talented."

It took a few more minutes of light conversation before we got down to business.

Helen sighed. "My husband just took the train back to Ohio on business, so he doesn't know I'm talking to you. I don't know where to begin..."

"The beginning is always good," I coaxed.

"You know that President Roosevelt signed an executive order after he took office, forbidding people from hoarding gold. Beyond a hundred dollars' worth, I think. It was part of taking the United States off the gold standard to fight the Depression. We turned in our coins, just as we were instructed, and the government paid us in paper money. Everything seemed properly done, I was sure of it. Anyway, the Camelback Inn, that's the name of the resort my husband is helping finance, well, it's all on the up and up. The Camelback Inn is going to be lovely," she sniffed, "not some dude ranch."

She knotted her fingers together before continuing. "But we received a letter in the mail saying the resort's financing included thousands of dollars in gold bullion. From us! And if we didn't pay fifty thousand dollars, this person would expose it, and we'd go to prison for up to ten years! John never owned bullion!"

At this point, she was in tears. Pamela asked to see the letter. Helen left and soon returned with an envelope. Inside was a typed letter saying pretty much what she'd told us, along with a threat against going to the police and a warning that they were being watched, not all the time, but they'd never know when. The envelope had been postmarked in Phoenix. The letter went on to say they would receive another letter with instructions as to where to deposit the blackmail money. Pamela copied the information into a notebook, writing in beautiful cursive.

I pulled out a handkerchief, and Helen dabbed her eyes. "Even though it's not true, the accusation would ruin my husband's reputation. We've tried to be good citizens here, donating to the Desert Mission. What a horrid reward!"

Pamela looked at me, so I went forward.

"Mrs. Lincoln, my experience is that this is only the start. If you give in to a blackmailer, he'll be back for more. He wants to bleed you dry. It never ends."

"My husband wants to pay," she said.

"But the person who wrote this letter doesn't offer anything in return," I said.

She looked at me quizzically.

"My point is that they don't claim to have compromising photographs or film." I thought about the peep spaces in Kemper Marley's whorehouses. He had plenty of compromising photos of important men in Phoenix, but he wasn't a blackmailer. He used them for political or business leverage. If someone crossed him, he'd pull out a photograph of them with a pro skirt and threaten to send it to the man's wife. That settled it. I continued, "They aren't offering anything in return. If you pay, what do you get?"

"They'll stop this threat."

I suppressed a sigh.

"John told me to wire him when the next letter came and withdraw the money from the bank and deliver it."

"But you said he doesn't know you're talking to us."

"That's true. But I don't feel confident enough to deliver it myself. I need someone trustworthy to handle it."

Here I was again. I didn't like the idea of being a bagman now any more than I had for the late "William Jordan."

I tried again to talk her out of it, but her tears evaporated. "Don't even try, Mr. Hammons. We are going to pay! This must go away!"

It wasn't going away, but I shut up.

"How is bullion even worth having, now that hoarding is outlawed?" Pamela intervened. Both women looked at me.

"Gold is always valuable," I said. "It can be sent to Mexico and exchanged for dollars, then brought back across the border. That's just one way to convert it to money quickly. Gangsters have even more inventive methods to use it. Gold is private and confidential. It's a tangible asset you can hold in your hands. What about your husband's partners in the Camelback Inn?"

"They're all trustworthy people," Helen said, raising her voice enough to bring the maid to the door. "I resent your implication that they might be involved in this or that we're somehow to blame!"

That's me: making friends, influencing people. I apologized. At least the maid refreshed our lemonade.

Still, Pamela coaxed a list of their names, promising we wouldn't contact them. Nobody on the list stood out to me. None had contacted Helen about receiving a blackmail threat.

I asked if the family had any enemies, if anyone in their employ was an ex-con, if someone had been lurking around or following them. The answers were all negative. Pamela still wrote down the names of their workers. I could get Don to check for rap sheets. If he was in a good mood, or distracted by his latest fight with his wife, or coming off his visit to a Chinatown opium den, he was at his most accommodating.

Helen said, "My question is whether you will deliver the money?"

"Of course," Pamela instantly answered.

I wished we could demand proof of how they knew about the outlawed gold, but it was too late. It wasn't too late to tell Helen Lincoln that we intended to open a quiet investigation into the case, so we'd be ready when the next letter arrived.

Instead, we left the way we came. Louise was playing Gershwin.

Seven

We drove back to town. I had a bad feeling.

"Is that black Dodge still behind us?" I didn't want to turn my head around to look.

"Yes," Pamela said, checking the rearview mirror.

"It's been following us for some time."

"I didn't even notice. You're sure it's the same one?"

I was. "Thirty-three black four-door sedan, right?"

"That's the one. I can see the driver and passenger. They're holding back. What should we do?"

I saw a dirt road between the citrus groves and told her to turn into it, then find a place to back up out of sight. She accomplished this flawlessly, and we were concealed between the freshly harvested orange trees.

"Now we'll see." I pulled out my gat.

Her eyes widened.

"Be prepared," I said, hoping that I was only being jumpy from this morning's assault.

Unfortunately, within three minutes, the Dodge came creeping down the dirt path. It stopped directly in front of us. The driver was a tough-looking lug with a scar running down the side of his face. He stared.

I stepped out, keeping the M1911 concealed beside my leg. I held out my Phoenix Police badge. There was no time to explain that the Chief of Detectives had returned my buzzer when I was working on that case where I first met Pamela three years ago, and he'd never asked for it back. I used it sparingly, for I wasn't a sworn officer anymore. Here, it might be a lifesaver.

"Police," I said, thumbing back the hammer of my semiautomatic, but still keeping it out of sight. "Step out of the car."

That was when I saw his friend show a Tommy gun. Thompson submachine gun. It was equipped with a drum magazine, which could hold fifty or a hundred .45-caliber bullets. If the drum didn't jam, the submachine gun was murderously powerful and favored by gangsters. I would have to shoot him first.

I whispered for Pamela to get down. She opened her door and slid out into the dirt with her revolver.

The man called, "We're FBI agents!"

"Show me a badge," I called back, and he reached carefully into his pocket and held out his credentials.

"It would help if your friend put down that Tommy gun."

I heard him say something to the other man, and the Thompson was lowered. I approached the Dodge.

Sure enough, his case showed a gold badge. I glanced at the eagle on top, "Federal Bureau of Investigation," U.S. on either side of an engraved woman holding scales and a sword, then, "Department of Justice." I handed it back and holstered my piece.

He introduced himself as Special Agent Hunnicutt Purvis and his partner as Special Agent Swigert.

"Where did you get that scar?"

"Machine Gun Kelly's wife," Purvis drawled. "She got me with a razor when we caught up with them in Memphis." He touched it lightly with his index finger. "They say I'll need plastic surgery."

"'Don't shoot, G-man, don't shoot!'" Pamela chuckled.

"The press made that up. He didn't say anything when we arrested him. But it's a great line."

I said, "What brings the G-men to our little town?"

He knew I had met with Hoover and mentioned a potential kidnapping. None apparently had materialized, and fortunately for me, Hoover hadn't clarified that I was no longer a Phoenix Police detective. But the man I knew as William Jordan and then George Parris was a federal fugitive. He had a long rap sheet for embezzlement, armed robbery, and murder. He was about to stand trial in Kansas when he killed a guard and escaped, crossing state lines.

"Your department sent out his fingerprints, and we matched them," Swigert said. "We have no idea why he was here. Now he's dead."

"I'm not working that case," I said, feeling the limb I climbed out on in danger of snapping. "That's my brother, Don Hammons, and Detective Navarre."

"We talked to them," Purvis said. "And we let them know he had at least one enemy, a partner in a bank heist in Wichita. Name of Andrew Jackson Poet."

"Poet?" Pamela asked.

"Yep. Believe it or not. When they were dividing up the loot, Parris cold-cocked him and took all of it."

I asked the value and fought back a gasp.

"It was gold and gold certificates," Purvis continued. "The local authorities arrested Parris, he escaped, and they never found the money or gold. The bank shouldn't even have had that much. It was to be transported the next day to the Federal Reserve Bank of Kansas City by train, in a sealed and guarded baggage car. It's amazing three years later, people are still turning in gold. If you ask me, it was an inside job. Otherwise, Parris and Poet wouldn't have known what the bank was holding."

"Poet isn't somebody to trifle with," Swigert said. "He'd been a triggerman for the Purple Gang in Detroit before he went freelance as a robber and hit man for hire. If he tracked Parris to Phoenix, I'd bet he was the one who put a bullet in Parris's brain. Detective Navarre thinks a Negro did it."

"He always says that about every crime. I'd go with your gut, Agent Swigert."

This made some sense. If Andrew Jackson Poet came to Parris's door, Parris might have been careless enough to step back inside, thinking he could talk his way out of it. Then he either turned his back or was ordered to turn and received the bullet in the back of his head. As I suspected, a .22 is a favored mob hit weapon.

"So, why were you on our tail?"

"The latest information we had was Poet driving this make, model, and color of car. Also, he had a moll with him with red hair."

Pamela, who had stood up and followed me to the Dodge, kept her mouth shut.

They showed us a booking photo of Poet: Wavy dark hair, narrow face, thin lips. Eyes of a stone-cold killer under unforgiving eyebrows.

"Keep it," Purvis said, and I pocketed the mug shot. "We carried the Thompson because this man is a killer, always packing heavy heat," Purvis said. "Shoot first, don't even ask questions, and known to carry a Chicago Typewriter himself. What brings y'all out here?"

"The Lincolns are looking for a tutor for some friends' children, and Miss Bradbury interviewed."

"I'm Gene's girlfriend." She smiled.

"With a pistol," Swigert said.

Think fast, Hammons. "I'm taking her target shooting in the desert."

This seemed to satisfy the G-men, and they drove off. We sat under the orange trees for several minutes before Pamela spoke.

"I carried the missing gold across the bridge that night, didn't I?"

I nodded. "But to who?"

"Whom," she corrected.

"I thought you didn't want to teach English."

Eight

I reached my brother at police headquarters and asked if he had time to meet. He climbed the stairs to my office half an hour later as I was still cleaning up.

Don examined my rifled room. "Doing some rearranging?"

"Somebody jumped me and ransacked the place."

"Anything missing?"

I shook my head.

He examined my face. "He did a number on you."

Except for his dark-brown hair, Don was easily recognizable as my brother. Tall like me. Long legged. I feared his vices were aging him prematurely.

"Know who it was?" he asked.

I speculated it might have been the man who killed George Parris.

"Turns out he was on the run from the feds," Don said, stretching out his legs and lighting a smoke. "Got a visit from the FBI."

While I lit a Lucky, he ran through the information I had already received from Purvis and Swigert. I listened anyway.

"But no gold," I said.

"Not yet. How was the execution?"

The execution. It took my brain a few seconds to process he meant Jack Sullivan's death. That seemed like a lifetime ago. I gave him the basics. "There's no good way to die."

"Don't go soft on me, Gene."

"You know what his last words were?"

Don opened his arms as if for an embrace. "Surprise me."

"He said he didn't get a fair trial."

"That's what they all say."

I hoped to nudge the conversation along. "Any chance Parris had a partner?"

Don blew a long cloud of smoke toward the open window. "Why do you care?"

"I'm a curious guy."

"Don't go playing cop, Gene."

I kept my big questions to myself. Pamela had likely carried the stolen gold and gold certificates from the robbery to someone across the bridge. But to who? Hell, whom? Someone who would have to be especially trustworthy.

"Did Parris have any family?"

Don slammed his fist on the desk. "Damn you! You're no longer on the force!"

"Don't be a jerk, Don. It was just a thought. Moving the gold might take two, one as a carrier and the other as a fence. Maybe that's why Parris wanted me to deliver the 'ransom money' on the Central bridge, the case I didn't take. Unless you and Frenchy have discovered a real kidnapping."

He sighed and shook his head. "Frenchy is busy rousting Negroes, but this was a premeditated murder related to the robbery in Kansas. The Sheriff's Office didn't find any bodies in the riverbed. No kidnappings or missing persons matching your case have been reported."

"You need to have Cyrus Cleveland give Frenchy an attitude adjustment." Cleveland was the most powerful Negro gangster in Phoenix and controlled the rackets in Darktown. Navarre, who was on the take from Gus Greenbaum, was afraid of him and was his occasional bagman. Frenchy led a complicated life. Don chuckled. "Parris only has a sister in Tulsa." Then, "Tell me about your new girlfriend."

I started to deny it but remembered how she introduced herself at the murder scene.

"She's smart and fun," I ventured.

"Pretty, too," he said. "I always went for redheads. She's a little young for you, but it's good you stopped carrying that torch for Victoria Vasquez. Marry her and have some kids, settle down."

My brother, with his drunken fights with his wife, Dottie, was not an advertisement for marital bliss. I steered the conversation back to the case.

I said, "Makes more sense that this Andrew Jackson Poet is the murderer."

"Agreed."

"Chasing the stolen gold and gold certificates."

"Agreed. But why do you care? If Poet attacked you, better be on the lookout. He knows you're connected to Parris. You were smart not to take the case, and I hope to hell you're in the clear."

"Not quite." I told him about the new case, blackmail against the Lincolns.

"Bullion to help finance the Camelback Inn?" He stubbed out his nail. "It keeps coming back to gold. Better watch your ass, little brother."

"I always do." Then I gave him the list of Lincoln family employees and Camelback Inn investors, asking him to check them for criminal records, wants, and warrants.

After cussing me, he agreed to help.

I went to the regular Tuesday night poker game with Barry Goldwater, Harry Rosenzweig, and Del Webb. Del was a fervent FDR supporter and donor. He'd been rewarded with many construction projects, making him one of the richest men in Arizona, second only to Marley. I was happy to take some of his money at the poker table.

With the presidential election coming up, he ran through all the New Deal money coming here from the Works Progress Administration, Bureau of Public Roads, Public Works Administration, Civilian Conservation Corps. The alphabet soup to soothe the Depression, plus farm aid and agricultural price stabilization programs. It was essential that Roosevelt win reelection this year, he said.

Three Civilian Conservation Corps camps were around town, including one building and improving hiking and horse trails through South Mountain Park, also erecting ramadas, building roads, and an entrance to the park. Hearing about that, I thought back to Pamela hefting that heavy bag to the middle of the bridge. Could Parris's partner have been hiding out in the CCC camp? I asked about the camp, just making conversation.

"They're good men, unemployed during the Depression," Del said. "They get thirty dollars a month for their work. It was organized by the Army."

It was a shot in the dark. South Phoenix was an enormous swath of land, mostly farmers, including Japanese, plus rural barrios. Plenty of places for the partner to wait to receive the gold.

We played five-card draw as usual. Ante up. Barry expertly shuffled the deck, and I cut it, then he dealt. He casually talked about the department store before Rosenzweig reminded him of the "no work talk" rule, but I was on guard. He was an excellent card player, and his handsome features presented a perfect poker face. He often took my money.

Harry, another downtown merchant prince, thanks to his father's jewelry store, talked about meeting a Jew who escaped from Nazi Germany. "Samuel Herzfeld?" I asked.

"Yes!"

"I met him at Otis's barber shop."

"I've introduced him to Temple Beth Israel," Harry said. "He's got a job at the Goodyear operation out in Litchfield Park as a chemist."

"Chemist?" Barry asked. "I thought they only had land for growing long-staple cotton to make tires?"

Rosenzweig shrugged and asked for three cards. "What about you, Gene? Where'd you get that shiner? From your pretty new girlfriend?"

Everybody laughed and raised a toast with their beer bottles. It was pointless to say Pamela wasn't my girlfriend. Gossip wasn't restricted to the church choir. I lit a nail and asked for two cards. Then betting began.

As the game progressed and the ashtrays filled, I tried to casually back into my case.

"Anybody know John C. Lincoln?"

"He's bought two suits at Goldwater's," Barry said. "That makes him okay in my book."

Rosenzweig volunteered that Lincoln brought in a watch to be repaired. A Glashütte. "That's a rich man's timepiece. Are you working, Gene? No work at the poker table."

"Alright, alright." I slid across two inches of chips. Webb sighed and folded, dropping his cards on the table like fallen soldiers. Barry saw me and raised by ten dollars.

"Call," he said. "But now I'm interested. What's up with John Lincoln?"

I laid out a full house and raked over my winnings.

"What if I said someone was blackmailing him?"

"Whatever for?" Webb asked. "He strikes me as a total square john."

I looked around at my friends. "Nothing I say leaves this room." They all agreed, and I laid it out.

"Bullion?" Goldwater said. "I've never even seen a brick of gold except in the movies!"

"Bullion doesn't just come in bricks," Harry said. "With that, you're talking about a gold bar weighing, say, forty-two ounces. It has a serial number and the location it was minted stamped on it. That's usually New York City. That one bar might be worth around two thousand dollars. But bullion can also come in ingots. They're smaller, twenty ounces or so, again with a serial number and stamp from the New York Assay Office. Both also have the purity of the gold stamped on them. Anything from New York is gold close to one hundred percent pure."

The card game was at a dead stop as I whipped out my pocket notebook and took notes.

I asked, "How do you know so much about gold, Harry?"

"FDR put a special clause in his executive order that allows jewelers to keep more gold than average citizens, because we still make gold jewelry. Now, time for Gene to deal."

I took the deck from Barry and went to work. Not that it did me any good. An hour later I left twenty bucks lighter.

Outside I saw a shadow moving behind my car a hundred feet away. A man squatted down. I quickly moved out of the illumination of the porch light and sidled against the darkened shrubbery in that direction. My gun was out and hammer thumbed back. If he was planning an ambush, I was going to ambush back.

If I was lucky, I'd come outside from the poker game before he could get in position. A pair of thick, low-hanging queen palms helped conceal me.

Now I was parallel to the squatted shadow and made my move.

"Don't even breathe if you want to live," I said, leveling the .45 at him.

A flash followed by a boom and my straw Panama flew off. I fell to the grass and returned fire, one shot that ricocheted off a car bumper. But the shadow was gone. I hugged the ground like an old infantryman until I heard a door open.

"Gene! Are you okay?" Barry ran to me.

"Get down!" A loud whisper. "Flat on the ground!"

For a good ten minutes I made him lie next to me on the grass as I listened and aimed the gun. Then, in the distance, I heard a car backfire and drive off.

"I'm okay." I stood and slid the gun into its shoulder holster. "Somebody shot at me. I bet it was the man who gave me the shiner."

But his possible identity was part of a growing list: Jack Sullivan's brother, George Parris's murderer, maybe the blackmailer of the Lincoln family. I was impatient for Don to check out those names.

Goldwater lifted my hat from the ground, poking his index finger through a bullet hole two inches above my brain. "We have a sale on these," he said. "Come by tomorrow and I'll fix you up."

He dusted off my clothes and focused on me. "Only one man in town could help you find out who's blackmailing Lincoln."

I hated to even say his name. "Gus Greenbaum."

Barry nodded. "You have to go see him."

"Unless he's the blackmailer."

"That's not his racket," Goldwater said. "Pun intended."

"I'll never understand why you're friends with him."

Barry shrugged. "I like a fast crowd." He let out a hearty laugh. "I'm probably friends with the guy you just shot at."

"I hope not."

I drove around the neighborhood for half an hour, but my assailant was gone. At a phone booth, I checked to see if Pamela was safe. She was but concerned about me.

"Why don't you come over?"

I demurred. Finally, I circled my apartment building three times and finding the street safe I mounted the stairs to home, where the door was locked and everything inside was in order. Turning off all the lights, I watched Portland Parkway for an hour without a single car driving by.

That night I slept with a chair propped against the front door, the M1911 beside me, and my snub-nose .38 Detective Special on the bedside table. I woke up at one point with a beer hangover adding to the pain of being assaulted in my office. More aspirin. Then I fell sideways across my bed and dreamed of the University Park Strangler. A feeling of menace fell over me like a dark robe.

———

We knew something big was coming. "Trench rations" had been cut back to "emergency rations": cakes with beef powder, cooked wheat, as well as chocolate bars. We nicknamed them "iron rations." It was less to haul to the front.

Now the bombardment shook the ground for what seemed like hours. But this time it was our artillery, hitting the Hun salient at Saint-Mihiel. The new "tanks" were attacking elsewhere. We were battle-hardened by this time, out of our trenches with their parapets for firing, periscopes, duck boards, mud, and rats.

Now we were forward in foxholes. The soldier beside me couldn't stand it anymore—he had all the signs of shell shock—and prepared to run away. I sensed his panic and upward crouch before he did it but pulled him down roughly. "Stay! We're going on the attack!" He stayed.

Amazingly, the usually fearsome German artillery didn't answer.

"Fix bayonets!" The lieutenant stood and moved forward. I did too and then we were hundreds, heading toward the Hun positions. My rifle felt light now, after so many months of drilling, training, and carrying it. My terror was under control as my legs powered me forward. I stepped over bodies and discarded rifles, helmets, and other equipment. Bodies were blown apart, a head detached neatly from a torso. Legs and arms severed.

Then the machine guns opened up on us. Men fell at my right and left. One was disemboweled, still alive, holding his intestines, strange looking, flowing out of his tattered uniform tunic before he collapsed dead. Another's head exploded not two feet ahead of me. The rest of us hit the dirt and crawled toward the machine-gun nest.

Maybe this was a forest once, but years of war had reduced it to nothing but stumps and twigs. Smoke surrounded us. I fired and reloaded, fired and reloaded, trying to steady my aim.

An American machine-gun team set up and sprayed lead. The surviving Krauts panicked and fled. I shot one in the back, reloaded, and got his comrade in the neck. My buddies finished off the rest, and we crossed the first line of sandbagged German trenches. Then we dropped into the second.

A soldier with a pump shotgun—one of General Pershing's innovations—took out the German infantry before they could even draw an aim. These trenches were luxurious compared with the wet, rodent- and lice-infested ones of the Allies. They were built with reinforced concrete and zigzagged more expertly so an enemy couldn't mow down an entire platoon while he stood topside.

I was suddenly alone, pulling out my three-by-five trench mirror to see around the corners, moving cautiously into the rooms that led off the main concrete entrenchment. Food was hot. They had just left.

Only they hadn't.

German voices and a big soldier came for me, his face obscured by the coal-scuttle helmet. I fired and missed. He did the same. I felt his bullet tug at my uniform. Then his bayonet was coming for me. I raised my rifle to fend it off and thrusted at his chest, but my bayonet melted and...

I woke up screaming.

Slowly, my breathing eased. "My apartment. Phoenix. It's nineteen thirty-six." I heard my voice. But I couldn't stop myself from reciting, "In Flanders fields the poppies grow/ Between the crosses row on row..." It was hours before sleep came again, this time without dreams.

Nine

Gustave "Gus" Greenbaum was the Chicago Outfit's man in Phoenix. He came up in New York's Jewish mob under Meyer Lansky, then moved on to the Windy City. They sent him here in 1928 to run the Southwest branch of their Trans-America News Service. On the surface it sounded legitimate, like the Associated Press or United Press. He made friends with respectable locals, including Barry Goldwater. Spreading money to the city commissioners didn't hurt.

But the "news service" was all about gambling: using Western Union at horse races, ball games, and prize fights to instantly transmit the results. So, the bookies who worked for the Outfit could keep taking bets, already knowing the outcome, before it became public on the radio or in the ticker tape in newsrooms.

Take a horse race. The basic race information was available to the Associated Press, United Press, and International News Service—they'd transmit it to the *Republic*, the *Gazette*, and the radio stations. But Trans-America was faster. At many tracks, maybe half, Trans-America paid for the exclusive rights to use a direct wire from the press box.

At other tracks, they had a spotter with a telescope or a

"wigwag artist," who could signal the racing results to someone on a telephone. Whatever way they received it, Trans-America had exclusive Western Union circuits leased. The distributors are given what they call a drop—a receiving station with a high-speed ticker. The radio might carry an individual race. The syndicate covered them all, coast to coast, two dozen major tracks.

The money was made by allowing the bookmaker to keep taking bets as if he didn't know the race results. The AP hadn't reported them yet. When the bookie already knew a horse had lost, he'd take the bets anyway.

Before the hour of the races, when customers lined up to place bets, they didn't know, say, track conditions, things like that. The bookie sure wasn't going to tell them. Most of the money went to the syndicate. Local bookies had to pay a percentage of net daily receipts, plus a fixed weekly fee to receive the results.

And the bookies who wanted to work their own show? They received a "friendly" visit from a syndicate enforcer: join us or see your pool hall burn down or your legs broken.

All this was completely illegal in Arizona—but only on the books.

I explained all this to Pamela on Wednesday morning after I found her waiting for me in the outer office at the Monihon Building. She insisted on going with me to see Greenbaum in his office atop the Art Deco Luhrs Tower, the most beautiful building of the 1920s booms, and diagonal across the intersection from Police Department Headquarters. I called for an appointment, and he invited us over.

At the corner newsstand, I bought an *Arizona Republic* and was greeted by a banner headline about an overnight crime. A burglar disarmed two police officers in a radio car behind the Arnold Pickle & Olive Company at Van Buren and Fourteenth

Street. But he was confronted by another cop who shot and killed him. He made every shot count, hitting the criminal six times as he ran one hundred-fifty yards. The officer was identified as Earl O'Clair. Yep, the rookie who nearly threw up at the murder scene of George Parris. The kid grew up fast. If it had been me, I'd have shot him with my .45, instead of the police-issue .38, and the criminal would have dropped after the first hit.

The last time I saw Greenbaum was three years ago when he broke into my apartment and found me waiting in the dark with a gun. Confrontation turned to conversation—he was tied to my investigation of the murder of Carrie Dell—and we'd parted ways. Not only Navarre, but who knew how many other cops were on his payroll. I wondered, but not too often, how my brother kept up his fine wardrobe. Kemper Marley, not content with the state's major liquor distributorship, vast land holdings, and whorehouses, wanted in on Greenbaum's gambling action. It was a small town.

On the fourteenth floor of the Luhrs Tower, a secretary ushered us into Greenbaum's office. It had a panoramic view of the city looking north. Our modest skyline was tiny compared with Chicago's and New York's, but it was much more impressive than the town I came back to after the war. And those big cities didn't have our spectacular mountains.

As for Gus Greenbaum, except for thinner hair, the man was much as I remembered him. Dark hair combed straight back. Bulbous nose. No goons with Tommy guns stood by to protect him. Still, he seemed built to hurt people. We shook hands and he gave me that bone-crushing grip. I returned it as hard as I could, maintaining a neutral expression with difficulty.

"Gene Hammons, my favorite doughboy."

I had never cared for that term. "That was a long time ago," I said, maintaining the handshake and eye contact. "Come to the American Legion Hall, and you can meet more of us. You can meet the ones who had parts of their faces blown off by Hun artillery. Some of them were so disfigured that their wives didn't recognize them. Their children saw them and ran away screaming. If stretcher-bearers placed them on their backs, they'd choke to death on their own blood."

Greenbaum winced and let go of my hand as if it were a hot poker.

He quickly regained his composure. "You ever kill anybody?"

I hated that question, but I wasn't going to use my usual dodge of claiming I served behind the lines. But in truth I had shredded that part of the Ten Commandments. I prayed for forgiveness.

Now I said, "Nobody who wasn't trying to kill me." I cocked my head. "How about you?"

"Same," he said. "But reading the newspapers we might have another war coming. Hitler. There's a real gangster and in charge of a country. My people are Jewish. This won't turn out well."

He changed the subject. "And who is your beautiful friend, Hammons?"

"Mr. Greenbaum, let me present Pamela Bradbury."

He took her hand and bent to kiss it. I resisted the temptation to be nauseated. She was wearing dark-blue slacks and a light-blue sleeveless top. I could see him undressing her with his flat eyes. It made me want to pistol-whip him.

A big predatory smile. "Call me Gus!"

He waved us to plush armchairs, sat behind an impressive desk, clipped one end of a cigar, struck a match, and lit it in a slow circle. The air-conditioning kept the office cool and less filled with the acrid smell of his spent Cubans.

"I know you don't partake, Hammons. Shame."

"I'll have one." Pamela smiled gamely.

"Of course." Gus pulled one from the polished wood humidor on his desk, snipped it, and handed her the cigar and matches. She lit it and wafted the smoke over her palate. I wondered how long it would take before she turned green.

"Excellent, Gus," she said. "Thank you."

"It's a Belinda Corona," he instructed. "Note the silky, dark brown wrapper. The flavor is flawless."

I lit a Lucky.

"How's business, Gus?"

He leveled that penetrating nowhere-to-hide look at me, then smiled.

"Better than ever. I do worry about Nevada."

I raised an eyebrow.

"They legalized gambling in 1931, you know. The old economy, the mining economy in northern Nevada, was wrecked by the Depression. The state needed new money. Now Las Vegas, this nothing stop on the Union Pacific Railroad between Salt Lake and LA, is going somewhere. The building of Boulder Dam nearby has also helped. Legal casinos may be the future, and that's bad for my business."

"I'm sure you can get a foothold. The Outfit will probably send you there to run their casinos. And Lake Mead will provide a convenient place for the mob to dispose of bodies."

He snorted. "You and your imagination, Hammons. Anyway, I love Phoenix. We're going to build a house in Palmcroft. It's been slowed by the Depression, but eventually Palmcroft will be the most beautiful neighborhood in the city, and right by the new Encanto Park." He let a half inch of ash drop into the glass ashtray on his desk. "I don't want to go to Las Vegas."

I got down to my business. "I was wondering if you knew of

men named George Parris and Andrew Jackson Poet." I showed him Poet's booking photo.

Greenbaum gave an unsettling chuckle.

"Poet?" he said. "That's what he's using now? You're talking about Albert Anastasia, otherwise known as the Mad Hatter and the Lord High Executioner. The man from Murder Incorporated. What's he doing in my town?"

I laid out what I knew: Parris making off with the gold and gold certificates after knocking Anastasia out. Parris ended up here and was now dead. Maybe Anastasia killed him.

Greenbaum chuckled again. "So much for Hoover's scientific law enforcement. The Mad Hatter created this entirely new identity and background, right down to his fingerprints."

"How could he do that?" Pamela asked.

Gus rubbed his thumb across his big fingers. "The long green, little dish. Money will buy anything, even within the FBI. So, the G-men are chasing a shadow. Hoover would blow his wig if he knew. The Mad Hatter was never involved with the Purple Gang in Detroit. How do you know he didn't take back the gold?"

Pamela said, "Because I lugged a locked suitcase to the middle of the Central bridge. It was supposed to be ransom money to get back the son of an important man."

"What important man?" Greenbaum demanded.

"There was none," she said, meeting his glare. "Parris hired me to do it. But the kidnapping was a hoax. I'd bet that suitcase held the gold, and it was safer to use a courier while Parris hid out."

"You're lucky the Mad Hatter wasn't waiting for you," Gus said. "You never would have made it back alive. But a lady shamus. I could use someone like you."

She smiled and set the rest of her Belinda in the ashtray.

The gangster leaned forward. "How much gold are we talking about?"

I said, "Forty million dollars."

He rose and walked back and forth like a caged lion, taking an occasional puff on the cigar.

"I don't know this Parris cat," he said. "He's got balls, though. Probably an alias."

"He used the name William Jordan when he came to me," I said. "I turned him down because he wouldn't tell me the 'important man's' name."

Greenbaum blew smoke in my face. "Still an alias. Have your brother check him out."

I waved the smoke away and lit another Lucky to steady my nerves.

He went on, pacing. "I'm a businessman, and having Anastasia and Murder Incorporated here is very bad for business. I have people in Chicago who are going to be very unhappy to hear this." He stopped and stared out the window. "He's not going to stop until he gets the gold."

I said it could be in Mexico by now.

Gus stared out the window. "Maybe. Parris had to have a damned trustworthy partner to receive the bag of gold you left on the bridge. They were going to meet up. Parris knew he was in danger keeping it in town. Sure enough, Anastasia caught up with him here, shot him dead. That's his style: .22 at close range, although he's been known to use an ice pick, whatever works. Interesting he left behind the suitcase of money."

Navarre must have told him the details of Parris's murder.

Gus went on, "If Anastasia's thinking like you, Hammons, he'd go to Nogales and sniff around, find nothing. But maybe he rifled around that suitcase and found the railroad ticket to Los Angeles. Parris wasn't going to Mexico, at least not immediately.

The meetup was in LA. It's easier to blend in and hide out in a big city."

He returned to his desk and leaned toward me with his concrete block of a head.

"Sure, the partner might be in Mexico, he might be on a train to the Coast, but I'd bet he's lying low here waiting for the heat to die down. You'd better find them, the partner and Anastasia, or the killing has only begun."

Ten

Outside, Pamela caught up with me as I stomped ahead across Jefferson Street, nodding at Torrez at his busy shoeshine stand, feeling as if I needed to shower Greenbaum off me. I massaged my aching right hand. Halfway down the block, she pulled on my tie so our faces nearly touched.

"Why didn't you bring up the Lincoln blackmail?"

I untangled her fingers. "One thing at a time. Nothing to do until they get another letter, or my brother finds something in that list of names."

"Was what you told him about the facial injuries true?"

"Every word."

"Those poor men."

I told her about plastic surgery being pioneered in Britain and making its way to the States.

She took it in. Then: "What next for us?"

It was a good question. We walked to Western Union, where I sent Deputy FBI Director Tolson a wire, that Andrew Jackson Poet was really Albert Anastasia. It wasn't intelligence about communists, but I was a patriotic kind of guy.

Next, I said, "Let's find Parris's landlord and talk to him.

We're getting ahead of ourselves and need to start at the beginning."

We hopped the Kenilworth line streetcar and rode north.

The two-story apartment house where Parris had lived looked better in the daytime, when you could see the cut grass, flower beds, and hedges in front, all well-tended. The manager's unit was directly below Parris's. I knocked and a reed-thin, middle-aged man opened the door halfway, looking us over.

"I have a vacant apartment to rent, but it needs cleaning," he said. "Are you two married? Because we don't allow any shacking up here."

I sidled closer to the door jamb. "We have some questions about your upstairs tenant who was murdered."

He reddened. "I've already talked two times to you cops about this. What now?"

"We're private investigators," I said.

He started to close the door, but my foot prevented it. "Just a few minutes of your time, sir. I'm Gene Hammons and this is Pamela Bradbury."

His eyes flicked to Pamela then back to me. "Same Gene Hammons who caught the University Park Strangler?"

I nodded, happy to have this morbid icebreaker help me again. "Come in. I'm Simmons, the manager here." He invited us in and introduced us to his wife Mildred, a stout woman with iron gray hair pulled back.

"Make some coffee, honey. This is the man who caught the strangler back when. And Miss Bradbury."

"Oh, my!" She disappeared into the kitchen. It was getting to be iced tea season, but I didn't want to turn down their hospitality.

"So, what can I tell you about Parris?"

"How long did he live there?"

"Only two weeks before this…" he struggled forward, "awful crime. I usually ask tenants for references, where they'd rented before. This is a respectable apartment house. But he paid me three months' rent in advance, cash. Said he was in sales, but I don't have any previous address or names of relatives. Now I don't even know who to send the rest of the rent money to."

"What kind of a tenant was he?"

"Quiet," he said. "The best kind. No loud radio or phonograph playing. Not a single complaint from his neighbors." Pamela took all this down in her notebook.

I asked if he had any mail that arrived after his death. The man shook his head unconvincingly.

I decided not to push it. "Did he have any visitors? Anyone come asking for him?"

"No one asked about him," Simmons said, furrowing his brow. Mildred arrived with coffee and sat with us as we thanked her and sipped. "He did have one visitor soon after he moved in. I'm not nosy, but I happened to see them talking on the landing, and Parris invited him inside. They seemed like old friends."

Pamela asked him to describe the man.

"Well, he was a big man, I noticed that. Not fat but muscle. Blond hair like yours," he nodded toward me. "About your age. Wore seersucker suits."

Parris's trusted partner? Maybe.

"So, you saw him more than once?" I asked.

"Yes, he came by at least three times, now that I think about it."

"Did you catch a name?"

"No."

Mildred started to say something, but her husband cut her off. "Don't the flowers need watering?" His eyes flicked again from me to her. She shrugged her heavy shoulders and walked out.

I pulled out the photo of Albert Anastasia and held it out,

covering the bottom that showed the booking number. "How about this man?"

"No," Simmons said. "I said I'd talked to police detectives twice. One came by yesterday, asking the same questions."

"Did he show a badge?"

"Sure did."

"Did he give you a name?"

Simmons shook his head.

I thanked him and we walked outside where Mildred was working the hose. Pamela approached her.

"Was there something you wanted to tell us?" Pamela asked.

"Well," she said, "my husband doesn't want trouble. I don't even know it matters."

"Even the smallest thing might help."

She squinted and thought. "That night. We heard a thud above us. I know now it was George hitting the floor. And the friend's name was Oscar, I remember that. He was from Wichita."

———

We walked a few blocks and got my car that was parked in front of my apartment on Portland Street.

"Where to?" Pamela asked.

"South Phoenix. Let's get the lay of the land." With my headache finally gone, I felt okay to drive. So I wheeled out to Central and turned right.

"Do you think Simmons was telling us everything he knew?"

I clenched my jaw before responding. "All my years as a policeman say no. For one thing, I suspect Parris had mail."

As we went south through downtown, past the nearly new Hotel Westward Ho, the Spanish colonial revival-style post office, the art deco Professional Building, Hotel San Carlos, and the older Hotel Adams—"fireproof" since its predecessor burned down in 1910, when I was a boy—she asked about the University Park Strangler and how I caught him.

That seemed like a long time ago, even though it was only seven years past. It was another time, though: the end of the Roaring Twenties, just a few months before the stock market crashed. Still, I was reluctant to tell her much. At the time, she was probably about the age of the victims.

"I'm not a baby, Gene. I need to understand how investigations work, and this was famous. Right here in Phoenix."

I tried to put her off. But the memories came flooding back, fast, close, almost overpowering.

He killed on nights with new moons. The national press called him "The Fiend of Phoenix," but the geography of his attacks gave the name that stuck and made my career: The University Park Strangler.

University Park was a neighborhood east of downtown named for a proposed Methodist institution of higher education that was never built. Too bad for Phoenix, too. The University of Southern California had been affiliated with the Methodist Church. We only got the Strangler.

It began with a single killing. At eleven thirty p.m. on Thursday, January 10, 1929, the westside patrol car driving east on Van Buren Street was flagged down by a frantic man. He led the officers to his house at 324 N. Twelfth Avenue, where his daughter was dead, murdered. The blue light and horn sounded at headquarters, and more officers headed that way. I was the sole night detective and arrived a little before midnight. It was cold outside and even most speakeasies were closed.

The victim was Edna Sawyer, seventeen years old, pretty, with flame-red hair. We found her in bed, in her own room, where she had been raped and strangled. Her periwinkle-blue flannel nightgown was pulled all the way up, exposing pert breasts, parted fair legs, a ginger bush, and a pool of semen on the white sheet.

I ran the gawking uniformed officers out of the bedroom, instructing one to sit with her parents—her mother had found her, and her father had called headquarters then run a block to busier Van Buren, where he was fortunate enough to find the police car cruising.

Captain John J. McGrath, the chief of detectives, arrived. With him was a beautiful, raven-haired female photographer. It was the first time I met Victoria Vasquez. Don and Turk Muldoon came soon after. I briefed them and, as the youngest member of the Hat Squad, prepared to step aside when Turk put a hand on my shoulder.

"You were here first, lad," he said in his rich brogue. "You're the primary."

I felt a thrill—and a terrible responsibility. I had never been the primary investigator on a homicide before, much less one this horrible.

After they left, I closed the door and surveyed the bedroom more carefully, making detailed notes and sketches.

Entry was obvious. The killer came in through an unlocked window facing the backyard and caught the girl sleeping. Her brothers and parents were also asleep but separated from Edna's room by the bathroom. A sock stuffed in the girl's mouth took care of any screaming as he prepared to go about his work. But she must have fought. Her nails were bloody and flakes of the attacker's skin were underneath them. In return, he punched her in the left eye. He must have been straddling her. Afterward, he exited the same window, leaving it fully open.

Through the door, I heard her mother's hysterical crying, while her father was angrily demanding a doctor. But Edna's body was cold.

We didn't realize it at the time, but she was the first victim of the University Park Strangler.

The postmortem confirmed the obvious: death by strangulation, genital bruising, penetration. She fought hard enough to break one fingernail. The killer would have received a nasty gash on his face. But he was very strong. Edna's windpipe was collapsed, as was the cricoid cartilage surrounding it. The pathologist said it took forty-five pounds of pressure to produce such damage. He also speculated that the killer had been in no hurry, slowly strangling her.

With the sock stuffed in the girl's mouth, I assumed the rape preceded the strangulation. But the doc, who had worked at the coroner's office in Los Angeles and seen such cases before, said it was possible that the murderer was raping Edna while he was slowly crushing her windpipe. "It's part of the excitement for him."

He turned her to show me a cross, two inches long, carved into the exact middle of the small of her back. It looked as if it was done with a penknife rather than from some injury, and it was fresh.

"He marked her," the doc said. "Mutilation is part of the MO of a lust murder."

I had never heard the term before, I told him.

"It was first used by the Austrian psychiatrist Richard von Krafft-Ebing in the 1880s," he said. "The killer receives intense sexual gratification by killing someone."

Almost a month later, on Saturday, February 9th, he killed again. Dorothy Jameson was raped and strangled in a Spanish colonial revival house on Taylor Street, a quarter mile from the first killing. She was an only child who lived with her grandmother, who was hard of hearing. The woman didn't discover her body until the morning when Dorothy, usually an early riser, wasn't already up and making coffee and breakfast for both of them.

Some elements were identical: The sock in her mouth, nightgown pulled up, and bedding folded. He came in by an unlocked bedroom window. The second victim was a redhead, although not a natural one. Dorothy had small firm breasts and delicate, "cute girl" features like Edna Sawyer. She had the same cross carved into the small of her back.

But the evidence revealed some differences, too.

He took more care and time with the assault. The girl's wrists were tied with rope to the headboard. The rope strands were cut to exact lengths and brought by the killer, as was the sock. No doubt the gash he received in the first attack made him want to restrain the victim. Had he spied on the house to know the grandmother was nearly deaf, thus giving him more time for the attack? Her thighs were raised and knees bent with her feet flat on the mattress, as if he arranged her that way after the rape. This time he didn't have to worry about being overheard by parents and siblings.

Dorothy had a cat that slept with her. Her grandmother said she always kept her door partly open so the animal could come and go. But Dorothy's door was closed while the cat was hiding under a chair in the living room. The killer somehow immobilized the girl, or she was a hard sleeper, then shooed away the cat and shut the door. This was the second victim whose family didn't own a dog. Did the killer know this in advance? Of course he did. He reconnoitered his targets.

Unlike the first scene, where the ground below the window was covered with grass, the Jameson home had a flower bed. We were able to get a clean cast of a footprint, a tennis shoe or sneaker, size eleven. My brother estimated that the wearer was a well-built man, at least a hundred-eighty pounds.

When I went through the bedroom with Dorothy's grandmother, she found that a pair of the girl's knickers was missing. So was a stuffed animal, a puppy with a red ribbon around his neck. I also went carefully through the girl's diary, but it gave no clue that she was afraid, being stalked, or had enemies.

The postmortem was similar to the first victim's. Genital bruising and bleeding, slow strangulation by a man with strong hands. It was possible she was raped and then killed. But the doc's comment, once again, about the penetration occurring along with choking her to death stayed with me. "Maybe it's the only way he can maintain arousal and orgasm," he said. "Classic characteristic of a lust murder."

Dorothy was another straight-A student at Phoenix Union High, a clarinet player in the band, member of the pep club, popular. She was sixteen, a year behind Edna Sawyer. Interviews with her friends indicated that she didn't know Edna, didn't have a boyfriend. She was hoping to attend the University of Arizona after she graduated.

Once again, detectives talked to neighbors, who saw and heard nothing. They hadn't seen any Peeping Toms, and the police call logs backed that up.

Once again, we rounded up potential suspects: ex-cons with rape or burglary convictions, single men passing through who turned out to have rap sheets in other states. But this went nowhere, either because of alibis or the most promising ones failing to break under heavy interrogation.

One whacky who was familiar to us came in to confess. But he didn't know even the basics of the crime, especially the parts we held back from the press: taking trophies, the penknife cross, and tying her hands with ropes. I sent telegrams to Tucson, Los Angeles, San Diego, and El Paso, asking if they had anything similar. Nothing close came back.

As for the rope lengths and socks, they could have been purchased anywhere. The shoeprint matched a Converse, but that was available in at least a dozen or more stores. Fingerprints from the second house produced no suspects, although they did match the ones from the windowsill of the first murder. It was the same killer, not a copycat.

Panic overwhelmed and the city was consumed by fear. The next new moon was coming up March 11th, so Captain McGrath canceled leaves and vacations, extended shifts with overtime, so we would have every possible officer on the streets. Officers worked in pairs, carrying tommy guns or pump-action shotguns.

Yet nothing happened that night.

After sunrise two days later, Wednesday, a homeowner at Thirteenth Avenue and Polk Street called. A girl was lying on his front yard, half-dressed, not moving. By the time I got there, the street was crowded with people, police cars, and an ambulance. But she was long dead. Her head was turned at an angle, ginger-red hair swept back, eyes staring at us reproachfully. On her stomach with her blouse off, I made an immediate check: the cross was carved in the small of her back. For a moment I lost my composure until Muldoon steadied me.

We interviewed everyone within two blocks of the body dump. Nobody saw anything. Not even the milkmen who were out that early.

More information allowed us to sort out the basics. She was likely Grace Chambers, sixteen, who never came home from the movies the night before. Her parents felt it was safe for her to see the pictures at the Rialto with her steady boyfriend, Ben Chapman. It was her birthday, and they also wanted to reward her for perfect grades this year. They felt safe because they lived in the Las Palmas neighborhood, north of McDowell Road, miles from University Park.

When neither Grace nor Ben came home by nine on Tuesday night, as agreed, her parents notified the police. Because of the letdown the night before, headquarters was short-staffed, the desk sergeant made a report and said he would send a car to interview the parents—but somehow it never happened. A drunken brawl in the Deuce distracted the patrolmen on duty.

Chapman was seventeen, a varsity athlete, choir member, and in ordinary times the prime suspect. That certainty borne of desperate policemen wasn't diminished when Ben's 1928 Buick was found parked outside the Arizona Citrus Growers warehouse on Jackson Street an hour later.

But it was not to be. Two hours after Grace's body was identified by her parents, Ben was found bludgeoned to death out in the county, in an orange grove. Mexican farmworkers discovered him. He was beaten badly. Don guessed a baseball bat. His hands were tied behind his back with rope.

As in the prior cases, Grace had been viciously raped and strangled, her underwear taken. But the killer had more time with her: She was not only tied up with a rope, but also with barbed wire. Her body had multiple cigarette burns. Her bottom had been whipped with a belt or bullwhip, hard enough to leave bruises and bloody welts.

The pathologist guessed she was first bound with rope, perhaps at the same time as her boyfriend. He was an athletic young man, capable of defending himself and his girl, but it raised the possibility the two had been forced to give in at gunpoint. Then the killer made Grace tie up Ben, and she was restrained by the killer. As always with victims, they held out hope: "This is only a robbery. He'll let us go if we do what he asks."

The fingerprint tech went over Ben's car, and the latents were sent off to other departments.

Here the evidence petered out into our speculation. Did the killer take them both somewhere and force the boyfriend to watch as he tortured and raped Grace? Then what? Beat Ben to death before her eyes, finish her off, and leave her in the University Park neighborhood? Then dump his body outside the city limits? Quite a night's work and plenty of risks of being discovered, our guy was highly confident, a risk-taker. Frenchy raised the possibility of two killers, one following the other who drove Ben's car. Then both could make a quick escape.

The heat came quickly, from the city commission, the chamber of commerce, the newspapers, and two sets of well-connected parents. It came from inside headquarters, too. Three members of the

fifteen-man Hat Squad had daughters around the age of the stran-
gler's victims. Senior patrolmen and sergeants, too. And those weren't
shy about voicing frustration and recriminations.

On Thursday, a typed letter came, addressed to Chief of Police
Matlock:

> The Phoenix Police can't solve the greatest crime ever to hit
> our city. Doesn't speak well for your new city hall and police
> headquarters building.
>
> It's me, you clowns. I'll get your tiresome little hidden
> tricks out of the way: I take their knickers and stuffed toys.
> I use a sock to keep them quiet. I carve my brand in their
> backs. I used barbed wire on the latest girl.
>
> Believe me now? I am HIM.
>
> You thought you had me all figured out. So predictable,
> you flatfoots. But I nabbed two lovers this time and had
> my way with both of them. Took them to my lair, isn't that
> what the reporters will call it?
>
> Made him watch while I did things to her. Nice and slow.
> Made her watch while I did things to him while he cried
> and pleaded, then killed him. Then it was only us. I was
> naked and bloody. She was screaming and begging right to
> the end. Nobody could hear her. I delivered her body to the
> neighborhood like the morning newspaper.
>
> Speaking of THAT…I'm sending a copy of this letter
> to the papers and radio stations.
>
> I'll kill again and you can't stop me. It will be worse
> every time.

Given the specifics, this letter was definitely from the Strangler.
The paper contained no fingerprints. Chief Matlock succeeded in
getting every news outlet to spike the letter. The one exception was

the Los Angeles Examiner, *owned by William Randolph Hearst. It printed the letter in full, headlined:* FIEND OF PHOENIX SPEAKS! I *took that letter apart sentence by sentence, word by word. "Talk to me, you bastard," I said under my breath. The person who wrote this was either the killer or intimately knew him, an accomplice. Very confident. "She was screaming and begging right to the end. Nobody could hear her." That indicated an isolated location or a soundproofed room, likely somewhere he could come and go with no notice by neighbors.*

I made notes. What did we know? All the victims went to Phoenix Union, none to St. Mary's or the colored high school, much less the schools in outlying towns. The killer was strong. He prepared his attacks in advance. For example, he never chose a house with a dog but did pick one with a deaf grandmother. He had a connection to University Park.

"He's neat, almost fussy," Victoria said, who by this time had become my friend and confidant. "The comforter or blanket and sheet wasn't thrown off in a heap. It was neatly folded. He took trophies from the first two, but otherwise their rooms were undisturbed. Barbed wire will hurt, but it won't cause extensive bleeding."

I made neat reports but after a week, the case went cold again.

McGrath assigned me, Don, and Muldoon to continue working on it full-time, while other detectives went back to cases that had been holding. We had four dead students, no viable suspect. The city commissioners, fearful of having to cancel the Masque of the Yellow Moon festival set to begin April 25th, fired Chief Matlock. They replaced him with David Montgomery, captain over the traffic division, who made it clear that nobody on the Hat Squad was safe from meeting the same fate. He stared at me, the youngest detective, as he made this announcement.

Dead ends multiplied: A second check found no previous arrests of the high school teachers, not even of the many deliverymen and tradesmen who spent time in University Park. The same was true of Phoenix Union High janitors and maintenance staff.

Prowler calls increased but arrests were few. In many cases, someone called after seeing a neighbor take out his trash or work in his backyard after sundown. One suspect had a burglary conviction in Texas, but he had the best alibi in town for the time when Grace Chambers and Ben Chapman went missing: he was in jail for drunkenness and vagrancy. None of the fingerprint reports to other departments matched their files.

Yet weeks went quiet. The Masque went off safely.

I was not fooled.

We had to make a break instead of waiting for one.

The Chief of D's McGrath blew up when I first took the idea to him. Only Muldoon agreed. Turk pulled me aside and said, "Always trust your gut, lad, and sometimes fight for what it's telling you. It's the best weapon a good detective has."

Finally, McGrath agreed.

I picked Juliet Dehler from the records department. She was twenty-one but looked much younger. She was petite, pretty, red haired.

In my work with Juliet, I'd been impressed by her intelligence, maturity, and most important, street smarts. Over lunch at the Saratoga, I laid out my plan and asked her to consider it, take her time if she needed. But she immediately agreed and helped me refine my idea. I issued her a .38 snub-nosed for her purse and took her to the police range to teach her how to use it. She also got a police whistle to hang around her neck, hidden below her blouse.

June arrived, and Phoenix Union High School graduated four hundred seven students; the Salt River Valley shipped its first-ever carloads of apricots on the Santa Fe Railway to New York City; people had to shake out their shoes for scorpions; and wealthy men sent their wives and children to California or Iron Springs. Juliet took to the streets of downtown and University Park two or three times a week. Although the summer heat was oppressive, the city cooled down at night.

She dressed like the victims the Strangler favored, feminine and middle-class stylish but never looking like a roundheel. She went to movies in air-conditioned theaters, shopped on Thursday nights when the stores stayed opened late, took the streetcar to the Carnegie Library, walked "alone" to a rental house in University Park we'd commandeered as her "home." Making herself visible was critical to the plan.

I was watching, of course, tailing at a safe distance. Sometimes Don or Muldoon joined the tail. Juliet attracted plenty of attention, whether from young whistling wolves or the "summer bachelors" freed of their wives and children during the hot months.

Nothing dangerous happened, however. Not a sign of a perv or rapist, much less the Strangler. That changed on the night of Friday, June 28th.

Friday, June 28th, 1929. Juliet took in a double feature at the Fox and walked west on Washington in a crowd as the other theaters let out. I followed half a block behind. It looked to be another fruitless night, and McGrath would shut down my attempt at baiting the killer.

Then a taxi pulled up and paced her.

I heard the driver lean out and call. "May I take you somewhere, pretty lady?"

She came two steps closer to the curb. I thought: Do not get in that cab!

It might have been innocent, but I realized here was one thing that had evaded our attention: a driver and vehicle that could go anywhere without raising suspicion.

Suddenly, he opened the door and started to wrestle her inside. She yelled and kicked him.

Then I was there with my Detective Special out. Don was soon at my side, and we braced him against the taxi with difficulty. Although he had a meek face and average build, he was strong as hell. It took both of us to get him in cuffs, with a nipper for good measure. He argued, then begged us to let him go. But we had our man.

In the back seat were ropes, barbed wire, a sock, and a rag soaked in chloroform. A penknife was in his front pocket.

We sweated him for twelve hours. Finally, under my continued questioning, catching him stumble through lie after lie, as he told and retold his activities on the dates of the murders, he broke. It happened when I lied to him and said his wife refused to support his alibi that he was home the nights of the murders. And when I told the truth: we found a soundproof room added to his garage on an acreage outside of town. Then he cracked and spilled.

By that time, other detectives had executed a search warrant at his home, finding the knickers and stuffed animals taken from the first two victims, as well as a bloody baseball bat. His typewriter matched the taunting note sent to the police chief. His wife expressed surprise, then outrage that we suspected her husband of such heinous crimes. But I suspected she was aware of what he was doing all along.

He wasn't a taxi driver—that cab had been stolen specifically to snatch Juliet, whom he had been watching. But previous cab thefts coincided with the dates of the other murders. It was a car that blended in anywhere.

He was a teller at a building and loan. Each of the female victims had opened passbook savings accounts with him. This was the link we didn't find.

Emil Gorman, forty-five, was a model employee at the building and loan, shy, kept to himself. He didn't have so much as a parking ticket. His neighbors near the acreage were similarly surprised that Gorman was suspected of being the Strangler.

With one exception: An elderly woman with a habit of watching the street saw him leave late at night on the date of Grace Chambers's disappearance. She remembered because it was also her daughter's *birthday. Few cars came that way at night. He didn't return until early the next day.*

His arrest and confession were national news. The Hearst Examiner's headline: FIEND OF PHOENIX CAUGHT!

Although Gorman confessed to all the murders, I always wondered if there were more. Maybe he got his taste for it on prostitutes nobody would miss. University Park seemed only sinister coincidence. The first girl lived there, and it was fertile hunting ground. Then he liked the name bestowed on him by the press. Maybe right up to the time he was hanged in Florence.

By that time, the stock market had plunged, and the Great Depression came upon us.

I didn't tell her all of it, leaving out the grisliest details and—why?—mention of Victoria. By the time I was done, we were well across the bridge and driving aimlessly amid the two-lane roads lined with tall trees, the fields, pastures, and rural barrios, across the San Francisco and Southern canals, with the South Mountains pacing us.

We pulled off Baseline Road and sat in the car beside the Japanese farm that grew tomatoes, watermelons, summer squash, and cucumbers. Kajuro Kishiyama emigrated here to America, soon to Phoenix, in 1928. He became so successful he was known as "The Tomato King." But his jealous Anglo landlord kicked him out. So he started again here a few miles away earlier this year. Phoenix was a city of fresh starts, even with the antipathy to the Japanese, which I didn't understand. The view north swept down to the river and then began its rise to the far bare mountains, the city gleaming in between.

"So that's it. The University Park Strangler." I sighed. "Ancient history."

Pamela took my hand and squeezed it. I squeezed back.

"Oh, Gene. You're a hero. How could they have ever fired

you from the police force? Couldn't this Detective Muldoon have protected you? He seemed so helpful."

My throat was dry. I told her that was a story for another day. Then she took me by the tie again and pulled me close. Our lips were an inch apart.

"I..." That single word contained so much. I was several years older than her. I didn't want to be hurt again or to hurt her. I didn't want her to hear me when I had nightmares of the war. I did need to snuff out the old torch. And I did want this, had wanted it for a longer time than I realized...

She whispered, "I swore I'd never give my heart until I was sure. I'm sure about you, Gene Hammons. Am I wrong?"

"No," I said, feeling her sweet breath on my face, everything suddenly clear. "You're right." My throat was full. "I promise to take good care of your heart."

I took her in my arms, cupped her beautiful face in my hands, and kissed her. She returned it. A long kiss. A nice kiss. More kisses followed.

Eleven

After Wednesday night choir practice, I drove home. Soon the Chancel Choir would begin its summer break. But instead of parking on Portland, I left the car a block north on the identical Moreland Parkway. I walked around the east side of my apartment house, stood beside the wall in the darkness, and watched. Looking for anything out of the ordinary, anyone who might be laying an ambush for me.

My neighbors were in for the night. No one was on the street. Climbing the stairs, I found the door locked as I had left it that morning. I let myself in but left the apartment dark until I closed all the shades and blinds. Then I turned on a solitary light, the lamp on my desk, and turned on the radio low, listening to Duke Ellington. There I laid out a blank sheet of paper and sketched out what we knew.

- George Parris. An almost unknown man, but someone wily and gutsy enough to outwit the next name I wrote.
- Albert Anastasia, the Mad Hatter, hitman for Murder Incorporated, Parris's accomplice on the gold robbery in Wichita.

Next came an X?, followed by a question mark. Parris's trusted partner in the gold handoff on the bridge. I lit a cigarette and took a long drag, as if the tobacco would provide an answer. Mister X had to be a close friend if Parris's only family was the sister in Tulsa. I drew lines connecting all three men. Then another line to a circle in the middle of the sheet. There I wrote one word: gold. Below this I wrote questions.

- Why did Parris come to Phoenix, much less rent an apartment and pay three months' rent ahead?
- Why did he concoct the fake kidnapping story in the attempt to hire me, and succeeding in engaging Pamela to carry the bag?
- Why the need for a courier? Why not hand it off himself?
- Why the partner? If I had forty million in gold bullion and coins, I'd never let it out of my sight.
- Why carry the suitcase of currency? Where did it come from and how did he intend to use it?
- Who attacked me in my office and ransacked the place, taking nothing that I could tell? It wouldn't be Jack Sullivan's vengeful brother. He would have killed me, end of story, me never living to kiss Pamela. No, this had to be someone who had connected me to Parris.
- Who murdered Parris? Greenbaum seemed sure it was the Mad Hatter's work. But the killing wouldn't get him closer to the gold. Why not tie him up and torture him until he gave it up? Anyway, someone had come to the apartment manager after the murder, after his initial interview with the detectives. Maybe it was routine. Or maybe it was a killer impersonating a policeman. If Anastasia wasn't Parris's killer, who was?

- Where did the FBI come in? Hoover summoned me to his Pullman, took my measure and assigned me to search for communists. But he never mentioned Parris, Anastasia, and the missing gold. I had to get that information from the two G-men who followed us. They also told us Anastasia had a red-haired girlfriend with him. Who was she?

Too many questions and too few answers. The smoke wrapped around me as if seeking some truth.

"Walk away." It was my voice.

I said the words in the darkened room. It seemed like a good idea. I called Pamela. It was half past nine.

"Tell me you're not having second thoughts about us." I heard her inhale sharply.

"None at all," I said.

Her voice caught. "I'm so glad."

Then I laid out my reasoning about the case. Why we should walk away.

"I agree," she said. I was surprised but relieved. "Come over and be with me."

I didn't take convincing. I said I'd be there in a while, to make sure no one was following me.

"I'm falling for you, Gene Hammons." Then she hung up. I thought about calling her right back to say the same about my feelings. But there would be time for that.

———

Back on Moreland, I started the Ford and glided around the parkway west with my lights off. No headlights followed me.

At Fifth Avenue with my lights on, I turned south and cruised through downtown for about half an hour. The Busy Bee was open, and I remembered being there with Pamela and her theory about pie. Suddenly, the siren went off at police headquarters in the new City-County building. Two squad cars and a detective car roared north, sirens blaring.

That was their problem. I was excited about the night to come.

I looked south on Fourth Avenue and the lights were on at Union Station, waiting for the late-night train arrivals and departures. Over to Nineteenth Avenue, I drove north to where it intersected with McDowell Road and Grand Avenue. A heavy steam locomotive was bringing in a Santa Fe freight train from northern Arizona into Mobest Yard. The state fairgrounds were on the northeast side. No one seemed to be following me.

East on McDowell toward Pamela's apartment near Central. I had never been there before. My nerves were bundled up.

But at Seventh Avenue I saw the police lights.

In.

Front.

Of.

Her.

Apartment.

I floored it, roaring to a stop in front of the squad cars. I jumped out and ran as fast as I could.

"Stop him!" My brother's voice coming from a second-story balcony. Nobody was going to stop me. My heart was pounding so fast it felt as if it would fly out of my chest.

Frenchy stood in front of the apartment house door.

"Geno, you don't want to go up there." He gently pressed his hands against me.

"Why?" I demanded.

"Don't," he said. "Please Geno, for the love of God."

I shoved him aside and took the stairs two at a time. Two

uniforms wrestled with me and failed. I stepped inside the apartment, Pamela's apartment, and smelled fresh blood.

"Damn it, Gene!" My brother took a swing at me, but I stepped inside his haymaker and punched him in the kidney, sending him down.

Pamela was on the floor, facedown, skirt up and underpants missing, legs parted. And her hair was gone. Her naked scalp was bleeding onto the wood floor.

"Ambulance!" I screamed, falling to my knees, feeling tears streaming from my eyes, searching for her pulse through what seemed like a gallon of blood. "Get a damned ambulance here! She can't be dead!"

By this time, Don and Frenchy were on either side of me, holding me up more than restraining me.

Don spoke firmly. "She's gone, Gene."

PART TWO

Men of Blood

Twelve

My brother washed off my hands and drove me home. I felt numb, my mind and body overflowing of grief and remorse, with "what ifs." *What if* I had driven to Pamela's apartment immediately after we got off the phone? *What if* I had never let her go home that night? We didn't speak a word, but I was already committed to tracking down the murderer and killing him the same way he killed Pamela, or worse. I'd stake him out in the desert and let the ants, coyotes, and Gila monsters have their way with him. And the unforgiving sun broiling him to death. I'd put a canteen of water, easy for him to see but just out of his reach.

This time, instead of taking the stairs two at a time, I dragged my feet up to the apartment, pausing to catch my breath.

My door opened, and Pamela stood there. I blinked. Not a ghost. I ran and took her in my arms.

"I thought you were dead!"

"I can't breathe," she squeaked. I relaxed my grip. Barely.

"Oh, baby, I'm so sorry you were so worried." She caressed my face and kissed me.

Don said, "I told you she was gone."

I turned back. "Asshole."

"You're gonna make me piss blood for a week from that sucker punch," he muttered.

"Sorry," I said, "You could have told me Pamela was still alive."

"I told you she was gone!"

"So what the hell did I think? That she was dead!" But all my attention was focused on her, wonderfully alive.

We sat down and both of them explained. A minute or two after we hung up on our telephone conversation, before I left, she heard a scream from her neighbor's apartment. Pamela peeked out her door, but the adjoining door, where the scream originated, was closed.

"It was the sound of terror," Pamela said. "It wasn't a love-making sound at all."

She tried to call the police, but the phone was dead.

"The lines had been cut from the outside," Don said. "It wasn't obvious where the phone junction was, so the killer must have cased the apartment house before the attack."

"I should have gotten my gun," she said. She paused and looked at the floor. "But I panicked and went out my back door into the alley. I ran to the corner and called the police and hid behind a building until they arrived."

"And I told an officer to bring her here," Don said. "I gave him the key you gave me."

"I'm ashamed of myself," Pamela said. "That I didn't go to help her. I swear I'll never back down again."

I stroked her hair. "You were smart to leave. The killer was after you."

"We don't know yet," Don said. "But it's a good possibility. Pamela is in apartment 6 and the victim in apartment 9, but the 9 had slid down so it read 6. Remember the raid we carried out and made the same mistake?"

I did. That was back in 1932. We kicked in a door looking for a bank robber, finding an elderly couple asleep. Meanwhile, the bad guy fled.

"She was a sweet girl," Pamela said. "She worked as a nurse at Good Samaritan. Had a boyfriend who works at Valley Bank. I can't imagine she had an enemy in the world."

Don wanted to know about Pamela's enemies. It was time to open up about Albert Anastasia, the Parris gold heist, the Lincoln blackmail threat.

I watched his ears turn red. Shaking out cigarettes, I gave him one first. He lit and inhaled. Then I lit two more nails and handed one to Pamela. No smoke rings this time.

"And it didn't occur to you to tell us about this Murder Incorporated assassin in town," he growled.

"I assumed the FBI told you," I said. "Special Agents Purvis and Swigert."

"The FBI cuts out local law enforcement all the time." His initial anger cooled to a simmer of frustration. He smiled at Pamela. "You doing better?"

"Yes, Don. Thanks."

It was the first time I had seen my brother directly turn on his considerable charm for her. Unlike so many unfortunate women, she wouldn't be taken in.

I said, "Or I assumed Frenchy told you because Gus Greenbaum told me."

He swung to me. "Stop assuming, Gene!"

I let it be.

He stubbed out his smoke. "I've got to get back to the crime scene. First thing is to round up all the Indians we can find. Go to the Indian School and see if any students were missing tonight."

"That's ridiculous," I said. "No Indian did this."

"She was scalped, you idiot! Who else would do it?"

I saw Pamela briefly cringe, then I turned back to my brother. "White men scalped, too. Back on the frontier. Nowadays? Homicidal maniac? Check the files for a similar MO. Send telegrams to other cities. Get your informants to work. Check the hospitals on the chance he cut himself. Spread out the uniforms in the neighborhood to see if he dropped the scalp nearby. Dust for prints. Keep the fact that she was scalped out of the press. And of course, check the boyfriend."

Don smirked. "There you go again. It's too bad you're no longer on the force, Gene, to save us from ourselves." He nodded to Pamela. "We can put her up in a hotel."

"She can stay here." I squeezed her hand. "If she wants."

She said, "I do."

We talked late into the night. She was an only child. I learned that her father had abandoned them when she was four, and her mother raised her while working as a legal secretary. She got straight As going through high school and won a scholarship to Arizona State Teacher's College. Then her mother passed away her sophomore year.

"I was so heartbroken, I almost dropped out," she said. "But I knew my mother wanted me to be the first in the family to graduate from college. So I grinded the books and was first in my class, valedictorian. I'm sorry she's not alive so I can show you off. If you'd go."

I kissed her. "I'd be honored to go."

"You're lucky to have a brother," she said.

I let that lie.

She wanted to know about my soldiering in the Great War, and I gave her a true but sanitized version.

"What's your middle name?" she asked.

I hesitated.

"Oh, come on, Gene. I told you mine was Sue. Pamela Sue."

"I like that. Well, okay. Don't laugh. Mine is Sherwood."

She only smiled. "Like Sherwood Forest, Robin Hood."

"You should have heard the ribbing I got over that in the Army."

"I love it," she said. "Eugene Sherwood Hammons."

"It was my grandmother's maiden name."

I told her how the 1918 Spanish flu killed both our parents while Don and I were overseas. They weren't much older than Don was now. It was a fluke because that influenza especially killed young people, spread overseas by American troops.

She hugged me a long time. "We're both orphans."

Had I ever been in love? I hesitated. "I thought I was, but she left me, and now I can't be sure if it was real."

"You have a good heart, Gene Hammons."

———

Early the next morning, Thursday, I got a call from Captain McGrath, summoning me to police headquarters. I reluctantly left Pamela alone in bed with my snub-nose .38 Detective Special on the table within easy reach. She fell back to sleep, exhausted. We had started off with me sleeping on the sofa. But at some point, she woke me and took me by the hand into the bedroom. The only interruption to what came next was a phone call at two a.m. I answered it, but the caller hung up. Wrong number.

"Any regrets?" I asked after I had dressed in my best summer suit.

"None at all, handsome."

"Me neither, beautiful."

For all the chaos and terror of the previous night, I felt happier than I had in years.

At 17 South First Avenue, I walked into headquarters and announced myself to the desk sergeant, a cop I didn't know.

Lefty Mofford came by in uniform and greeted me warmly. It was nice that some cops still remembered me decently. Lefty's real first name was Thurold, but he'd played baseball, pitching as a south paw for the Washington Senators.

McGrath, still the chief of detectives, came out to get me and led me back to his office. Most of the detectives weren't at their desks after the event of late last night, but I still felt curious eyes on me. I looked straight ahead, following McGrath. Even though the building was air-conditioned, he had his suit coat off, his snub-nose revolver in a holster on his belt.

"Gene, it's been too long."

I sat, feeling both at home and yet also on the other side of the gulf that opened three years earlier when I had been cut loose. The reason was ostensibly city budget cuts during the worst of the Depression, but the real cause was me speaking up for Ruth Judd, the infamous "Trunk Murderess." I knew she didn't kill and cut up those women by herself.

Jack Halloran was the accomplice if not the sole murderer. He was having affairs with three women who worked at the Grunow Clinic: Judd and her sometimes roommates Anne LeRoi and "Sammy" Samuelson. Those were the two murdered, dismembered, and stuffed in trunks taken to Union Station for Judd's trip to Los Angeles. When baggagemen found blood leaking from the trunks, Judd was arrested, extradited back to Phoenix, and convicted.

Halloran was wealthy and connected. Another man, one with surgical skill might also have been involved. I wouldn't let it go, so I was let go. The only officer laid off because of "budget cuts." Because of my bullheadedness, Halloran was tried but exonerated. Even so, he was shunned by Phoenix's elite and moved to Tucson. At least Ruth avoided the death penalty and was confined to Twenty-Fourth Street and Van Buren: the state insane asylum. She had already escaped once and probably would again. She was our local bogeyman. Parents would compel their children to bed by the threat that Winnie Ruth Judd would come for them if they refused.

McGrath lowered himself into his chair behind a desk cluttered with files. The crinkles around his eyes were deeper now. "Do you still have the badge I gave you three years ago?"

"Yes, sir." I had even brought it along in its leather case, suspecting he would want it back.

"Good." He leaned forward. "I want you to investigate the scalping last night. Maybe the killer was after your girlfriend."

Now I didn't dispute the term.

He continued. "Maybe it was this Anastasia thug I heard about. But it's entirely possible this was random, done by a lunatic who will do this again. God help us when the papers and city commissioners get the details of this. Mayor Udall is new and is focusing on the police. You know Pelham Glassford?"

The newspaper told me he'd been named police chief for ninety days to reorganize the department.

The local press didn't dwell on the fact that as chief of the District of Columbia police, he was largely responsible for the violent dispersal of the "Bonus Army," ex-vets who wanted their promised bonuses paid early. That was rich considering he was a West Point graduate and brigadier general in the Great War.

"He got a mandate to root out corruption, increase efficiency, and get results," McGrath said. "Everyone was under pressure, especially me. Glassford left and 'Brack' Morrison was named chief. But let's just say he's not my friend. That's why I need results in a hurry on this case."

I took in a deep breath. "Does that mean I'm back on the force?"

"Unfortunately, I can't make that happen, Gene." He sighed.

"Too much water under the bridge. You made too many enemies here."

I felt my face flush and looked away, feeling like a fool for even asking.

If McGrath noticed, he didn't let on. He said, "I want you to use the badge, run a parallel investigation on the side. I can pay you."

"You don't have to pay me, sir," I said, thinking I'd rather have McGrath owe me something for later should the need arise. It was distasteful to be so calculating, but I'd learned my lesson the hard way. I continued: "But why don't you trust your own people?"

This got the rise I expected. "Who says I don't, Gene?" he growled, boring those gray eyes into me that had brought many confessions from hardened criminals.

"It's implied, sir. I used to be a detective, remember?"

He smiled and the deep crinkles around his eyes reappeared. "Gene, the only thing that got in the way of your brains was your smart mouth. Anyway, you have the most experience in investigating a lust murder, which this certainly qualifies as. It became your specialty. You also know the weaknesses and blind spots of some officers."

"Yes, sir."

"Keep this on the quiet," he instructed. "Report only to me. Not a word to your brother."

"Of course. But I expect you to have my back."

He rose, squared his shoulders, and pursed his lips. "I will."

Then he passed across a file. "This is for you, carbon copies of the initial reports and detectives' notes. It's a start."

I took it.

Outside, I sat on a bench in the shade and leafed through the reports McGrath handed me, including the autopsy by the county physician. Carbon copies and photostats. The victim's name was Caroline Emma Taft, twenty-six years old, five-four, red hair, pretty—all similar to Pamela. For that matter, except for being older, she bore an eerie resemblance to the victims of the University Park Strangler. She wore a necklace with a heart attached. Her door had been jimmied. The murderer had time with her. She was hit in the eye. Her hands were tied to the headboard. Genital bruising and semen showed evidence of rape. If she was conscious, which was likely, she perhaps thought the rape would be the end of it and he'd leave.

When did she give the scream that Pamela heard? When she saw the knife that stabbed her thirty times, then scalped her? Several of the stab wounds would have killed her, but not instantly. It's possible she was alive when the killer started to scalp her. The time between Pamela's call to the police and the arrival of the first officers was seventeen minutes, add in a few more minutes for her to leave the apartment first. And he was gone. But that doesn't include the time before, he was alone with her, had her bound up.

Her boyfriend had an alibi: He was in Globe on bank business, a fact corroborated by the hotel where he was staying and his boss at Valley Bank, as well as the manager in Globe, a declining mining town east of Phoenix. He didn't return until this morning. The fingerprint dusting showed none besides Taft, her boyfriend, and landlord. The killer had been careful, wiping down surfaces, or he'd worn gloves.

As I expected, the overnight dragnet for Indians had yielded nothing. All the students at Phoenix Indian School were accounted for. Frenchy had questioned the girl's coworkers at Good Sam. She worked in the emergency room as a nurse, was known as competent and caring. No enemies. No spurned lovers. No threats from patients.

Pretty thin stuff to begin with.

As I closed the file, I saw Gus Greenbaum walking toward his office. I jaywalked and caught up with him from behind. He gave a start.

"What the hell, Hammons?"

"Tell me more about the Mad Hatter?"

"Whatayawana know?" he rattled. "He worked New York, controlled the Longshoremen, did some work with Lansky long after I left. I never knew the cat. He was indicted for murder at least twice, but the witnesses disappeared."

"Funny thing, that."

His flat eyes looked beyond me. "Lucky Luciano put him in charge of the Syndicate's muscle, Murder Incorporated. Contract killers. They've probably committed thousands of murders."

"How does he kill people?"

"He usually orders the hit. If not, he uses a gat or an ice pick. Look, Hammons, this is what I've heard. I'm a..."

"Businessman, right. I know. What about scalping?"

Greenbaum winced. "You mean like Indians?"

I nodded.

He involuntarily ran a big paw over his thinning hair. "I've never heard of a mob hit that involved scalping. Anyway, Anastasia doesn't like blood, and scalping would mean lots of blood, right?" A hitman who didn't like blood. I'd heard of stranger things. "Why do you ask?"

"A woman got scalped last night." I gave him a few details.

The news knocked him off-kilter for a few seconds, then he flicked his eyes at me and focused hard.

"That sounds like a lust murder, Hammons. Your area of knowledge, right? Before you got kicked off the force. Hitmen are cool characters. Otherwise, they're not trustworthy. They do the job quickly and get out. It's nothing personal. What you're talking about sounds very personal, a frenzy."

Back at my apartment, I fetched Pamela and a passionate kiss. We went back to her place and packed suitcases. She suppressed a shiver when she saw the Phoenix Police seal covering Caroline Taft's front door. I could see how a crowbar or other tool had slipped open the lock.

"Do you have your pistol?" I asked.

She opened her purse and showed me.

"Put on some slacks and sturdy shoes. And do you have some empty bottles?"

She pointed to a bag of them in her kitchen.

"Excellent. We're going for target practice."

Thirteen

After buying extra ammunition, we drove across the river again and through south Phoenix. I took a dirt road that led us all the way into the mountains, where a sturdy outcropping of granite provided a safe backstop. To her kit she had added a smart straw hat with a bright red band.

"Walk heavy," I instructed.

"Why?"

"So the rattlesnakes can feel you coming and get out of the way."

She gently punched my arm. "You picked a great place for our first date, Gene. I'm afraid of snakes."

"They're afraid of you, too."

We hiked fifteen yards and set up the bottles, about five feet apart. Then we walked back to a level spot. I took her revolver and inspected it. Then I laid out the basics. It was a snub-nosed Colt Detective Special, same as I owned. Chambered for six .38 special rounds. Here's how you swing out the cylinder, reload, and swing it back. Here's the firing pin. It's a double-action revolver, so you don't have to cock it. Just pull the trigger. Here's how to hold it and line up the sight.

Never point a gun at someone unless you intend to shoot him. I handed it back. "Have a try."

She pulled the trigger and a small geyser of dirt rose behind the bottle.

"Damn!"

"Here." I aligned her feet, one straight in front of her and the other turned at a ninety-degree angle behind her for best balance. I inhaled her fresh scent, sweeter than any perfume. "Now, align the sight but aim a little low. Trust me. Then, take in a breath and as you let it out, pull the trigger."

This time she hit the middle bottle straight on, shattering it.

"It worked!" She expended four more rounds and demolished four more bottles.

Of course, a real-life situation would be harder. It might be dark. The bad guy would be shooting back. Your adrenaline would be shooting to the moon.

Here, the sun was beating down on us. But I made her run in place for thirty seconds and try a shot. It went wild to the left. Again. This time she took a bottle at the neck. Overall, she did well. We'd have time for more challenging shooting. And I needed to teach her how to clean and oil the gun to keep it in good working order.

Driving back, Pamela pointed to some shacks off Baseline Road.

"Those are for migrant cotton pickers," I said. "They'll be empty until the harvest this fall."

I instantly slowed and turned the car around, stopping.

She read my mind. "A good place to hide."

I slipped off my sunglasses, pulled binoculars from the back seat and looked the place over. The camp was made up of a dozen wooden shanties, outhouses, and a water tank perched precariously on stilts holding a metal tower in the middle. All the structures were barely standing, and the place reeked of despair. Only one car was parked by the nearest shack, an ancient Ford Model T with bald tires and an Oklahoma tag tilting off the rear bumper. Two dirty, blond children, a boy and a girl, played in the dirt nearby. It was a reminder that however much the economy had improved under the New Deal, plenty of people were still suffering.

I stopped behind the Model T and shut off the engine. A thin, sunburned woman in a homespun dress emerged, pushing aside the door. It lacked hinges or a doorknob. She might have been thirty years old, but her face was cratered with lines caused by worry, tragedy, and manual labor.

"Police." I flashed my buzzer.

"We're not trespassing or gas moochers," she drawled. "We were picking grapefruit and the landowner said we could stay here a few days before moving on to California."

"Not a problem," I said. "Is anyone else in these houses?" I used the term loosely, as the shanties looked as if a strong dust storm could blow them down.

She hesitated, shook her head.

"Where are you from in Oklahoma?" Pamela asked.

"Cimarron County," she said. "It's at the west end of the Oklahoma Panhandle. Dust Bowl hit us hard. Bank foreclosed on our farm. We've been working our way west to California. My husband died in Gallup, New Mexico, and since then we've been on our own. I taught school in Boise City while he worked our land." She pronounced it Boyz, not like the capital of Idaho. "But nobody wants to hire an Okie teacher."

"I trained as a teacher, too," Pamela said. "And who are these cuties?"

"This is James, named after his father," she said. "And this is Mary."

Pamela knelt and shook their little hands. "My name is Pamela, and this is Gene." She nodded toward me.

"Well," I said, touched by how easily Pamela had charmed the children, "we'll leave you be." I whipped out a couple of twenties and held them out. "Maybe this will help."

She hesitated then snatched them.

"Just one more thing," I said. "You're sure you've been out here alone."

I waited while she made up her mind. Then: "There was a man. He was in that cabin." She pointed at one fifty feet away. "He didn't look like he belonged here. He was well dressed."

Alarms went off inside me. I glanced at Pamela. "Is he here now?"

She shook her head. "He comes and goes. Drives a new Buick Roadmaster, black."

I wondered: Could it be this easy? I showed her the Anastasia photo. She said she couldn't be sure. She had never seen him close up. "He certainly wasn't neighborly."

"When did you last see him?"

She furrowed her brow. "I'd say two days ago."

The day after Caroline Taft's murder.

We thanked them, said goodbye, and walked to the cabin the woman had identified. I took off Pamela's hat and walked it back to my Ford, tossing it in.

"I don't want you to be an easy target with that red band."

No Roadmaster was visible. This shanty was more substantial with doors in front and back, held by new hinges. I told Pamela to walk to the backside corner in case someone tried to escape that way.

"If you have to shoot, aim low," I said. "A bullet could come straight through that wood."

She gave me a worried look. I squeezed her shoulder and

nodded for her to take her position. Then I sucked in a sharp breath and drew the .45 from its shoulder holster.

Kneeling low, I pulled at the hole in the door that substituted for a knob. It creaked five inches open.

"Phoenix Police," I called. "Come out with your hands up!"

Not a sound. I pushed the door until it swung fully open. Then I stepped in and traversed the room with my pistol. Empty. I called Pamela and she joined me inside.

The only light came from the open doors. The room was maybe eight feet in each direction. A cot with a pillow and blanket sat on the floor. A chair sat flush against a wooden table where an ashtray was filled with butts and a kerosine lamp was half full. No closet or clothes.

"Oh, my God!" Pamela whispered. Then I saw it.

A mane of red hair was nailed to the wall like a devilish work of art—or a trophy. I pulled out my penknife and carefully examined it: blood and skin on the other side. On a nail below it hung a simple silver necklace with a heart attached. Another trophy.

Pamela kept her distance. "The Mad Hatter?" she asked.

I shook my head. "Based on my conversation with Greenbaum this morning, we have another killer at work, and he'll kill again. I've been hired to track him down."

"We've been hired," she said.

It was time to find a phone and report to Captain McGrath.

Fourteen

Pamela directed me to the best parking on the campus of Arizona State Teachers College in Tempe. It looked much the same as when I first met her there three years before.

"Take you back?" I asked as we walked across the shady campus.

"It does," she said, "but I can't say I miss it. Here we are."

She pointed to a building marked SCIENCE HALL. We stepped inside, grateful for the air-conditioning.

It was almost the end of the semester, so we were lucky to find Professor Horace Scott in his office, between classes.

He remembered Pamela. She introduced me, and they made small talk. He was tall and slender, balding with reading glasses that slumped to the tip of his nose. His specialty was anthropology.

"We're investigating a murder that involves scalping," I said. "Pamela said you might be of assistance."

"A scalping now?"

I nodded.

His eyes widened. "Well, scalping is an ancient practice," he said, steadying his voice. "There's evidence of it all over the world going back centuries. In America, it was common among Indians, particularly among the Plains tribes in intertribal conflicts as well as against Whites."

"Counting coup?" I asked, using an expression I thought I understood as the same as taking a scalp. I was wrong.

"No, counting coup is getting close enough to strike an enemy."

I stood corrected.

He continued, "But it wasn't confined to Indians. Early colonies offered bounties for the heads of warriors, then just their scalps."

"What about modern times?"

"I assume you already know about the Butcher of Hanover or the Vampire of Hanover in Germany?"

I felt foolish but admitted I hadn't heard of him.

"Fritz Haarmann," he said. "He was found guilty of twenty-four murders of boys and young men in 1924. His methods involved rape, torture, mutilation, and dismemberment. This included scalping. He probably killed more, stalking from at least 1918. He went to the guillotine in 1925."

Pamela took notes while I took it all in.

"How would someone scalp another person?"

"It's fairly easy once the victim is subdued," the professor said. He pantomimed. "Grasp the hair, make several quick cuts in a semicircle on either side of the scalp, yank hard. It separates from the skull along the connective tissue. It's not necessarily fatal. I know of a woman in Mesa who was scalped as a baby in a Comanche attack on the Texas frontier. She wore a wig for the rest of her life."

We walked back to the car in silence, and I took stock. McGrath told me he would arrange surveillance of the cotton-pickers' camp. It gave me morbid comfort that the murder might well have been random and not aimed at Pamela. Still, the killer was out there and might kill again. It was a good chance he had stalked Caroline Taft. We would need to talk to her coworkers, covering the same ground as the PPD detectives, looking for any sign that someone had been after her before the attack.

I brooded over Fritz Haarmann, "the Butcher of Hanover," and how I could have missed this case. I would need to research this one.

And none of it got us closer to the Mad Hatter. He was out there, too.

"I want to check with my answering service," Pamela said, stopping at a pay phone.

"Answering service?"

Her green eyes sparkled. "You don't have one? Come into the twentieth century, Gene. How else can clients contact you whenever they need to?"

She fed a coin in and talked. Then she made a second call. When she hung up, she said Helen Lincoln had received a second blackmail letter.

"We really don't need this distraction," I said.

"Don't pout, Gene." She took my hand. "We can walk and chew gum at the same time."

"Tell me that when another girl gets scalped."

———

We drove north out of Tempe across the three-year-old Mill Avenue Bridge and up to the Lincoln place. This time the door was opened by an attractive middle-aged woman with her long blond hair pulled back. She introduced herself as Louise Lincoln Kerr.

"Please have a seat," she said. "Helen is upstairs."

"You were playing the piano when we were here before," I said. "Beautiful."

She smiled and shook her head. "You're very generous. The violin and viola are my main instruments."

"And you're a composer," Pamela said.

"I try to be." She lit a cigarette in an ivory holder. Her face turned serious. "We received another letter."

At that moment, Helen Lincoln joined us, and the Mexican maid served lemonade.

"Thank you for coming so quickly," she said. Then she handed Pamela a letter. Pamela scanned it and passed it to me. It read:

Lincolns. Are you related to Honest Abe? Because we know you haven't been honest about the bullion. Deliver the money to Union Station on Saturday night. Fifty thousand in unmarked twenties in a dark hatbox with an unmarked white luggage tag. Be there at 7 p.m., sit on the bench nearest the newsstand and put the hatbox on the floor. Then walk away and leave the station. Remember, we're watching you. Not all the time, but you'll never know when. If you go to the police, we'll release the scandal information to the newspapers. You will be ruined.

The address on the envelope was typed, too. It could be dusted for prints. We could also match the keyboard strikes on the note to the typewriter if we ever caught the letter-writer. But I was thinking like a policeman, not a paid courier.

Nobody spoke for several minutes. I played it out in my mind. The blackmailers were clever, not least in choosing a gullible mark. They offered nothing in return for the money. That meant they would be back again soon, demanding more money.

But there was no way to contact them, negotiate, demand a quid pro quo. They chose a busy place for the handoff, with plenty of ways in and out. With the police, we could swarm the station with undercover officers. But without them, it was only Pamela and me. It was beyond foolish for the Lincolns to give in. And in the back of all this was the image of the girl's scalp hanging on a nail and when the killer might strike again.

Helen said, "I'll get the money. I have a hatbox. Will you deliver it?" She was focused on Pamela, ignoring me.

I started to try again to talk her out of it, but Pamela beat me to the punch.

She said, "Of course. I'll come by at six on Saturday evening and pick it up."

Fifteen

The rest of the week unspooled quietly. Sure enough, the fact that Caroline Taft had been scalped had been withheld from the press. So stories in the *Arizona Republic* and *Phoenix Gazette* only reported that a nurse had been stabbed to death. A suspect was at large. "Police are baffled," the stories said. We weren't baffled, but the killer was ahead of us, clever and dangerous.

Captain McGrath and I had lunch at the Hotel Adams coffee shop, which also served as the unofficial meeting place of the state legislature. As I suspected, the surveillance stakeout of the shanty village had yielded nothing. But he had news.

"Two other murders are similar to Caroline Taft's," he said. "Last year, a twenty-year-old student nurse was murdered in El Paso. She was raped, stabbed to death, including wounds to the head. The MO matches a case from 1933 in Little Rock, Arkansas. The victim was a young nurse. Her hair was torn off."

"Not quite scalped," I said, "but maybe he's evolving."

"That's a distinct possibility." He slid across a file with carbon copies of the police reports from El Paso and Little Rock.

I let out a long breath. "He's working his way west."

"Looks that way," McGrath said. "More cases might show up. I'll keep you in the loop."

The only relief I felt was that the killer hadn't targeted Pamela. Without her permission, I told him the latest on the Lincoln blackmail plot. He listened through fingers folded "this-is-the-church-this-is-the-steeple" style. Then he asked how we intended to play it. I told him.

"You know they'll be back," he said. "Blackmailers always are. Unless the victims murder them. I've seen that happen more than once."

"I've tried to convince them. But they're determined to pay."

I felt the need to say the Lincolns were incapable of murder.

"Of course not," he said. "These are important people to the city's future. Keep them satisfied; you're doing all you can."

At the Carnegie Public Library on Washington Street, I learned more about Friedrich Heinrich Karl "Fritz" Haarmann, the "Butcher of Hanover." Kodak had developed an ingenious product that filmed and published the *New York Times* on 35-millimeter "microfilm." I used a reader machine to learn about his trial and background.

As a child, Haarmann was quiet and kept to himself—how many times had I heard that of murderers, more so as adults? It was the same with Emil Gorman, the University Park Strangler. Usually, they tortured and killed pets, too. Haarmann committed his first known offense at age sixteen, molesting young boys. He was confined to an insane asylum as "incurable deranged," yet escaped to Switzerland. This was in 1898. A year later, he returned to Hanover, a city in northern Germany. He served in the army but was discharged for mental issues. Worked for, and fought with, his father. Then he settled into life as a petty criminal. He also became a police informant.

After the Great War, he began his known career as a

murderer, preying on young male runaways, train commuters, and prostitutes. They were raped and strangled, sometimes given what he called his "love bite," biting completely through the victims' tracheas and Adam's apples. Many were stabbed, dismembered, and beheaded. Some victims were scalped with a small kitchen knife.

Had Haarmann not been executed in 1925, I would think he might be loose in Phoenix, or he might have inspired the killing this week by a copycat. But as I walked out of the library into the sunlight, I realized it was a stretch. Caroline was a woman, not a young man. That was only one of the many differences.

But to be sure, back at the office, I phoned Goodyear and spoke with Samuel Herzfeld, the German Jewish emigree I met at the barber shop. I recalled that he came from Hanover.

"I remember that time well," he said in accented English. "It was a time of great fear. They also called him the Vampire of Hanover or the Wolf Man. Did you know he also claimed to be a grave robber?"

"I didn't."

"In May 1924, as I recall, some children playing by the river found a human skull. Back in those days, Berlin's Kripo—the criminal police—had the finest homicide detectives in the world, led by a Jew, by the way. Hanover wasn't as lucky, so the police wondered if it had been left by grave robbers or even as a prank by medical students. But more skulls turned up on the riverbank, all severed with a sharp instrument. At least one had been scalped. I hope I'm not boring you."

"Not at all."

"He prowled the central railway station looking for young men." He sighed. "The Weimar Republic had much to recommend it. Not least being a democracy. But it produced some—what's the word?—lurid killers. Peter Kürten was another, in Dusseldorf. The newspapers called him the Dusseldorf Monster, the Vampire of Dusseldorf."

"Teenage boys again?"

"No," Herzfeld said. "He killed women and men, stabbing and strangling. Mostly women. It's how he reached climax."

This was a characteristic of a lust killer.

"He raped a servant girl and beat her to death with a hammer. Awful, simply awful. Kürten was executed in 1931. He had a Hitler mustache. Haarmann, too. Isn't that funny?"

He didn't laugh.

After he hung up, I began my interviews with people who knew Caroline Taft. The boyfriend was first. I met him at the bank. He looked and reacted like a square john banker, which didn't mean anything, of course. Looks often deceived. Unfortunately, solid alibis didn't, and he had one. He seemed genuinely broken up about her murder.

"I've already been through all this with the police," he said, a statement I expected to hear again and again. "I even talked to a Detective Hammons."

"That's my brother." I lit us each a cigarette and a few puffs seemed to calm him down. "I want to go over things again. How long had you dated?"

"Two years," he said. "I gave her a necklace with a heart. I was going to ask her to marry me…"

This led to another crying jag. I handed him my handkerchief and let the grief machine run down.

Then I asked the usual: "Did she have any enemies, anyone make a threat, any patients she treated who might be stalkers, Peeping Toms, violent?" All the answers were negative.

"What about before the two of you got together?"

I let the question hang to see if he would pick it up. And he did.

"She had a boyfriend before me. He didn't treat her well. Had a temper. Slapped her more than once when they argued. So she broke up with him."

"When was that?"

"Soon before we got together. We never even had a disagreement, much less an argument. I was taught never to hit a woman."

I asked if he had a name for the former boyfriend. He did: Bill Sherman.

"He delivered milk," he said. "They knew each other in high school. I only saw him once when we came out of the Fox Theater, maybe six months ago. He came up and wanted to know who I was and whether I was Caroline's new boyfriend. We tried to go around him, and he shoved me to the sidewalk."

I wrote all this down.

"Did you tell my brother about this?"

He handed back the handkerchief and shook his head. "He didn't ask."

———

On Saturday afternoon, Pamela and I strategized in her office. Located on the sixth floor of the Heard Building a little north on Central from Adams Street. It was also home to the *Arizona Republic* and *Phoenix Gazette*, plus KTAR radio, with tall towers on the roof with the station's initials in neon. It was air-conditioned and on weekdays had an elevator operator, a friendly ancient Negro man named Paul.

Across the street was the Hotel Adams. If we didn't need reminding that the blackmailer had chosen the railroad station for the handoff, the Santa Fe Railway ticket office was on the corner at Adams and the Southern Pacific's ticket office was on the first floor of the hotel across the street. And a green Railway Express Agency truck was parked at Vic Hanny's men's store, making a delivery.

Even on the weekend, Central was busy with traffic. Commerce was everywhere around the intersection, and shoppers walked the sidewalks under awnings. It was an alarming contrast to the bleak cotton-pickers' camp.

I told Pamela how the bad guy—or bad guys—had made a smart play. Southern Pacific's eastbound *Apache* passenger train was due a few minutes before seven, headed for Chicago. At 7:05 p.m., the westbound *Golden State Limited* would arrive on the way to Los Angeles. Both stops were scheduled to last ten minutes. This offered a quick escape out of town on either train. On the other hand, the person who snatches the hatbox could walk out and get in a car or taxi.

"You want to follow him," Pamela said.

I nodded.

"Ideally, I'd follow him to see if he takes the money to a handoff with another blackmailer," I said. "Then I can nab them both."

She lit a snipe and blew smoke rings. "It's risky, Gene. We're only supposed to be couriers. If something goes wrong, the blackmailers will follow through on their threats."

"So what?"

"'So what' is this isn't how we should treat clients. We're partners now. In fact, you should move in here with me. There's plenty of room for another desk. Anyway, I don't want us to be responsible for the Lincolns being ruined by these allegations."

"The allegations are bogus," I said. "Unless they're not telling us the whole story…"

I let that float inside her smoke rings as she considered it.

"Are you always suspicious of clients?" she asked.

"Always. Remember the part of the latest note about them not being honest like Honest Abe? What does that mean? Maybe they really did use bullion to finance the Camelback Inn."

"You're serious?"

I held out my hands, empty.

"I don't know," I said. "But something about this case stinks. My brother ran the names of their partners, and all came back with clean records. All upstanding citizens. But that's what people thought about Jack Halloran in the early stages of the Winnie Ruth Judd case. An upstanding, prominent citizen. Yet as time went on and details accumulated, he appeared more and more guilty of something, even though he was acquitted. I gathered plenty of evidence against him—it ended up costing me my damned job. But the prosecutor wouldn't push it. This made me forever suspicious of clients."

"I don't believe that about the Lincolns. Not for a minute."

"I don't want to either," I said. "But we need to be prepared for anything tonight."

Sixteen

While Pamela drove out to the Lincoln place for the hatbox full of money, I went to Union Station and hung out. It reminded me of my days on the Hat Squad, when the detectives would watch who got off the trains. More than once, we caught a criminal on the run. More often than that, we questioned a suspicious-looking passenger stepping onto the platform. If he didn't have the right answers—*Why are you in Phoenix? What job do you have?*—we escorted them back onto the train. It helped give Phoenix a reputation. We were not to be messed with. Beware the Hat Squad.

But none were here now, although as I expected, the place was busy. Out front, blue-and-white U.S. Mail and green Railway Express Agency trucks with advertisements on the sides were backed into the long express section on the west end of the station. Most of the sliding doors were closed at this time of the evening, but a couple of them were raised as expressmen wrestled cargo to or from the trucks. Two additional mail trucks pulled in, presumably bringing letters and parcels to go out on the arriving trains and pick up mail bags the trains delivered.

Trackside, just inside the arches to the waiting room, the

schedule board was marked with both trains on time. Fifty feet south, a freight slowly rumbled along the bypass track that separated these trains from the passenger tracks trailing smoke from the big locomotive. It sounded two long and a short whistle to warn cars on Third Avenue, then Seventh Avenue. The headlight of the eastbound *Apache*'s locomotive was emerging from the west.

The oncoming sunset painted the western sky deep, burning orange with an echo of pink to the east, all intermingled with the exhaust of the locomotives. For just a moment, I let my mind wander to my father, a veteran Espee conductor, with blond hair and blue eyes like mine. And mother, with raven black hair—Don got his hair from her, but not so dark. When they died from the Spanish flu while we were overseas in the Great War, Don and I were notified by letters from neighbors that arrived weeks after they were in the ground. I missed them desperately, still. I felt guilty that they were dead from a flu carried by the war, and we weren't here for them. It was irrational, sure. But human.

On the east side of the station, passengers sat on benches of the open-air waiting area, catching a breeze through the arches as the warm day cooled down. I lit a cigarette and pretended to read a newspaper as I scanned the two dozen or so people. Families, mostly. A middle-aged traveling salesman lugging a heavy suitcase. Red caps handled luggage for most passengers.

A young tough with no suitcase leaned against a pillar, his left leg crooked and foot casually propping himself against the stucco pillar, smoking. In Hat Squad days, I would have pulled him aside and braced him, looking for weapons or wallets he'd lifted from unsuspecting passengers. Tonight, I only cataloged him in my memory: slicked dark hair, medium height, open-collar shirt, jittery.

Past the dispatcher's office with TRAINMEN ONLY engraved on the glass door, I walked around front again and through one of the three sets of double doors. My watch read 6:55.

Pamela was right on time, wearing white slacks, high-fitted at the waist, and a short-sleeved blouse. At my suggestion, she wore a blue beret so I could easily notice her in a crowd.

The hat box was no cardboard job from the Boston Store but an expensive piece of leather luggage, a rich dark brown. A white luggage tag was attached. She sat on a bench near the newsstand and snack bar on the east end of the high-ceilinged waiting room.

On the west end of the big room, people lined up at the ticket counter. In between, the benches were crowded with travelers.

She held onto the hat box until the clock hit seven and the stationmaster began to announce the trains. Then she stood and walked away, the hat box sitting on the floor beside the bench. I kept my eye on the box, where it sat unattended for maybe five minutes. Then it was gone. I scanned the crowd and saw it in the hands of the tough who had been standing outside.

The public address boomed: *"This is your final call for Southern Pacific's Apache. All aboard on track two for all points east, Tucson, El Paso, Tucumcari, Kansas City, and Chicago. All aboard."*

"Now arriving on track three, Southern Pacific Train Four, the Golden State Limited, for Los Angeles, via Yuma and Indio. Passengers holding tickets for the Golden State Limited, please proceed to track three."

People moved toward the three sets of double doors that led to the tracks, holding hats, purses, and suitcases.

But the man with the hat box wasn't among them. My pulse jacked up as I tried to see him.

There: He wasn't going for a train or the front doors to the street. He was walking past the ticket counter through doors that led into the baggage-express rooms. I pushed past a family waving to arriving passengers, provoking a protest. I ignored them and slammed through the swinging doors.

I heard Pamela's admonition in my head: We're only couriers. We've done our job.

The blackmail money was handed off.

I was not admonished. The heavy doors closed behind me, and it took a few seconds for my eyes to adjust. The baggage-express-mail wing of the depot was about two blocks long, lit unevenly by hanging fixtures. Workers pushed and pulled dark-green baggage carts toward trackside. Through the open roll-up doors, I could see the cars of the *Golden State*. Suddenly, I was blinded by the headlights of a small tractor towing carts laden with mail and express. Then, maybe fifty feet ahead, I saw the man lugging the hat box. Nobody challenged either of us. They were on a schedule.

He slowed and glanced behind him. I hung back and knelt below a stack of mail bags, took off my hat and gingerly looked toward him. He couldn't see me in the relative darkness where I hid.

At that moment, he met another man, well dressed in a dark suit. The handoff was seamless, and the well-dressed man slipped through an open door, heading to the street. The sliding door nearest me was closed. I yanked it, but it was locked down.

"Hey buddy." I turned and saw the first man, the younger one who first snatched the hat box. He smiled, several teeth missing. "Looking for something?"

At that second, I saw a dark object heading toward my face. A slender pipe, maybe. There was only time for quick reaction. I raised my left forearm and let it absorb the blow. Then I had my blackjack out, swinging it hard against his other arm, connecting with the elbow squarely enough that it made a distinct crunching sound.

"Ah! You bastard!" He dropped the pipe.

A click and a flash caught my eye. Switchblade.

A second swing of the leather sap connected with his left knee, dropping him sideways, then a third swing, carefully aimed and timed, hit his temple. He fell as if a trapdoor had opened under him. Years of experience taught me how to use the sap in a way that stopped a man without killing him. He was now facedown on the dusty concrete floor. I rifled his pockets and took his wallet. I confiscated the switchblade, too.

Then I ran toward the door that led me out to the street.

But the expensive hat box, its more expensive contents, and its dapper carrier were gone.

So was Pamela.

—

I ran back into the waiting room, which was now nearly deserted. Another passenger train wasn't due for several hours. I scanned the room. No woman with red hair and a blue beret. The newsstand operator had no memory of her. I dashed out to the parking lot, dark except for a few streetlights, seeing no sign of her car.

But, in a bit of inspiration, I went back inside and closed myself in a phone booth. I called her answering service, identified myself as her partner, and sure enough she had left a message for me. It directed me to an address on west Van Buren Street, several blocks past the Santa Fe Railway tracks.

Her car was parked a block away. She flashed her headlights, and I pulled in behind her, then climbed into her car.

"What happened to being a courier?"

She shrugged. "I couldn't find you, but when I went to the car, I saw a man carrying the hatbox. He got in a car. I followed him. He parked over there and went into one of the cottages."

I scoped out the sign for Pickwick Gables. The cottages were laid out as duplexes, with mature shade trees and grass in front, framed by hedges.

"That one," Pamela pointed to the cottage nearest the road. It had chairs on the porch and the lights were on inside.

"There were two," I said. "A young man who ran into the baggage room. He made the handoff, then attacked me with a pipe. I took him down with my blackjack." I showed her the leather-covered sap, nine inches long, with a heavy piece of metal inside and a strap for me to securely hold it.

"Ouch!"

"Better than shooting him. I took his wallet and this." I flicked open the switchblade.

"He came prepared."

"Me, too." I opened the black wallet. It contained twenty dollars, a sawbuck, and singles. No identification. A piece of paper with the address to the Pickwick Gables scrawled in handwriting. Another with directions to the Lincoln place. And a business card. I ran my thumb across it and wondered.

After a few minutes, she asked to see the knife.

I pressed the button in the middle of the handle and the four-inch blade swung out.

She used a penlight to examine it.

"Gene, it has blood on it."

Again, I thought: Could it be this easy? This was an ideal blade to make the cuts on Caroline's scalp before pulling off her hair. I was getting ahead of myself. The blood could have come from a fight—or another murder disconnected from our case. It wasn't necessarily the weapon used on Caroline. We still had the abusive boyfriend to check out.

"How should we play it?" she asked.

I smiled. "I thought we were only couriers?"

"Hypothetically."

I again showed her the growing bruise on my forearm where the pipe had struck me. Add that to my black eye and the knot on the back of my head, and I was growing impatient.

"Well, hypothetically, we could break down the door and pistol-whip the hell out of them. Find the incriminating information they have on the Lincolns, if they have any, which I doubt. Take it and either threaten them with death if they ever came back or turn them over to the cops."

"The subtle approach," she laughed. "Hypothetically."

"Hypothetically." I looked at the lighted room again and scanned our surroundings to make sure no one was watching us or sneaking up from behind. All clear.

I asked her how she thought we should proceed.

"I think we should fulfill our promise to the clients," she said. "They asked us to deliver the money and we did. We'll collect our fee and be gone. Meanwhile, we know where the blackmailers are."

I handed her the business card from the tough's wallet. "Do you know this guy?"

She read aloud. "Walter Humphrey, Attorney at Law. No. I do work as an investigator for lawyers, but never this one. You?"

"Unfortunately, I do," I said. "He defended Jack Sullivan, the young man who was convicted of murdering the railroad bull in southern Arizona. He was executed in the gas chamber earlier this month. I was there."

She stroked my face. I leaned into her soothing touch. "Was it as bad as it sounds?"

I nodded.

"And this Humphrey hired you?"

"No," I said. "His mother hired me to find him before the police did. She was afraid they'd gun him down. So, I did. But the trial went against him. She couldn't bear to see her son put to death, so she said goodbye to him, and I took her to the train. I was a witness at the execution on her behalf."

"Did he do it?"

"That's the thing. When they were strapping him in the gas chamber, he thanked his lawyer. Humphrey wasn't there. But the last thing he said was that he didn't get a fair trial. That stuck with me. If Humphrey had hired me, I would have dug much deeper. He didn't hire an investigator at all. 'Reasonable doubt' is what a defense attorney wants to present before a jury. I might have been able to find some. The other people pilfering the box-cars all testified against Jack Sullivan, but I bet they all had police records. They were trying to save their own skins from being charged as accessories to murder. One of them might have been the real killer. At the least, they were unreliable witnesses. But Humphrey never brought this up at trial. He never asked for my help, and I didn't volunteer it. I was trying to hold the mother together through all this."

"You can't blame yourself, Gene."

"Jack's brother vowed to kill me." I shook my head, more out of exhaustion than bravado. "Between the Mad Hatter, whoever ambushed me in my office, the guy who took a shot at me outside the poker game, the scalper… Get in line."

"You need pie," she said. "And a movie. Fred Astaire and Ginger Rogers are playing at the Rialto. We can sit in the cool and make out."

I kissed her. "That's the best idea I've heard all day."

Seventeen

On Sunday, Pamela went with me to church. Afterward, she told me how beautiful the choir was and how she could pick out my rich baritone. She had been raised a Methodist but hadn't been to church in years. This made her want to return.

We walked down Central, holding hands.

"Did the war make you question your faith?" she asked. "Or your time as a policeman? How could God allow such violence against innocent people?"

"They say there are no atheists in foxholes," I said. "But that hasn't been my experience. My brother lost his faith for just the reason you describe, especially the Great War and losing our parents to influenza."

"And you?"

I lit a cigarette and handed it to her, then one for me. "I don't judge. I'm not a better person than my brother. Faith is a gift. I kept mine. The war strengthened mine. And I love to sing in the choir."

She took my hand again. "I'm glad."

We crossed the street and enjoyed brunch at the Hotel Westward Ho.

That afternoon, while Pamela reported to the Lincolns, I turned my attention back to the Caroline Taft murder. I found Don where I expected. Where I feared I would find him. He was in a basement of Chinatown, beneath a small grocery on Second Street and Jackson. This was the heart of the Deuce, Phoenix's skid row.

I paid a bribe to the Chinaman behind the counter, and he allowed me to descend the dark stairway, then walk through a narrow hallway all made of aging bricks and adobe. These tunnels were older than statehood and cooler in hot weather. At six-foot-two, I had to bend down to make it. The passage opened onto a larger room. I could smell the opium before I stepped inside.

My brother was half falling out of an armchair, a pipe in his mouth. His suit coat was off and tie undone. He was alone in the room. It was Sunday. Anyway, who wanted to be smoking opium with a policeman? Bleary eyes aimed at me with little reaction.

Then: "What are you doing here, Gene?"

"Looking for you. I knew you wouldn't be spending Sunday with your family."

"Dottie and I fought, and she kicked me out."

I sighed. "You said you'd kicked the pipe, but obviously that was a lie."

"I've got a piece of Kraut shrapnel in my side. I hurt all the time. The shell killed five men in my platoon. Boys I was responsible for, and I let them down!"

"From an artillery shell? That's not your fault, Don. Your valor resulted in being decorated with the Silver Star and Purple Heart."

"Pawned them."

I knew that. I also went to the pawn shop and bought them

back, along with the citations for his bravery and leadership. For now, they sat in a cushioned box with my Purple Heart and identification card as a member of the American Expeditionary Forces, with a photo of me looking impossibly young in a high-collar uniform. We also had our Victory Medals with multiple battle clasps. If Don were ever sober again, I would return them to him so he could pass them on to his children.

"You were decorated by Pershing himself."

He started to yell at me, but I held out a finger.

"Don't. I fought in the same damned war."

"Yeah, the 'War to End All Wars.' How's that working out?" He momentarily focused. "Italy's conquered Ethiopia, China, and Japan. Hitler's marched troops into the Rhineland, same place we were stationed after the war, in violation of the peace treaty. The Frogs didn't do a damned thing to stop him. Big words, then they backed down. You watch…"

"I know, Hitler's going to start a war."

"You're damned right. We should never have let Germany survive the Great War intact. Belgium and a swath of France were ruined, but Germany was untouched. To hell with the armistice. We should have kept going and shelled their cities, leveled them—make them pay the price for starting the war and never forget. Never have the ability to start another one! But Black Jack Pershing and the Limeys and the Frogs wouldn't do it. Woodrow Wilson was a fool. Now, we'll pay the price, and the Japs are going to jump on us, too. MacArthur is trying to build the Filipinos into an army, but that won't work out."

I let him run on. How Roosevelt had signed a bill to expand the Army to 165,000, but it was way smaller than what we'd need. How three years ago U.S. Navy carriers had success-fully carried out a mock bombing attack on the battleships at Pearl Harbor in Hawaii. He was remarkably well-informed and, when he wanted to be, highly functional, for a gowed-up dope fiend.

Finally, I said, "That doesn't mean you need to be slowly killing yourself with opium."

"The doctors couldn't get all the fragments out of me. They gave me morphine. Stop badgering me! I'm hurting!"

Sober, he might have taken a swing at me. But he remained slumped, nursing the pipe.

I lit a cigarette to cut the pervasive smell of opium. "You've got a wife and two boys who need you."

He sullenly stared at the wall.

"Why the hell aren't you working on the Caroline Taft murder?"

He shook his head. "We're not getting anywhere. I'd be happy for Navarre to be the primary and Woodward and Littlefield helping."

"Frenchy is busy with the vice squad." I chuckled. "So you're the primary."

He shrugged. "McGrath had us watch a farmworkers' camp beside Baseline Road. Inside one shack was her hair and necklace. Don't know where he got that tip. But we spent three days watching, and the killer never came back. After that, it's been dead end after dead end." He inhaled deeply. After holding the opium in his lungs for what seemed a couple of minutes, he let it out and coughed. He and the other detectives didn't know about Bill Sherman, the former boyfriend. Possessive and violent, Sherman had motive, means, and opportunity.

"What does this matter to you?" he said. "This is police business."

"A client hired me to look into it," I lied.

"Well, Marley can go to hell," he said. "I'm surprised you still take his money."

I kept my expression neutral, not that he would have noticed. But my brain cells screamed, *Kemper Marley!* Now I had to decide how to play it.

I said, "How did you know?"

"Because we know he was pitching woo with the nurse. Her twit boyfriend didn't know. Given Marley's temper and violent past, we're looking at him as a possible suspect. Maybe she tried to break it off or threatened to tell his wife. So, he offed her and made it look like a lust killer. If I were you, I'd refund his money and stay clear. Knowing Marley, he could find a way to pin it on you, make you an accessory. He's got plenty of pull in this town, and you've got none."

I stubbed out my nail and changed the subject.

"What do you know about Walter Humphrey?"

"The lawyer? Not much. Didn't he defend Jack Sullivan?"

I nodded.

"Cop killer. The gas chamber was too good for him. I hope he died hard."

I let that pass. "Is that the kind of case he takes?"

"Fuck, I don't know, Gene. He's a criminal defense lawyer who does a share of pro bono work for the county Superior Court. Also practices some water and real-estate law. Why do you care?"

"I found his business card in the wallet of a goon who came at me with a switchblade. I dropped him with my blackjack."

"I would have shot him," Don said.

"That would have required more explaining if I'd have done it."

He took another long hit on the pipe.

"You're too sentimental, little brother. Still going to church. Don't get trapped by this little chippie you're seeing."

"She's not 'a little chippie,' and I'm far from trapped."

"I remember you wouldn't even go to the whorehouse when we were overseas. It's a lot healthier, no commitment."

It was true about me, and the healthy part was what put me off. The Army put out pamphlets warning us about venereal disease. It didn't stop most soldiers, but the prospect of catching some disease scared the willies out of me.

Finally, he said, "I do remember one thing about Humphrey. He's supposed to be an investor in that new resort they're building out in the desert."

"The Camelback Inn."

"That's the one."

———

I drove back to Caroline Taft's apartment. I badged the manager, and he let me in. The door had been repaired but otherwise nothing had been touched since the night of her murder. I sent him away and had a look around.

The bedclothes and mattress were dark with dried blood. The bedroom closet contained dresses, nurse uniforms, shoes, nothing remarkable. A bedside table drawer yielded nothing unusual, same with her bureau and the bathroom.

In the living room, her bookshelf held a mixture of popular fiction and nursing textbooks. I reached behind each shelf, searching for anything hidden. No luck. The same was true in the kitchen, all ordinary except for milk gone bad. It reminded me that Bill Sherman, the former boyfriend, was a milkman. The dining table held a stack of newspapers that had accumulated outside her front door, presumably brought inside when the door was repaired.

Could she really have had an affair with Kemper Marley? He was a moralist who owned whorehouses. Anything was possible. But the apartment held no expensive gifts or love letters from Marley, only some from her banker boyfriend tied in a blue ribbon on the bedside table.

I went back downstairs and asked the manager to open her mailbox. It was in a steel frame that held the individual tenants' mail behind separate metal doors, each opened with a key. He swung the entire frame open.

Pamela's box was stuffed. I grabbed those bills and magazines. "Evidence," I said, which seemed to satisfy him. Caroline's mailbox held a phone bill—reminding me the killer had cut the lines to the entire building from the outside. Otherwise, a few other bills and a letter with no return address. I slit it open and read:

Why aren't you returning my calls? No second thoughts, I hope. I want to see you.

Your Admirer.

Was the admirer Marley, Bill Sherman, or someone else?

I brought the mail back upstairs and put it on the dining table.

Again in the bedroom, I retraced my search. Reaching behind the bedside table, I found a framed photograph of Caroline and the banker boyfriend. It was color, Kodachrome. They looked very happy. She was a memorable girl, halfway between cute and beautiful. Her red hair fell over her shoulders, just like Pamela's. The photo must have fallen during the violence of the attack, otherwise the murderer might have taken it as yet another trophy.

I couldn't believe the detectives hadn't found it.

Next, I raised the mattress and saw it. A diary.

I sat in the living room and paged through it. The entries in the days leading up to her murder were mostly ordinary. She was hoping her boyfriend would pop the question. She would say yes. But she worried that Bill Sherman was still harassing her, demanding she come back to him. In one entry, she said Bill made a threat to kill her boyfriend and kill her if she didn't return to him.

I found an empty grocery bag in the kitchen and wrapped the diary, photo, and letter in it to lock in my office safe, then take it to McGrath. There would be time to go over the diary more extensively. For now, I needed to find Sherman.

Eighteen

Monday morning, I called headquarters and got Lefty Mofford, who happily gave me Bill Sherman's rap sheet. Multiple arrests for assault, including assault with a deadly weapon.

"One of our fine citizens, Gene. Somehow, he never went to prison, but he went under glass in the county jail a year ago, three months. He attacked his ex-wife with a knife. Ask me, he should have gone to Florence. He works at Central Dairy."

"Any new murders, especially like Caroline Taft?"

He lowered his voice. "I've got to be careful, Gene. But no, we're in the clear."

"So far. Thanks, Lefty."

Next, I leaned on one of my old informants, who fortunately didn't know I'd left the police force. I threatened to violate him if he wasn't straight with me, a one-way ticket back to prison. He knew Sherman and told me where I was likely to find him.

The tip led me to a pool hall on Washington Street, on the north edge of the Deuce. I knew the place. They ran numbers as well as providing legal recreation. It was secretly owned by Cyrus Cleveland, although all the patrons were Anglo or Mexicans. Cleveland paid bribes to certain detectives to keep the police away or warn him that a raid was coming. The vice raids were necessary to make the taxpayers believe their fine city was a moral one.

As my eyes adjusted to the dimness, I checked out the room. Six pool tables, a bar, pool cues in holders on the wall, although the sharks brought their own custom cues. Behind a partition were several slot machines, illegal but protected with bribes. They could be wheeled into a closet if a raid was scheduled. Fans overhead dispersed the smoke from cigars and cigarettes. The distinctive smell of reefers added to the mix. A Wurlitzer jukebox was pumping out music. Benny Goodman's orchestra was playing "Get Happy".

I didn't fit in: too well dressed, too much looking like a cop. No matter. I walked over to the bar and asked if Bill Sherman was there.

"Who wants to know?"

I discreetly showed my buzzer.

He leaned in. "That's not right. We pay our taxes, if you get my drift."

"I get your drift," I said, "but I'll shut you down if you don't answer my question. Then you can explain to Cyrus why you're short of receipts for the day."

He sighed and subtly pointed.

The man was in his late twenties, muscled up, thick wavy haircut, handsome in a thuggish way, but he looked like a hard package, his eyes threatening even the billiard ball. I let him take his shot then walked over and asked if he'd talk to me.

He looked me up and down, feigning unimpressed. He stood up straight with his cue held like a rifle at order arms. "Now why would I want to talk to you?" he smirked. His two pals laughed.

"So you don't go back to jail," I said, showing my badge.

"Ah." His face hardened into a scowl and I sensed what was about to happen.

He suddenly brought the heavy end of the cue at my head. His friends laughed, but I stepped out of the way just in time. His momentum brought it down on the pool table, twisting his body sideways, leaving both his hands on the edge to keep from falling. That's when I pulled my blackjack and slammed the supple leather encasing a steel bar onto the top of his left hand. Hard.

He bent over in pain. "You broke my fucking hand!"

"Move and I'll give you a matching pair," I said. The sap went in my belt and my right hand pulled out my M1911 pistol. I thumbed back the hammer and aimed it at his buddies.

"Any of you want to be part of this conversation?"

They fled out the front door like Bill Sherman carried typhoid. I holstered the gun, then grabbed him and hustled him out the back door into the alley to the sound of Tommy Dorsey.

"Do I have your undivided attention?" I braced him face-first against the wall, pushing him hard enough that I felt his shoulder blades fold in.

He nodded quickly. "My hand!" It hung uselessly at the end of his arm, blood leaking out of the knuckles.

"You're not used to your victims fighting back, Billy."

He made one last attempt at defiance. "It's Bill."

"Okay, Billy." I patted him down, finding a set of brass knuckles. "These are considered lethal weapons, genius. Come at a cop, and he'll shoot you." He also had a folding knife. I slid both in my pocket and turned him to face me.

"You like to hurt women," I said. "Why is that?"

"I never hurt nobody that don't deserve it."

I punched him in the stomach. He bent over, gasping for breath. Now he's crying.

"You're really starting to piss me off, Billy. Time to pick on someone your own size."

"What...what do you want?"

"I want to know about Caroline Taft."

"She's my girlfriend."

"No, she's not, Billy. She made that clear, but you were stalking her. Now she's dead, and guess who's the prime suspect?"

"Dead? What?"

I raised him up and forced him against the wall, facing me. Then I asked him where he was on the night she was murdered.

"I don't remember!"

"You're going to have to do better than that, Billy. I saw a man die in the gas chamber last month, and it's not pretty. I'm picturing you being strapped in for the killing of Caroline Taft."

I slapped him with my open hand. He gave me a shocked look, then the pain set in. "Is that how you like to hit women?" Then I slammed the heel of my hand into his nose until I heard cartilage snap. This time he let out a scream. He tried to hold up a hand to staunch the bleeding, but I wouldn't let him. Red flooded down on his shirt.

"I have to get up early for work," he stammered and moaned. "That night...that night I shot some pool here, then I had a woman..."

"Paid for it?"

He painfully nodded.

"Good-looking man like you having to pay for it?" I smirked. "Where?"

He didn't want to say. Red Light Row in Phoenix ran from First to Sixteenth streets and Van Buren to Jackson streets, a good neighborhood for bad habits. It contained at least sixteen whorehouses. Mark's Place, Irene's, the Cozy Room, and the Dunbar were among them. They paid bribes to detectives—I wasn't among them, which caused suspicion among some of my colleagues when I was a policeman—and some of the money also went into the city treasury. As usual, they were warned when a vice raid was coming.

But when he realized I wasn't going anywhere, he gave me the address. It was a disreputable house on the east side secretly owned by Harry Rosenzweig.

I demanded the prostitute's name and the time he left.

He let out a moan. "Then I was arrested for being drunk. They put me in the drunk tank and didn't let me out until the next morning."

If true, he was completely in the clear based on the time of Caroline's death. I could easily check all this out.

I grabbed his bloody nose and shoved him against the wall.

"Don't leave town. I can find you again, and things won't be as friendly next time." I wiped the blood on his shirt and stuck my card in his pocket. "Call me if you decide to talk."

Walking away, my pockets heavy with Bill Sherman's weapons, I was heavy with worry. If Sherman's alibis checked out, then we really did have a lust murderer. Maybe passing through. But maybe homegrown and only getting started.

Back at the Monihon Building, I took my time with Caroline's diary and typed up a report for Captain McGrath, carbon copies for my files.

Nineteen

The next week passed quietly. The high temperatures were in the low nineties, the lows in the sixties, normal for June. Since spring, we'd been shaking out our shoes for scorpions but rarely finding one. The tiny clear ones were the worst. The dry heat and cool nights were comfortable enough that we didn't use the sleeping porch. Pamela and I shared my bed, I spooned her through the night and slept better than I had in years. Happily, I didn't have nightmares to spook her. We also began sharing her modern office in the Heard Building. I prepared to let my Monihon Building lease expire.

If any progress had been made on the murder of George Parris case, I didn't know about it. Parris's gold was gone—to Mexico, I guessed. Special Agents Purvis and Swigert might have left town for all I knew, which meant the Mad Hatter wasn't here, either.

The Lincolns seemed satisfied with our services, although I knew this would boomerang sooner or later.

A check arrived in the mail from the FBI for services rendered. I assume it was for my tip about the misidentification of the man from Murder Incorporated. I had yet to find a communist for J. Edgar Hoover. I told Hoover I didn't expect to be paid, so I put the check in the outgoing mail, returning it to Washington.

McGrath seemed satisfied with my "parallel investigation." If he was embarrassed that his detectives didn't find the diary or photograph from Caroline's apartment, he didn't let on, but I knew him well enough to be sure he was steamed. He handed me a copy of Bill Sherman's rap sheet.

Between help from Harry Rosenzweig and Cyrus Cleveland I was able to validate Bill Sherman's alibi. I asked Harry if Sherman had ever hurt one of his girls. Surprisingly, the answer was no. I still didn't like him.

I interviewed Caroline's coworkers at Good Samaritan Hospital, going through the "I already spoke to the police" rigamarole. But they weren't helpful. No one had threatened her, either a patient or employee. She was a good nurse. A "good girl." What happened to her was horrible. They didn't know the half of it because the police still managed to keep the scalping out of the newspapers. If anyone brought it up, he'd automatically become a suspect.

On Thursday, Kemper Marley agreed to meet me for lunch at the Arizona Club on the top floor of the Luhrs Building, east of Gus Greenbaum's lair at the Luhrs Tower. Marley was a member.

I arrived first and was seated at a corner table. The dining room showed no signs of the Depression: The ceiling looked more than twenty feet high with elaborate chandeliers. Large arched windows gave views in every direction. I picked out a bank president, a couple of judges, expensive attorneys, all at their own tables with powerful companions, including Mayor Udall.

The sky was cobalt blue and the distant bare mountains

looked as if you could reach out and touch them. Where the city tapered off, citrus groves and farmland spread out, then empty desert. The farms grew everything from alfalfa to cabbages, lettuce, cantaloupes, and grapes, and especially cotton. The six hundred thousand orange, grapefruit, and lemon trees of the Salt River Valley outnumbered the population of the state. Date palms added to the assortment. Everything grew in the rich soil, watered by the dams on the Salt River northeast of Phoenix.

Kemper came in wearing a dark-blue business suit and cowboy hat. He was barely thirty but carried himself like an older man. Unsmiling thin lips set off his harsh features. If he had a sense of humor, I never saw it.

"I'm surprised you contacted me again so soon, Hammons," he said. "I let you use the peephole to find your murderer. Now you're back. As I recall from three years ago, my money wasn't good enough for you. Are you looking for work? If so, get it on."

We ordered. He asked for his usual, a New York strip steak, "bloody rare," with a baked potato. I was content with a burger and fries. I'd see if they did a better job than the Nifty Nook across from Phoenix Union High School, my favorite burger joint and cheaper, too.

After the waiter left, he said, "Well?"

"I am working, Kemper," I said. "Tell me about Caroline Taft?"

He didn't even blink. "Who?"

Class and money will go a long way, miles and miles. I couldn't knock him around and brace him against a wall, as I did with Bill Sherman, a lowly milkman working for wages from Central Dairy. Marley was the richest man in Arizona.

I pulled out a photo and slid it across the table.

"Caroline Taft," I said again. "Your girlfriend."

"I've never seen or heard of the girl. What kind of game are you playing, Hammons?"

"No game. You sent her a note signed 'Your Admirer.' Had it dusted for prints and yours are on it."

I actually was playing a game. Marley's prints weren't on file. But maybe he didn't know that. The next few seconds would tell. I pulled out a Lucky and fired it up.

"That's really a disgusting habit, Hammons. Unhealthy, too." I blew a plume of smoke to the side.

"I've also been through Caroline's diary. She mentions you several times, with the initials K.M." That part was true.

Finally, he leaned in. "So what do you want, Hammons, money? I can't have my wife find this out. The girl came on to me, I swear."

"That's why you were writing her, wanting to know why she wasn't returning your calls? You, who always get what you want. From the diary, you came on to her. An older man, powerful, wealthy, but like a modern-day cowboy out of a movie. She wrote that last part. For reasons I can't fathom, she found you irresistible."

He reached in his suit and for a moment I thought he was going to bring out a gun. I wouldn't have been surprised. But it was a checkbook. He pulled out a pen and started to write.

"How about five hundred dollars and we keep this between ourselves?"

"Put your money away," I said. "I'm no blackmailer. What I want to know is whether you're a murderer."

His mouth opened but nothing came out.

Finally: "Murderer?"

"She was killed. Stabbed to death."

"What?" he hissed. "Dead?"

If the man was capable of shedding a tear, I swear he would have started bawling.

I asked him where he was on the night she was murdered.

Any emotion fled from his hard face. "How dare you accuse me."

"I'm doing more than accusing. This is a homicide investigation, and you're the prime suspect." I opened my coat to reveal my badge. "Don't think this is something you can phone a city commissioner and waltz away from. You had motive—maybe she was pressuring you to marry her or she'd rat you out." Unfortunately, she made no mention of making such a threat in the diary. But he didn't know that, so I pushed ahead. "You had means, a well-documented history of violence. It's not a reach from using a baseball bat on farmworkers to stabbing your girlfriend to death. And you had opportunity unless you tell me where you goddamned were that night. I had this meeting out of courtesy, not that you deserve it. But the next one will be in the interview room of police headquarters."

Unfortunately, I lacked much evidence, even circumstantial. But he didn't know that.

"You son of a bitch," he growled. "My daddy would have dragged you out and horsewhipped you in public! I might do it, too, right down on the courthouse steps. Frontier justice."

"Your frontier justice might be the gas chamber. I saw a man die that way last month, and it's not pretty."

He glared at me while I serenely smoked.

Finally, "I was at a Masonic meeting, and plenty of people can vouch for me."

"Until when?"

"I don't know. Nine p.m. or so."

"That's inconvenient for you because she was killed after that. You'd better come up with an alibi for after nine, and if it's home with your wife, too damned bad. Both women deserve better than you."

"I loved that girl!"

"Fine line between love and hate," I recited. "If she broke it off or threatened to tell your wife if you didn't leave her, you might have lost your cool and murdered her. Or you might have planned it. A search warrant and interviewing some of your employees can prove it. That's first-degree murder, a death penalty ticket. I can imagine a county prosecutor eager to make his name on your conviction."

He stared into his lap, his fingers fidgeting.

The waiter glided in with our food.

"I'll take mine to go." I stood. Looking down at Marley, I said, "Enjoy that steak, bloody rare."

———

Sitting on a bench in the shady park surrounding the six-year-old City-County Building, I ate my lunch from the Arizona Club and watched thin feathery clouds overhead. I'd have been happy with a burger from the Nifty Nook.

Marley was capable of anything. Yet for all his machismo about "frontier justice," he might not have had the guts to kill Caroline Taft the way she was murdered. Unless it was in a fit of anger after they fought. Otherwise, I could see him hiring out the bloody work, make it look as if a lunatic had done it.

But he seemed genuinely surprised when I told him Caroline was murdered. I'd type up a summary of our talk for Captain McGrath, but there didn't seem to be enough probable cause to arrest him or even interrogate him further. I'd bet Marley wasn't done with me either way.

After dropping my lunch bag in a trash can, I crossed the street and let "Mechudo" Torrez shine my shoes. We made small talk. He was adding a bedroom to his house in the Golden Gate barrio, doing the work himself by hand. He owned his land, bought from Victor Steinegger who owned most of the area, and Torrez was steadily improving it, including digging his own well to provide running water for his home.

Golden Gate, located off Sixteenth Street south of the tracks, was like most of the Phoenix barrios: outside the city limits with unpaved streets and no utilities. It was populated by people from Mexico seeking a better life. Others had been there for generations. Many worked in the packing sheds and icing platforms by the railroads.

Torrez had told me how during the worst of the Depression, Anglo vagrants had set up little camps nearby—*campitos* under the mesquite trees and near the railroad tracks. They begged the Mexican families for food, and many worked for them, tending their farms.

The Anglos looked down on the barrio dwellers, as opposed to the "respectable" Mexican Americans such as Vicente Canalez, who operated the Ramona Drug Store on Washington Street, or Victoria Vasquez's family, her parents owning businesses and a handsome bungalow near Eastlake Park.

"Hope you don't mind me asking," Torrez changed the subject, "but anything new about the murder of that nurse?"

"I don't mind at all," I said. "But, no, a bunch of dead ends and not enough leads."

"Your *hermano* is in a bad way about it," he said. "He told me the police think the murderer was passing through. He'd killed the same way in other places. But he worries that's wrong, and we might have another murder again here."

I nodded. My brother was in a bad way, period.

It amazed me again how cops, lawyers, and judges vented, gossiped, and philosophized for Torrez, who was completely trustworthy. These were the ones he trusted, too. Others, deceived by his rough looks, doubted he even spoke English. He was satisfied to let them enjoy their prejudices, always speaking Spanish and a few English words, while they talked freely to companions and he gathered intelligence. It was the lingua franca of the courthouse and police headquarters.

He sighed. "What a terrible thing." Then he went back to talking about his house.

I listened, and my mind wandered.

Too many loose ends were flapping in the dry, warm wind.

It began with George Parris, using a false name, trying to hire me to carry ransom money. Then Parris turned up dead, a bullet in the back of his head. I turned down the job, too many unknowns, but Pamela took it. And we reconnected after three years.

Who killed Parris? I only had the FBI agents telling me that it was Albert Anastasia and connected to gold stolen in a robbery in Wichita. But I hadn't read about this crime. They didn't even know the real identity of Anastasia. What if other parts of their information were wrong or incomplete? That was a loose end to tie up.

Another one: who knocked me in the head when I came upon them rifling through my office?

I wasn't usually that careless. The inside door was already jimmied. I saw that. Why was I so damned unaware that somebody was in my office waiting for me? But who? And why? They dug around but nothing appeared missing. What were they looking for? By the time I came to, they were long gone. It was a reasonable guess that it was connected to Parris. But only a guess. I didn't like that this loose end was still fluttering.

I bought a paper from a boy wearing an apron full of them and shouting headlines. A ninety-year-old Civil War veteran had died in Phoenix. Then I walked back to the Heard Building and shared what I knew with Pamela. She offered to call New York City about Anastasia while I called Wichita. We had enough money in the bank to call the long-distance operators and enrich Ma Bell.

Long distance to the Wichita Police put me through to

the investigation division that housed the detectives. Using McGrath's delegated authority, I identified myself as Detective Gene Hammons with the Phoenix Police in Arizona.

"I'm interested in talking to whoever is investigating the bank robbery involving George Parris."

"That would be me, Detective Hammond," came the scratchy voice on the other end of the line. "Hank Nelson."

It was wasting long-distance time to correct him on my last name, so I got down to it.

"Can you tell me what happened?"

"The Fourth National Bank on Douglas Avenue was robbed on the afternoon of March 17th, a Tuesday. The robbers made off with cash, gold, and gold certificates, mostly series 1928. Who is this Parris fellow?"

The cigarette almost fell out of my mouth.

I said, "That's the name I was given by the FBI as the robber, along with someone named Albert Anastasia, who might have been going by the name of Andrew Jackson Poet. Parris was supposed to have a long rap sheet, was arrested there, about to stand trial, and killed a guard to escape."

"Whoa, Hammond," Detective Nelson said. "No offense to Mr. Hoover, but nothing like that happened here. I'll look through our files and wire you if anything shows up." I gave him the Heard Building address so a telegram wouldn't go to police headquarters. He accepted it without question.

He continued, "I don't know anything about a George Parris, certainly not robbing the Fourth National Bank, much less killing a guard and escaping. I'll see if he's got a sheet. We have very low crime here. A woman shot her son-in-law the other day. That's a big deal here. The bank robbery was over the top, in the newspapers for days. Otherwise, people want to know about wheat prices and whether Governor Landon has a chance against Roosevelt. The Dust Bowl is hitting the southwest part of the state hard, but that's a long way from Wichita."

"Do you have any suspects in the bank robbery?"

"We believed it was Alvin Karpis, based on the description of the witnesses. The creepy smile he was known for. Two months later, he was arrested by the FBI in New Orleans, led by Hoover himself. But we're still tying things together, especially locating the loot. Cooperation with the G-men isn't great."

I had stopped writing information and taken to doodling. "Oh, one more thing," I said. "Would you mind checking your files for a William Jordan?"

"No problem."

I thanked him and hung up.

Pamela sat on my desk and swung her shapely legs. It was a pleasant distraction, but I told her what I'd learned from Detective Nelson.

"It gets worse," she shrugged. "Or is this where the plot thickens, as they write in my mystery novels? I talked to a crime reporter for the *New York Daily News*. He said Albert Anastasia has been cooling his heels in jail for allegedly being part of a plan to murder the special prosecutor, Thomas Dewey. He's been there since January. There's no way he could be in Phoenix."

I put my hand on her knee. "All of this is what? Misdirection? Or did I have it wrong from the beginning, based on what the G-men and Greenbaum told us?"

She tousled my hair. "Maybe it's a legend."

"Legend?"

"Parris or Jordan is real. We know that. But the rest is made up. In the dime novels I read about spies, that's called creating a legend, a false identity and background."

"But by who?"

She kissed me. "Whom."

Twenty

Somebody went to a great deal of trouble to create the legend. I couldn't get out of my memory that Parris had paid three months' rent ahead in cash when he was ready to blow town for Los Angeles. Pamela suggested we return to the apartment.

The landlord, Mr. Simmons, wasn't happy to see us again.

"I don't know what else I can tell you."

I flashed my buzzer. "Indulge us. This is a homicide investigation."

"I thought she was a private investigator?"

I was getting caught in my multiple assignments. "She's on the force."

"Oh, well good. I haven't rented the place."

"Have you seen the friend, the one in a seersucker suit?" Pamela asked. "Oscar from Wichita?"

He shook his head.

"And no other policemen have been by?"

"Not until you," Simmons said.

"May we see the apartment again?"

He reluctantly agreed, taking us upstairs and unlocking the door.

"Take your time," he said. "Lock it on your way out."

I closed the door and sat on the sofa.

"What are we looking for?" she asked.

I shrugged. "Inspiration?"

She walked around. "George Parris or William Jordan. Has a friend from Wichita named Oscar. Only he has never been to Wichita himself, based on your conversation with the police there."

I prowled from the bedroom back to the living room. "A rap sheet would have included 'known associates,' only he didn't have one, at least not that the Wichita cop knew. He's going to check their files."

"And he's lugging gold and cash," she said. "He tries to hire you with the ransom story. When you turn him down, he comes to me, and I carry it to the middle of the bridge. Only there's no missing boy. But missing gold that I left there."

Turk Muldoon was wandering around in my head. I hadn't told Pamela what happened to him. How he turned out to be a killer of her college friend—only I realized it and could prove it—and he attacked me on the Sunset Limited as it passed the Salton Sea at night, headed for Los Angeles.

We were alone on the back of the open vestibule of the observation car, and he grabbed me by the throat and tried to throw me off as the train moved at ninety miles an hour. I still remember his words, his rich brogue. "Go easy, lad," he said, "and at this speed it will be over in no time at all. Only a little pain, then sweet oblivion."

But I broke his grip, swung him around, and he fell over the brass railing. I reached for him, held one arm, told him to grab my hand with his free hand.

I shouted his real name. "Reach up, Liam, and take my hand!"

I remembered the ties and ballast flying beneath him. His eyes were full of terror. He said, "No, lad. But thank you for trying." And he let go.

I didn't know if I would ever tell her that story. The case was officially still open and people thought Muldoon skipped town because of gambling debts. But my brother knew and had begun to suspect him, not realizing we were boarding the same train together that night.

But I also remember better times when he had my back on the strangler case, when I looked up to him. He said, "Always trust your gut, lad, and sometimes fight for what it's telling you. It's the best weapon a good detective has."

And my gut focused on the fireplace.

"What are you doing?" Pamela asked as I got on my knees and looked up the flue.

"Playing a hunch."

I reached up. Nothing.

"Hand me that poker," I said. Pamela passed it over.

Then I pushed it higher and it touched a hard surface. Something moved. It felt heavy. Suddenly it came crashing down. I got my head out of the way just in time.

It was an ordinary rucksack. I used my handkerchief to protect fingerprints and undid the clasp to open it.

Inside was the gold.

———

We sat on the carpet, cross-legged, staring at the treasure.

"I can't believe it, Gene!" she clapped. "How did you know?"

"Just a guess. I kept coming back to this apartment, thinking how he'd paid rent months ahead in cash. At first, it seemed so bare, barely lived in. Yet…" I spread out my hand. "He was armed, clearly afraid, but he expected to live, so he hid the gold.

He was going to Los Angeles on the train but intended to return and retrieve the gold."

"But he was shot in the back of the head," she sighed. "We still don't know who the killer was. He sure never found the gold, but he left the money in Parris's suitcase."

"Maybe he was disturbed and fled," I suggested.

She pulled a face, still a pretty face. "What was I carrying across the bridge?"

"It might have been rocks, for all we know. And, like you say, the money in his suitcase. That's another mystery."

Again, I used the handkerchief for counting and sorting, while Pamela wrote an inventory in her notebook. One gold bar. Several ingots. All stamped with serial numbers and the seal of the federal New York Assay Office, perfect gold coins, and gold certificates, including one with Woodrow Wilson's portrait—Don's favorite president, made him a Republican—and denominated at a hundred thousand dollars.

I held it up as Pamela studied it. "One note, same size as a dollar, worth a hundred grand."

She added up the tally in her notebook twice. "Forty million dollars."

She smiled. "Nobody else knows this is here. We could run away, live a good life in Mexico together."

For a moment I felt the way bank robbers must after a successful heist.

"I like the run-away-and-live-a-good-life-together-with-you-in-Mexico-part," I said. "But this gold isn't ours, and it has a bloody trail. I'm afraid it would follow us, no matter where we went. I'd never forgive myself if you were hurt or worse because we tried to glaum it."

She looked deflated. "You're right, dammit," she said. "And it's sweet you worry about me. So, what to do?"

"Call Captain McGrath."

The chief of detectives arrived in ten minutes. I introduced him to Pamela. She said I should be back on the force. He smiled and shook his head. Then he walked around the loot twice before bending down to examine it closer.

"Good job, Gene," he finally pronounced. "You're a third of the way home."

"A third?" Pamela asked.

I said, "Finding the gold is one third. Then catching the scalper is the next third."

She filled it in. "And finding Parris's killer is the last third."

"Your friend is quite astute," McGrath said. He pulled out a handkerchief and picked up the phone. "It's still disconnected. I'm going down to use my car radio."

It didn't take long for the apartment to be crowded with uniformed officers and detectives. My brother was conspicuously absent. They once again interviewed Simmons and his wife, trying to get more information about Parris and his friend Oscar.

"Well done, Geno!" Frenchy said, shaking my hand with both of his. Then he started clumsily flirting with Pamela.

Next an armored car arrived, and the gold was boxed up for a ride to headquarters. It was accompanied by cops armed with shotguns and Tommy guns, and McGrath personally.

Pamela took my elbow. "I'd say our work here is done."

Twenty-One

For the next third, I wanted to double back on Bill Sherman. I asked Pamela to check out Walter Humphrey at the courthouse: what kind of cases he took, what his record was, and any notable clients. It was especially notable that he was an investor in the Camelback Inn.

But Sherman beat me to it. He called using the Heard Building office phone I had scribbled on my business card.

"It's Bill Sherman. You said we could talk more," he said.

"Any time."

"I want to do it now." His voice quavered, a change from the tough who attacked me in the pool hall. "Please."

"Are you okay, Bill?"

He didn't answer besides a groan. Then he gave me his address.

Sherman lived in a territorial-era single-story apartment on the corner of Jefferson and Twelfth streets. The dried-out little postage stamp of a lawn matched the dried-out color of the building. A rusting chair sat on the tiny front porch. On the corner, a dying palm tree sat alone.

Caroline's diary did more than corroborate Kemper Marley's

romance but repeatedly mentioned how Sherman had stalked and threatened her in the months before her death. In one particularly telling passage, she wrote how he cornered her outside the hospital and showed her a Bowie knife, saying he would "cut off that pretty hair" if she didn't come back to him. Scalping didn't require a Bowie knife, but it wasn't on him when I confiscated the brass knucks and folding knife earlier. Had he ditched it after killing her? If I found it, would it contain her blood and remnants of her scalp?

Another piece of information came when I read Sherman's file. At least up to his most recent arrest, he not only worked at Central Dairy but also part-time at the huge Tovrea feedlots and slaughterhouses on the east end of the city. He worked on the "kill floor" cutting huge steers into pieces. Good with a knife? I'd say so.

I parked a block away and walked along the sidewalk until the adobe building came into sight. His apartment faced Jefferson and the door was slightly ajar. But as I got closer, I saw the frame had been shattered. I pulled my gun and flipped off the safety, concealed it at the side of my leg, and approached with a combination of casual and caution.

I stepped onto the porch.

"Billy, it's Detective Hammons. Are you in there?"

No sound.

I slowly pushed in the door with my left hand and leveled my gun into the room. Suddenly I heard a tiny sound, a ping. And a louder sound of a spring being knocked off. A long-ago sense memory coincided with me seeing the wire attached to an oval-shaped metal object attached to the inside of the doorjamb.

As I ran toward the street and fell on the hot sidewalk, four seconds ticked off, and the doorjamb exploded, sending fragments everywhere.

I rolled over and pointed my gun toward the apartment. As the smoke cleared, I only saw a splintered door and bits of metal sprayed several feet onto the lawn and sidewalk. It was a booby trap made from a grenade, likely American made. I used many as an infantryman in the Great War. It was handy to drop one or more into a Hun pillbox. Count correctly so they couldn't toss it back. Count wrong, and you lost your hand or your life.

A woman opened her door and leaned out.

"What's going on?"

"Get inside," I yelled. "Call the police!" The door slammed.

But I wasn't waiting. I rose to my haunches and then slowly approached Bill Sherman's apartment again. The threshold was shattered. I stepped inside, mindful of wires strung across the floor and other signs of additional booby traps. Finding none, I stepped farther. The grenade had shredded a second-hand sofa, collapsed an armchair, and blown a coffee table to bits. The living room walls were decorated with fragments from the grenade. A framed "Employee of the Month" certificate from the Central Dairy was lying shattered on the wooden floor.

"Bill?" I called. "It's Detective Hammons. You called me. Are you here?"

Silence.

I carefully moved into the bedroom. Only a mattress on the floor with two pillows. But that wasn't what caught my eye. Even with my memories of the war, it was one of the most brutal sights I'd ever seen.

Bill Sherman was nailed to the wall with railroad spikes, hammered deeply into his body. The heads had numbers on them—marking the dates manufactured, I guessed—and they were long enough to go all the way through him into the wall, keeping him in a standing position. His head was turned to face the left, eyes and mouth open. And his hair was gone. He had been scalped. I avoided stepping in the huge pool of blood around his upright corpse.

I went back out and made a check of the kitchen as I heard sirens coming. The kitchen was free of lunatics, but the back door was open, with only the screen door closed. Then I saw it. Another booby trap. This was a second grenade, secured near the screen door with a wire connecting the door to the pin that secured the pineapple-shaped "hand bomb," as we also called it in the Great War. Open the screen, the pin would be pulled by the wire, then the long safety lever attached to the grenade's body popped off, setting the fuse. Four seconds to detonation. If everything worked as it should.

The Krauts liked to use booby traps with their "potato masher" grenades attached to a war souvenir. A Luger or old-fashioned spiked helmet that an unsuspecting Yank might imagine taking home to show his friends and family. Only it was wired to explode when the item was lifted. I'd even seen them do it to dead bodies.

I carefully unstrung the wire as I heard the cops yelling at the shattered entrance.

The next order of business was to identify myself so I wasn't shot by jumpy officers and warn them of potential booby traps I might have missed.

———

First, I was treated like a suspect. My story that Bill had called me didn't persuade anyone, much less my brother. He smiled as he handcuffed me from behind, tight, and sat me down on the hot curb.

He smirked. "Never thought I'd see my baby brother going down for a murder. Maybe you should have tried the opium pipe instead of the church choir."

I was about to respond, but something in his eyes told me he was itching to use his blackjack on me. Six years older, Don was plagued by demons. I had only an inkling: the war, a marriage where he felt trapped, his opium addiction. I'm sure there were more, and I figured into them.

Captain McGrath arrived, undid the cuffs, spent several minutes inside, and came back to sit next to me.

"What a fucking mess," he said. The Chief of D's was not given to such salty language. "What really brought you here?"

"I wanted to put the heat on him again," I said. "See if I could get him to crack, admit to killing Caroline. But he called me first, said he wanted to talk. He sounded different, made a groaning sound."

"Satisfied with Bill's alibi?" He wasn't smiling. "What's your guess as to how this went down?"

"Maybe the killer was waiting for him and overpowered him. Forced him to phone me. Then started nailing him to the wall." I hesitated. "Emasculated him, to top it off. He would have had to be incredibly strong. Sherman looked like somebody who could hold his own in a fight. Or he knocked Sherman out and held him against the wall and did it. But a lust killer would have wanted him conscious for as much of it as possible. Maybe that's the only way he can achieve climax. Several spikes could have killed him, but slowly. Then he scalped him."

"The scalp is gone, same as the Taft girl. Did he have a decent head of hair?"

I nodded. "The murderer took his tools with him. A hammer, maybe, but I'd guess a mallet. The knife he used to cut through the scalp. I assume he used all the spikes he brought with him."

"Railroad worker?"

"Maybe," I said. "But anybody can find spikes lying around alongside the roadbed where track work is being done."

"The booby traps are new. Good thing you sniffed them out."
I said I was lucky. But he was right about the grenade rig.
That didn't happen at Caroline Taft's apartment. The killer was
expecting me to come. "The grenade would be the bloody icing
on the cake. Neither of the scalping murders in Arkansas and
Texas involved this. That part made me think the killer had military experience. This was carefully planned."

McGrath pulled out a Chesterfield and lit it. I'd never seen
him smoke on a crime scene. He inhaled like my brother in the
opium den. "We didn't get any fingerprints from the Taft girl's
apartment except for her and the boyfriend."

"And we won't here. He either wears gloves or is incredibly
careful in wiping down surfaces he touched."

McGrath cursed again. "Prime suspect dead. Where does
that leave us?"

"Marley is still viable, but proving it will be hard," I said,
rubbing my wrists from the handcuff bruising. "You can bet
Marley's already complaining about me to the big cheeses at
city hall."

I looked back at the shambles of Bill's apartment. "My guess
is that the murderer isn't just passing through. He's growing
more violent, including the booby traps." I thought about it
more. "We also need to consider that more than one individual
attacked Bill Sherman. But they knew about the scalping, which
hasn't been in the papers…"

McGrath tossed his smoke and clenched his fists. "You need
to get cracking Gene."

That steamed me. *I need to get cracking,* but I can't be put
back on the force. I kept my composure.

He went on, "Sure, it might have been more than one killer.
But something connected Taft to Sherman. The murders in
similar fashion, the scalping. They hadn't been boyfriend and

girlfriend for two years. So, it's something else. Find it. That's where you need to start."

We both stood. "Yes, sir. One other thing..."

"Go ahead."

"Make sure the detectives do a more thorough search here than they did at Caroline's place."

Twenty-Two

I got back to the Heard Building, and Pamela greeted me with a kiss and nose nuzzle. We were still at the nose-nuzzle stage of our relationship. I liked it. She looked pleased with herself, so I hung up my hat and coat to listen.

"I've been at the Courthouse," she said. "Walter Humphrey is a one-man practice, no partners. I watched him argue a case in court and asked around about him. Discreetly, of course."

"With a little bit of flirting," I teased. "All honey, honey."

"Don't be jealous, Gene. It's not as if I can brace them against a wall or knock them about with my blackjack."

After all I'd been through, it was sweet to laugh and feel safe.

"Humphrey is broke," she said. "He's got a major gambling habit. His wife left him over it, and he had to sell his house last year. I checked that at the Recorder's Office, the house I mean. He's behind on alimony and child support payments. So how is he able to invest in the Camelback Inn?"

"By blackmailing the Lincolns."

"That would make sense. Why else would his business card be on the hood you got into the scuffle with at the train station?"

I folded my arms. "It still doesn't explain the gold bullion."

"No," she said. "Unless it never existed, and the Lincolns were spooked."

"Now you're thinking like me."

She stuck out her tongue.

"The other piece of information I got was that Walter Humphrey represents Kemper Marley. He's the attorney of record on several lawsuits over land and water rights, on the purchase of some land far north of Scottsdale, empty desert, whatever that would ever be good for. He's not the only lawyer Marley uses, but there's definitely a connection."

Marley kept popping up. But we knew from talking to the Lincolns that he wasn't an investor in the Camelback Inn. I asked her what Humphrey looked like, since she had seen him in court.

"Wimpy," she said. "'I will gladly pay you Tuesday for a hamburger today.' That Wimpy. But as you've taught me, looks can deceive." She dusted off my clothes and examined my bruised wrists. "What have you been up to?"

———

I felt at loose ends. One by one, leads evaporated—or were murdered. That night Pamela and I drove across the bridge again, this time for surveillance.. When in doubt, watch the suspects. Kemper Marley was the target.

He had a ranch on Broadway—named after the pioneer Noah Broadway, not the famous, theater-lined boulevard in Manhattan—at Fourteenth Avenue. The lights were on, and I recalled a visit there three years before.

Then, I had delivered a report on Gus Greenbaum that he had paid for, an assignment I had foolishly accepted. But I had been laid off from the police and times were tough as a new P.I.

His wife, Ethel, had served tea and struck me as a gentle and charming woman. Kemper had definitely married up. His young son played happily in the front yard. I remembered thinking: No man could be a son of a bitch all the time. Still, I had handed him back his money and was done with him.

Or so I had hoped.

Now, he was the only suspect left standing in the murders of Caroline Taft and Bill Sherman.

I swung around, parked a quarter mile west and shut off the car.

"What now?" Pamela said.

"Now we wait and watch," I said. "This is the boring part of police work, until it isn't."

"You take me on the most unusual dates, Gene."

We unwrapped ham and cheese sandwiches from the Nifty Nook—open twenty-four hours—and popped open cold bottles of Coke. When this was done, we each enjoyed a Lucky. She blew a smoke ring. I really needed to learn that trick.

It was the best surveillance stakeout company I'd ever had.

But I read the concern in her face.

"What?"

"You were almost killed today, Gene! You were targeted from the time Sherman was forced to call you until that grenade went off!" She wiped tears from her eyes. "I can't lose you. I just can't."

I squeezed her hand. "You're not going to."

Then for a good half hour, we settled into silence.

"What's Marley's motive?" Pamela challenged me. "He's rich from his liquor business, ranching, and land holdings."

"He wanted this young, pretty plaything. But Caroline was going to tell his wife."

"Her diary doesn't mention threatening to reveal their affair," she said. "It does say she needed to take a break from him. It doesn't say why. But putting myself in her shoes, she's young and naïve, but she's feeling her wild oats cheating on her banker square, can't make up her mind between the two. Meanwhile, he misses her, tired of the ball-and-chain but can't divorce her. That causes him to send the 'admirer' note. But say your theory is true. Why kill her? Why not pay her off?"

I said, "Maybe she didn't want money. She wanted him, or at least more time with him than he was willing to give."

Pamela said, "Then we're back to where they fought at her apartment, and he killed her. Maybe he lost his temper, or maybe he planned it."

I could buy that. Marley was certainly strong enough to stab Caroline to death and make it look like a lust murder with the evidence of rape and her scalp taken. Throw the police off the track. Bill Sherman was a harder challenge. Marley needed help. Men who would keep their mouths shut. He could certainly find them based on his attack of the union organizers, men with baseball bats. But killing Bill Sherman was several degrees of intensity higher. It raised the risk of somebody talking, even going to the police and turning state's evidence against Marley.

It was nearing eleven, and Pamela nodded off. I watched the house, surrounded by the cottonwood trees and stables in the back. No one came or went the entire time we'd been on stake-out. One by one, the lights in the house went out.

Suddenly, a dark car pulled out on two-lane Broadway and drove east toward Central. I followed at a distance with my lights off.

"Wake up, sleepyhead."

Pamela came up with a start.

"We're following a car that just left Marley's spread."

"With our lights off."

"That's how we stay concealed." As long as I didn't drive off into an irrigation ditch.

When it turned north toward town on Central, I made out the car's silhouette. It looked very much like a late-model Buick Roadmaster, sleek, four doors, outside spare tire, running boards. The same make and model of car that brought the man to the farmworkers' shantytown where Caroline Taft's hair and bracelet were hanging on the wall.

I turned left, let distance gather between us, and switched on my lights. After crossing the bridge, we picked up more traffic, and I felt comfortable closing in and not being detected. We bounced across the railroad tracks without being stalled by a train and entered downtown and the comfort of neon. Pamela wrote down the tag number, California. The big Buick turned on Monroe Street in front of the Hotel San Carlos and stopped. Three men got out and handed their luggage to a bellboy on the sidewalk. I pulled up on Central in front of the ornate eagles carved above the entrance of Valley Bank in the Professional Building. It was easy to find a parking place this time of night. Our office in the Heard Building was half a block south.

"They're big," Pamela commented.

"The right size and number for a hit squad hired by Marley, maybe from out of town." Such a hit squad would be much more reliable and trustworthy, for the right price. The driver stepped out, easily six feet four with a suspicious bulge in his sports coat. He handed the car keys and a tip to an attendant and followed his friends into the hotel. Even under the streetlights, it was impossible to make out their faces.

I gave it twenty minutes and then got out of the car and walked into the hotel. They were gone, which worked for me. I showed my buzzer to the desk clerk and asked for their names and addresses. He twirled the registration book to face me, and

I wrote down the information I asked for. Not one name was familiar. All were from Los Angeles. I told him not to mention I'd been there and passed him a twenty.

I was tempted to do the same with the garage attendant. But what would I find in the car? Any guns, grenades, or—Lord help us—other ordnance they possessed would have been carried inside. In case they needed to shoot their way out.

Back in the car, I showed the list to Pamela.

"Tomorrow, I'll ask McGrath to run them for police records."

Twenty-Three

The next morning, Pamela and I arrived at the office to find a short, cigar-chewing man waiting by the door.

"Name's Lewis, I'm your downstairs neighbor."

We opened up the door, and he made himself comfortable in the client chair. He looked familiar, but I couldn't place him.

"I'm a reporter for the *Arizona Republic*, 'The State's Greatest Newspaper,' as we say."

When he saw the dubious expression on Pamela's face, he pulled out a press card, showed it to her, and then stuck it in the band of his straw fedora. The all-caps PRESS stood at an angle.

I said, "And how can we help, neighbor? Want a match for that stogie?"

"Nah. Trying to quit. My wife hates them. Anyway, I'm a crime reporter. Do you have your morning paper?"

I unfolded it.

He recited, "Death dealt by two shots from a snub automatic wrote the closing chapter here yesterday in the romance of Donna Mary Park, beautiful blond Rendezvous Park dancer, and Irving LaZarr, former dance member of Sally Rand's troupe."

My eyes went to the news story on the front page from which he was reading. I held up my hand, but he was only getting going.

"They sat in steamer chairs on the north porch of a rooming house at 324 North First Avenue and chatted in the darkness for more than two hours." He adjusted his cigar. "Switch to indented boldface: Then LaZarr pressed the automatic to his sweetheart's head and shot her dead. As she toppled from her chair, LaZarr shot himself in the head with the second of nine shots in the small gun and died before an ambulance arrived."

I handed the paper to Pamela.

"I wrote that," Lewis said, eager to prove himself. "They don't allow us bylines like some papers do. Frosts me. But I cover crime."

"Which brings you to our humble abode," I said.

"A little bird at police headquarters says you're asking questions about the stabbing of the nurse. No arrests. Police are baffled, or so it seems. Maybe you have answers, too. Maybe we can help each other."

I said, "Your little bird is wrong."

He tossed the stogie into the trashcan. "I don't buy it. The police are holding something back. Then the explosion yesterday on Jefferson Street. They said it was a natural gas leak, but my source said it was the apartment of the nurse's former boyfriend and he was killed there."

"Well," I said, "it's news to me. Pun intended. Put it in the paper."

"My editors won't let me without corroboration. C'mon. Play straight with me and I will with you."

"What do you think the cops are withholding about Caroline Taft's murder?"

"See, you know her name!" He took out a notebook and slid a pencil from behind his ear.

I said, "Answer my question."

"I don't know, but it's big. The detectives won't talk."

"That's because they always hold back important facts that only the killer would know."

"Just like you did when you nabbed the University Park Strangler."

"And your paper agreed to withhold it."

"We would this time, too. Unless it makes it to the Hearst paper in LA. Can't control them, but I wish they'd hire me."

"I have a hard time believing you. Otherwise, you wouldn't be here. With the University Park Strangler, I was on the force Now, I'm not. I don't have anything to do with this murder. You're barking up the wrong tree."

Pamela said, "What can you offer us?"

I could see the gears turning in his head.

He said, "Welllll… Everybody loved her at the hospital. But I talked to her neighbors, and they said she had two lovers. One her age who worked at a bank, and another man who was a few years older." He looked me over. "Maybe your age or a little older. But tough-looking. Wore a cowboy hat. Two lovers are dangerous; jealousy might cause a murder."

He didn't know that under the cowboy hat was probably Kemper Marley. I was also relieved to hear that he didn't know that Caroline Taft was scalped.

"That's news to us," Pamela said.

"Oh, come on!" He pulled another cigar out and stuck it in his mouth, unlit. "There's got to be some give and take here. I gave. What can I take from you?"

"Have you talked to Walter Humphrey?" Pamela asked.

"The lawyer?" Lewis said. "He defended Jack Sullivan, for all the good he did. I covered the trial and the execution."

That's where I'd seen him before.

"Might be worth your time to look into him," Pamela said. "Give and take, your turn."

"I'm flummoxed," he confessed. "My editor is after me about this murder. Can't you give me anything?"

"Have you talked to my brother, Detective Don Hammons?" I asked. "He's the primary investigator on this case. That's who you need to see."

He wrote it down.

"May I use your name?"

I stuck a Lucky in my mouth and lit it. He looked envious. The *Republic* wasn't particularly aggressive, and McGrath could shut down any attempt by Lewis to dig deeper. I said, "Sure. Why not?"

"Will that help me or hurt me?" The cigar wiggled.

"Depends on his mood."

After he left, I swung around to the typewriter to fill out a new report for the Chief of D's on the stakeout and the visitors who came from Marley's place to the Hotel San Carlos. I called for a messenger boy and paid him to send the sealed envelope to McGrath at police headquarters.

———

Pamela wanted to watch the San Carlos for the men we followed from Marley's. But I thought we might have more success visiting another of Phoenix's gangsters. We put the top down on the Ford and drove south of the tracks. There, I found a familiar building with peeling paint, rusting "Barq's" and "pool" signs, and screen doors. In this part of town, few of the streets were paved. Running water and sewer service were rare. We parked and went inside.

Black faces shot our way, especially at Pamela.

"You're a long way from home, white girl," one said, tapping his pool cue in his hand, then making an obscene gesture, running it up and down through his circled fingers. He smiled widely.

"You, too, cracker boy," another chimed in. "Looooong way from north of the tracks. Wrong place, wrong time."

"That's enough of that." The deep voice came from a milk chocolate-skinned giant in a smart suit and vest, with a pocket watch on a chain, not a bead of sweat on him. Cyrus Cleveland. The other men turned sullenly away and went back to shooting pool. Cleveland invited us back to his office and shut the door.

"I was wondering how long before you came around, Hammons," he said. "And who is your lady friend?"

Introductions were made, and he invited us to sit on a luxurious leather sofa. He sat in a wide leather chair across a coffee table from us. His office also held a desk, chair, bookcases, and a wall of photos. From previous visits, I knew some of them were of him in uniform from the Great War. He served in the Harlem Hellfighters, the 369th Infantry Regiment.

Unlike most colored troops in the Great War, who were consigned to menial tasks in the segregated Army, they were attached to the French and saw combat. Cleveland was awarded a Silver Star and the Croix de Guerre. The regiment's motto was the wonderful, "Don't Tread on Me, God Damn, Let's Go." The war was a bond we shared.

"Navarre's already been down here," Cleveland said. "I'm surprised he showed his face. 'Course he gets protection money from me. And you, Hammons, shook up one of my pool halls. Same business?"

I nodded. "The murder of the nurse."

"You know damned well a Negro didn't do it."

"Of course, I do. Frenchy's just being Frenchy. But we're at a dead end, and I was hoping you might have heard anything about it."

Cleveland lit a Dutch Masters cigarillo.

"Stabbed to death," he said. "That's what Frenchy said. And then she was scalped."

I silently cursed Navarre for revealing confidential information. Who else had he told?

He exhaled the cigarillo smoke. "Are you telling me the cops had a sudden epidemic of good sense and hired you back?"

"No." I shook my head.

"They're idiots."

I agreed. Then I told him that Captain McGrath had engaged me to run my own investigation because this had the signs of a lust murder, my unintended specialty because of the Strangler.

"Who are you looking at?" He asked.

"Kemper Marley."

He inhaled sharply. "And you think this why?"

I gave him the shorthand version, at least as we'd figured it out. "Marley was having an affair with the nurse. She fell for him. When he wouldn't leave his wife, she cut him off. He sent her at least one note, which I found, asking why she wasn't talking to him. Maybe she threatened to reveal the affair to Marley's wife. Or maybe he couldn't have her on his terms. They fought and he stabbed her. Then he scalped her to make it look like a maniac at work."

The cigarillo wiggled in his lips. "You're taking on one powerful white boy. He wants in on Greenbaum's gambling wire. He'd like my rackets if he had the balls to show his face in Darktown. Both Marley and Greenbaum would like to sell narcotics down here, but I won't have it. Any dope seller down here is going to get a beat-down. I provide gambling, prostitution, and booze, but I don't want a bunch of colored zombies addicted to heroin."

Pamela steered the conversation back from Cyrus's high-mindedness. "Is Kemper Marley capable of murder, Mr. Cleveland?"

"Sure, he is," Cyrus said. "What about the young man who died in the natural gas explosion? I hear it's connected?"

From dirty cops in his pay to the quiet intelligence network made up of Negro domestic servants, janitors, and Pullman porters, Cleveland was always in the know. I told him the truth about Bill Sherman's murder and how I was lured to his apartment which was booby-trapped.

"Grenades?" He whistled. "That take you back to the war, Hammons?"

"Not in a good way."

"It shouldn't. You've made a powerful enemy in your investigation. Might be Marley. Might be someone else. Frenchy told me they found the nurse's scalp and necklace in a shack in a cotton-picker camp. Not a Negro one, either. They make the coloreds live in tents. White man in a Buick left the shack, but their stakeout didn't turn anything up."

It amazed me how Navarre played both sides, always rousting Negros but also in Cyrus Cleveland's pocket. Meanwhile, he was Gus Greenbaum's man, protecting his rackets. All the while he was in charge of the vice squad. It was a neat trick with the risk that Frenchy would end up with his throat cut someday south of the tracks or a bullet in the brain on the north side.

Pamela told him how we followed a similar Buick from Marley's, and how it disgorged three toughs at the Hotel San Carlos.

"You'd call that strong circumstantial evidence, Hammons. Or probable cause? In the cops-and-niggers game down here, probable cause is 'driving while colored.' Anyway, McGrath ought to roust them."

"I hope he's doing that now," I said.

"So, what do you want from me?" Cleveland said. The Dutch Master was at its end, and he diligently stubbed it out in the ashtray.

"It's been an odd few weeks, Cyrus," I said. "Three unsolved murders. The third was a man with hidden gold, and I don't mean the Lost Dutchman. The millionaire John C. Lincoln being blackmailed. We're in the middle of all of it. If you hear anything, I'd appreciate you passing it along." I gave him the phone number in the Heard Building.

"I'll tell you one more thing to complicate your life, Hammons," he said. "Your brother is hitting the pipe more and more. That's a liability. Get himself killed. Get you killed, as if you're not already at enough risk. And since I've got you here, where's the colored police officers the city negotiated with the NAACP back in 1919? W. H. Williams was hired then but didn't stay. Now, nobody. You tell your masters they need to rectify that. Joe Island is a good man. He'd make a fine policeman. Here's his address." He passed over a note.

"I'll put in a word."

"Do more than that," he said. "I'll be in touch."

Outside in the car, I lit a nail for Pamela and another for me.

She blew a perfect smoke ring that kept its shape far outside the window. "You continue to take me on the most interesting dates, Gene Hammons."

———

It was about to get much more interesting. I happened to look in the rearview mirror and saw a man approaching from behind. He was twenty feet away. He was carrying a sawed-off shotgun at his side.

I shoved Pamela down onto the floor of the car without a word. Then I rolled out onto the dirt and pulled my gun.

"I shoulda known I'd find you in Niggertown, Hammons," the man said. He was enough of a resemblance to photos I'd seen of Jack Sullivan's brother that I knew one of us was dead.

"I've been looking for you. Followed you. You're the one who killed my brother. Now I'm going to kill you."

Raising to a crouch, I kept the car between us.

"You don't want to do this," I said.

"Oh, I do. This time you're not getting away. And I'm going to kill his lawyer next."

"If you kill me, you'll get the gas chamber."

"If they catch me. After I kill you, I'll drive down to Mexico and slip across the border."

"They'll catch you," I said.

"If they do, it'll be worth it to know you're worm food."

Any hope I had for help from Cyrus Cleveland ceased when I heard the double doors of the pool hall slam shut. This was white-men's trouble.

"Stay down," I whispered when I saw Pamela start to raise up.

I suddenly came up over the car, aimed, and shot him in the shoulder. The impact of the .45 caliber slug knocked him down. A little cloud of dust rose from his backside. But the shotgun stayed in his hand.

Keeping my distance, I did the calculus of the shotgun. At ten feet or less, its two barrels of double-ought buckshot would put a hole in a man. But because it was sawed off, the buckshot would spread wider than a conventional shotgun if fired from farther away.

I kept that ten feet, gun still drawn.

"Stay down," I commanded. He was bleeding badly from the exit wound. "Let go of that shotgun. I did everything I could to save your brother. Your mom knows that. Your brother knew it, too."

But he gripped the sawed-off more tightly and his arm started to move.

"If you hurt my man, I'll kill you deader than dead, you bastard!" Pamela was standing up in the car seat, a ferocious look on her face, her revolver drawing a bead on his head. I'd never heard her use that voice before.

The brother and I were each so surprised that we both hesitated.

"Put that gun down now!" she commanded, honing her aim. And he did.

Twenty-Four

We drove back from Darktown in silence, Jimmy Sullivan hand-cuffed in the passenger seat of my two-door Ford and Pamela literally riding shotgun in the back seat, the sawed-off still loaded. Add in Bill Sherman's brass knuckles, the switchblade from the punk at Union Station, and I was accumulating quite a collection of illegal weapons.

Part of me was tempted to merely take him to a hospital and let him go. But I knew his vendetta would never end. So I made a citizen's arrest—or maybe with the badge McGrath gave me, it was a real arrest.

We drove to St. Joseph's Hospital downtown, and I hauled him inside, where an alarmed nurse saw both the gunshot wound and his handcuffs. I told her he was under arrest and stayed with him, keeping him cuffed to the gurney as they treated him, including starting a blood transfusion. After a phone call to police headquarters, Don and Frenchy arrived with uniformed officers. Explanations were made. So was a formal arrest. I was thankful Pamela wasn't detained for killing him. Frenchy pulled me aside and whispered excitedly. I nodded and patted him on the arm.

Outside, I saw my passenger seat would need major cleanup. But that could wait. Pamela hopped in back.

"Thank you for saving my life," I said.

"I told you I can't lose you, Gene," she said calmly. "Now I need pie."

Inside the Presto Lunch, we both ordered generous portions of cherry pie.

"Things are starting to come together," I said. "Now we know who knocked me out in my office and who took a shot at me outside Barry Goldwater's house after the poker game. We also know where the gold was hidden. Back at the hospital, Navarre told me the money in Parris's suitcase was all counterfeit."

Pamela stopped mid-bite.

"Counterfeit?" she whispered.

I nodded.

"Who the hell was George Parris? He was hiding gold and carrying thousands in counterfeit currency."

"Every time things seem to come together it opens new mysteries," she said. "If Sullivan would have confessed to scalping Caroline and Bill Sherman, blackmailing the Lincolns, and passing along counterfeit cash to George Parris before killing him, we could call it a day."

She had me there.

———

So did Captain McGrath's order to "get cracking." So far, I'd heard nothing about the men who drove into town in the Buick from Marley's spread and checked in at the Hotel San Carlos. Until then, Marley was untouchable.

"Where do we begin?" Pamela said. "We have to start somewhere."

"Let's say Bill Sherman was an outlier..."

"A big if."

"Sure. But maybe he was killed to throw us off the track. Maybe he was killed by someone else, for a different reason. He was the kind of guy who made enemies."

"But he was scalped, just like Caroline Taft. Only the same killer knew that."

"Except we know Navarre was running his mouth with Cyrus Cleveland. I'm not saying a Negro did it. But who else did Frenchy or other cops tell? Lurid crime. Cops talk, same with the coroner's office."

Pamela shrugged. "Okay, we'll do it your way. Tell me how."

I said we'd go back to my methods when the University Park Strangler case was going cold. I went piece by piece of information.

Talk to me.

Tell me something.

What's been missed?

We had to start somewhere: MOs that came close. McGrath gave me files on the Texas and Arkansas murders. The twenty-year-old student nurse in El Paso last year lived alone. She was raped, stabbed to death, and her hair was pulled off after getting off the night shift at the hospital and coming home. And in 1933, the young nurse in Little Rock. She had a roommate, but that girl went to visit relatives in Tennessee. Once again, the nurse worked nights and the same horrible drama played out. Both had red hair. Their underwear was found, one in the bushes outside the apartment—this was the 1933 murder. In El Paso, it was hanging on the wall of a shanty. No fingerprints at the scenes.

I talked to her about my experience with the University Park Strangler and my study of killers like him. As I told her before, I always wondered if he had killed other women, prostitutes who wouldn't be reported missing. But there was more to it. Every lust murderer evolved differently. Some began as rapists before becoming murderers. Or it started by them as Peeping Toms, then burglars, before getting a taste for more—breaking in and raping, then killing.

"Based on that," she said, "those murders in El Paso or Little Rock might have been preceded by those kinds of crimes. We should contact those detectives and see if they followed that trail." She thought for a moment. "Call it the headwaters."

I liked that. But in the meantime, we had more immediate business.

Pamela and I made the rounds of the hospitals, talking to the head nurses. The badge opened doors and mouths. After two days, we compiled a list of nurses and student nurses in their twenties at St. Joe's and Good Samaritan. Four were redheads, six blonds, and twelve brunettes. Of the twenty-two, six lived alone, eight had roommates, and the remainder were married. We put tacks on a map in the office of each nurse's home. All worked night shifts.

We interviewed each one separately. Pamela was invaluable. They were more comfortable talking to a woman, as she had told me when we first talked that night beside Riverside Park. We were straight with them: they might be in danger. All knew about Caroline Taft. We urged them to take sensible precautions, such as having a family member or boyfriend bring them home and make sure their place was secure. Better yet, move in with family or a friend. We asked each if she had noticed anything unusual lately.

A pretty strawberry blond, appropriately named Ginger, said she was sure a man had been following her after work, and her boyfriend was out of town for several days. She caught a late streetcar on Washington Street home to her apartment near the state capitol. Her family lived in California.

That night, we followed Ginger when she left St. Joe's at eleven. Pamela wore a nicely fitting cotton suit with a straw slouch hat. I dressed in black, with my snub-nosed revolver tucked in the small of my back. Ginger removed her cap but otherwise was in her nursing whites. She walked toward Washington Street. We kept half a block behind and stayed on the other side of the street. The city seemed quiet except for a train whistle and no one else was walking. No cars passed until we got to Washington. I let Pamela pace her while I hid behind a palm tree and fell a full block behind. No one appeared to be trailing Ginger.

At Washington, pedestrian traffic picked up. The movie houses were letting out from double features. The echoes of that last night when I caught the Strangler sounded in every footstep. By the time Ginger caught the streetcar, Pamela was aboard, and I ran to reach it. I was the last person to step on, and I remained standing, making a careful inventory of passengers. Single men. How were they dressed and carrying themselves? Knives were easily concealed.

Looks deceived.

Passengers stepped on and off at each stop. By the time we passed Seventh Avenue and headed toward the state capitol, the crowd had thinned out considerably. Ginger's apartment was on a side street half a mile away. I gave Pamela a nod and hopped off, walking slowly west on the deserted street. This way, I could get a sense of whether anyone else had left the streetcar—they hadn't—and be ready to assist if trouble arose when Ginger and Pamela got off.

They left the streetcar three blocks farther on. Nobody followed. We eventually connected and walked Ginger safely to her apartment and made sure it was secure inside. No one followed her this night.

But back home, another call came at two a.m. This time I could hear someone breathing. My "hellos?" went unanswered and they hung up after a few seconds. It was unsettling.

Otherwise, our protection of Ginger went for the next week. The same routine. No stalker behind her. I couldn't tell whether he had sniffed us out and stayed away or Ginger, jittery from the killing of Caroline Taft, was mistaken that she'd been followed. We put this surveillance stakeout on hold.

Meanwhile, I was summoned to headquarters, where McGrath shot down my Marley theory. His detectives interviewed the men in the Buick. They owned land in California's Imperial Valley, and they were visiting Kemper in hopes of selling him property outside El Centro. He didn't take the deal, and they drove back to Los Angeles. I wondered why they didn't take the train: safer and quicker. Safer unless a murderer was trying to throw you off the back of the observation car of the Sunset Limited going ninety miles an hour past the Salton Sea.

I told him about our strategy with the nurses, and his face reddened.

"You used that girl Ginger as bait!" he shouted. "Just like you did with Juliet."

"Juliet got results," I worked to keep my own anger under control. "As I recall, you were opposed at the time. But without my work with Juliet, we never would have caught the Strangler."

He started to speak, but I cut him off. He wasn't accustomed to that.

"Ginger thought someone was following her home when she got off her shift from the hospital," I said. "She wasn't bait. We only trailed her at a distance, then made sure she got home and her apartment was secure. She was never in danger."

We simultaneously lit cigarettes to steady our tempers, and in my case, at least, my nerves.

"It got you nowhere," McGrath said. "You're assuming the killer is the same one as in Little Rock and El Paso. That doesn't explain Bill Sherman, another scalping."

"It's not like the scalping is a secret anymore," I said. "I know Navarre told Cyrus Cleveland about it. That means he also told his buddy Gus Greenbaum."

McGrath winced.

I went on. "Why Frenchy is still on the force is beyond me. He lives above a bar where gambling goes on, for God's sake. Sherman might have made enemies, or had gambling debts, so it was a hit made to resemble the nurse's killing. It made sense to set him aside for now."

"Sense to you," McGrath said.

I shrugged. "We had to start somewhere. You can take me off this case anytime." I had thirty seconds of relief that he'd agree.

"I can't," he said. "Look, Gene, we're stacking up here. Speaking of nurses, we have one on trial for performing an abortion and the mother died. If she's convicted, she faces ten years to life. That's three days or more of the detective who investigated being called to the stand to testify and being cross-examined."

That was a part of the job I didn't miss.

"Had a murder overnight, an oil company executive from Tucson," he continued. "He was held up off Central north of the Arizona Canal. Had a woman with him, she lives on Moreland near you. A married one. The two had stopped for a drink, then came and parked. Make of that what you will. They were sitting in his car when the suspect came up and demanded money. The man refused and got shot. All over seventy-five bucks. Kicked the woman out, then stole the car, abandoned it in a field near Twenty-Fourth Street and Washington."

"That was where the holdup and murder of Bye Oliver took place in '32. My case."

"I remember. This one, he abandoned the stolen car and bent another one, drove north. Coconino County deputies just apprehended him at Mormon Lake. Sheriff McFadden is sending two deputies to bring him back to Phoenix. For now, they're sweating him in Flagstaff."

"That's good," I said. "Can the woman identify him?"

"No," McGrath said. "He was masked. This has the same MO, as the 'petting party' robberies we've seen in the same area. Man and woman in a car petting, get held up. This time, the robber shoots and kills one. We're still sorting out the stories. They were ordered out of the car. Maybe the victim lunged at the gunman, maybe not. Maybe he only argued with him. We don't know yet. The woman was so panicked she ran away and at first wouldn't even let another petting couple help her."

I stubbed out the Lucky Strike. "At least he didn't get scalped."

One corner of McGrath's mouth tilted up.

I said, "Maybe we need to go back to basics."

"Meaning?"

"Meaning, which detective did the death knock to Caroline Taft's parents?"

The death knock was notifying the next of kin in a homicide, then questioning them about pertinent details such as whether the victim had enemies, voiced concerns about being in danger. The basics.

"Your brother is the primary," he said. "But we sent Bill Randall to notify her parents that evening. Mother's dead."

I remembered Randall as a patrolman. He struck me as barely capable, hardly Hat Squad material.

"What about Murphy or Dan Jones? Woodward and Littlefield. They're all solid."

"Working other cases, including two boys firing shots into a house, some rivalry over a girl."

I sighed. "Is Caroline's father alive?"

"He works as an engineer on the Santa Fe."

"What about brothers?"

"She had one, a man three years older. His father got him hired on as a fireman on the Peavine, firing locomotives between Phoenix and Prescott. They both took it hard."

I took it in. Railroad men, railroad spikes in Bill Sherman's body. Could it be that easy? Revenge was the oldest motive in the world, besides envy. Cain and Abel. Don and Gene. I suppressed a shiver. I asked if I could interview them. Then asked the same about Sherman's family. McGrath agreed. I wrote down names and addresses, then stood to leave.

"One more thing," he said.

I sat back down and chain-smoked another nail.

"I received a parcel in the mail today," he said. "It was actually addressed to you, here at headquarters. Marked 'personal.' No return address, of course. In it was a man's head of hair, dark brown, torn from the top of his head. My guess is it's Bill Sherman's scalp. That, on top of Sherman being forced to call you and lure you to his booby-trapped apartment."

I said, "I suppose that's the other reason you won't take me off this case."

He nodded. "This killer is after you."

PART THREE

I Go Down to the Pit

Twenty-Five

The temperature crossed one hundred one degrees on Tuesday. The newspaper told me I'd receive six hundred dollars for being a Great War vet, part of the bonus we'd been promised, and the bonus marchers had demanded in 1932, before a bloody dispersal outside Washington, D.C. A fire destroyed the Cisney planing mill on south Third Street, killing a deaf and dumb Mexican man who lived in a nearby shanty. He lived until midnight at the hospital, horribly burned. No good way to die, but this was the worst. I prayed for him. Republicans held their national convention in Cleveland. They didn't stand a prayer against FDR.

The police swooped up five Chinese businesses for running illegal lotteries. Three downtown nightclubs were raided, too, with the *Republic* stating, "'When we had evidence that gambling was happening, we took action,' said Leonce Navarre, head of the anti-vice squad." Frenchy, head of the anti-vice squad! I laughed until my stomach hurt. Bribes hadn't been paid. The Chinamen were fined one hundred-fifty dollars and no doubt were back to business.

Pamela and I put our heads together about approaching the father and brother of Caroline Taft. Henry was the father. Her older brother was named Carl. Both worked on the Santa Fe Railway.

"Spikes," she said.

"Let's check their backgrounds first," I suggested. "I looked at headquarters and neither has an arrest record. But we can talk to people who know them."

She stood and grabbed her purse. "The railroad yards."

We locked the office and drove to the Santa Fe's Mobest Yard. Unlike the Southern Pacific, which ran straight through Phoenix from San Francisco and Los Angeles to Chicago, San Antonio, Houston, and New Orleans, the AT&SF built a branch to Phoenix from its mainline through northern Arizona. Because of its twisty profile with many spurs, it was nicknamed the "Peavine." Past Wickenburg, northeast of Phoenix, another line branched northwest to Parker and into California.

Santa Fe passenger trains ran south to Union Station. But except for a small freight yard to the west of the depot and tracks to serve warehouses, their freight station downtown with the neon SANTA FE sign on the roof, and to exchange cars with the Espee, most Santa Fe freight trains stopped at Mobest. The roundhouse was here, too, and a passenger-car-servicing facility.

We parked in front of the homely one-story railyard office facing McDowell Road, where it crossed Nineteenth Avenue and Grand Avenue. The air was full of dust and engine exhaust. Some trainmen sitting on a bench out front said the man in charge was appropriately titled the Yardmaster. As a small locomotive chuffed past, they fetched him and appreciated my colleague.

A barrel-chested man came out, sunburned bald head except for a remnant of brown hair on the sides and back, and I showed him my buzzer. He led us to a small office with an evaporative cooler hanging in the window. His desk was cluttered with paperwork and a two-piece telephone on a scissors extension.

Unlike the men out front in their overalls, work shirts, bandannas, and blue-and-white-striped caps, the Yardmaster wore a tie, a white short-sleeve shirt, and a vest that contained a Hamilton railroaders watch. He checked it against the clock on the wall, which also contained a chalkboard showing train movements. Don had pawned our father's Hamilton. Unlike his medals, it was gone by the time I realized it and reached the pawnbroker too late.

"Sorry to seem distracted," he began. "We had a fire take down a bridge fifty miles east of Winslow. Shut down the main line. Thirteen passenger trains and twelve freight trains are stuck in Gallup. They're holding our eastbound trains in Ash Fork." He shrugged. "What have Henry and Carl gone and done?"

I asked why he wondered they had done anything.

"You're the police, for one thing," he said. "Plus, they both have short fuses, and they've been broken up about the girl's murder. But they're good workers, reliable. Henry Taft has seniority and can bid on any train he wants. Carl's a decent fireman. If he keeps his nose clean, he might make engineer, too."

"Tell us about the short fuses?"

"Henry's a drinker. Never on duty. But I've seen him get in a bar fight when he thought someone insulted him or cheated at cards. Carl takes after his dad. He punched a conductor six months ago, not that the man didn't have it coming. But it nearly cost Carl his job. The union saved him."

"Has their behavior changed since Caroline's death?" Pamela asked.

"Well, not my place to go digging at a time like this…" he began and stopped himself.

"Of course not," Pamela encouraged.

"Mind if I smoke?" he asked. We didn't and he carefully packed tobacco into a pipe and lit it.

After a couple of drags, he said, "They've been quiet, to be expected. Done their jobs. Carl fired a train down from Prescott this morning, thirty-nine empty reefers." Refrigerated boxcars carried the citrus, lettuce, cabbages, cantaloupes, and other bounty of the Salt River Valley back east. Sometimes I thought it was the only part of the local economy that wasn't infested by corruption. But, of course, Marley owned plenty of farmland.

He exhaled heavily. "I can't even imagine losing my daughter, much less to have her murdered. And the killer's still at large, am I right?"

I told him he was.

Then I asked whether either had been in the service and whether they were working the day Bill Sherman was killed. Henry was in the American Expeditionary Forces and saw combat in France. Neither had been working on the day of Sherman's murder.

I showed him black-and-white photos of the spike heads that had been driven into Sherman.

"Those are ours," he said. "Why do you ask?"

"It's routine," I said.

"I'm surprised you're not here about the gold train?"

Alarm bells went off in my head.

"What gold train?" Pamela asked, her notebook at the ready.

"That's what we called it. About a month or so ago Train Forty-Seven came down from Ash Fork to Phoenix. The brass from Chicago alerted us that a courier was aboard carrying gold and he was armed. It was part of the gold confiscated by President Roosevelt." He pronounced it ROOsevelt. "Only me and a handful of others were told, just in case there was trouble."

"Was there?" I asked.

"Not a bit. He got off at Union Station. I have no idea what he was doing here."

I asked him to describe the courier, and it was a dead ringer for the very dead George Parris.

———

There was nothing to do with the fresh information about Parris but file it away. McGrath wanted to know about the two homicides. Were they the random work of a lunatic, a lust killer, or something more mundane: Bill Sherman killed Caroline Taft, and her father and brother took revenge? That latter scenario made sense if they knew Caroline was scalped—probable, considering her body had been released to the family. So much for Sherman.

But he wasn't the well-dressed man who left Caroline's scalp and necklace in the shanty, then drove away in a Buick Roadmaster. Her killer.

By now, however, it was a process of elimination. Time mattered. And hope. Hope like hell the scalper didn't strike again.

"I think we should split up," Pamela said once we were in the car.

I said it was a bad idea.

"Why?"

"There's a chance one or both of them are killers," I said. "Look at what they might have done to Bill Sherman. Remember, his murderer forced him to call me and lure me to his apartment. It was rigged with booby traps. If they're accused, especially because you don't have a badge, they might kill you."

"I can take care of myself." She sounded heated.

To get away from the sound of locomotives and freight cars coupling and uncoupling, I drove east on McDowell.

"I'm not saying you can't, dammit," I said. After a pause. "I can't lose you, Pamela. We came damned close outside Cyrus Cleveland's."

"And who came to the rescue!"

I had to admit it was her.

She smiled. "Are we having our first fight, Gene?"

"I suppose we are."

She laughed. "True love. Let's flip a coin. Heads we go together, tails we split up." She produced a quarter, flipped it, and slapped it expertly on the top of her hand.

"Heads," I said.

It was tails.

Pamela suggested she contact Carl. He was close to her age and might be willing to open up to her. I knew she could turn on the "all honey, honey" routine, too. I hoped it worked and she would be safe.

I knocked on the door of the Taft residence on Culver Street, a small bungalow with well-watered grass on the parking lawn between the curb and sidewalk, and the larger lawn set off with flower beds. Tall oleander hedges rose in the backyard. Out of habit from being a policeman, I didn't stand directly in front of the door.

The top of the head of the man who answered the door came up to my eye level. He had thinning sandy hair and wore a stained, sleeveless undershirt revealing muscled arms. Short as he was, I'd have trouble taking him down in a fight. For that matter, so would Bill Sherman, much less him and his son. Both had access to railroad spikes. Both, because Caroline's body had been released to the family, knew she had been scalped. I tried not to get ahead of myself, tried to assess Henry Taft. The resemblance to Caroline was hiding under the older features of his face.

I showed my badge. "I'm Detective Hammons," I said. "I wonder if you could spare a few minutes?"

"I suppose so." He turned away, and I followed him inside. We sat down in front of a coffee table crowded with half a dozen stubby beer bottles. Him on one side, me on the other.

"I don't know what else I can tell you people," he said, suppressing a belch. "Unless you're here to tell me you caught the murderer of my daughter."

I filed away that reaction in my mind. Did it mean he was genuinely curious or covering up his involvement in the revenge on Bill Sherman?

I told him I was very sorry for his loss, couldn't imagine what he was going through, the usual Hat Squad routine to build empathy. If it worked.

It didn't.

"Sorry?" His voice raised. "Sorry won't cut it." He swigged a beer. "Do you have children, Hammons?"

"No."

"Then how can you understand? How can you understand outliving your child? Much less have her murdered. I saw her body sewed up from the autopsy!"

I waited a few beats before I continued. "Did your daughter tell you anything that made you sense she was in danger?"

"I already answered this!" He paused and ran both hands across his head. "The truth is, we hadn't been close for some time. She disapproved of my drinking. She wanted me to get help, and I didn't need it. The last time we met, we argued. It breaks my heart. She had her mother's beautiful hair. Some son of a bitch scalped my daughter!"

"We're working very hard to catch him."

He just looked at me like I was lying to him.

"What about her brother?" I said.

"Carl? They were close. He's really taking it hard. He's not the same."

I took the interview in a different direction.

"I hear you were in the Great War."

"Fortieth Division," he said. "From the Arizona National Guard. Hundred Fifty-Eighth Infantry Regiment. We were in the Meuse-Argonne offensive."

"Handy with a grenade?"

"I sure as hell was," he said. His eyes focused suspiciously on me. "Why?"

"Just always happy to talk to another vet," I said. "I was in the Second Division."

He slightly relaxed. "You saw heavy fighting."

I asked about her boyfriend.

"You can't suspect him," he said. "Struck me as a good man. Way better than that hood she was with. That cured her of being attracted to bad boys. Bill Sherman."

He knew his name.

I said, "Do you think Sherman was capable of murdering her?"

"He sure as hell was," he muttered, a flush overtaking his face. "I can't say I'm sorry he was killed in that gas explosion."

"You read the newspapers closely," I said.

"I read that."

His face was unreadable. So I tried to drop it light as a feather, where was he the day Bill was murdered?

"I was at work."

"Are you sure?"

He watched me closely. "I think so. All this mess, the funeral planning, all of it. I think I was at work."

He looked different now from when he was in a suit, when I only saw him at a distance. The funeral was conducted in the

First Presbyterian Church on Monroe Street last week. Pamela and I attended, sitting in the back. This was typical Hat Squad procedure: Who was there, who wasn't, any suspicious characters? It looked routine and was hideously sad.

I said the boss told me he was off that day. His eyes flicked away. He finished off the beer, rose, and headed to the kitchen. "Want one? Nope, you're on duty."

My muscles tensed. I reached inside my sports coat and touched my gun, clicked off the safety. Its metal was the only cold thing in the room. He might emerge from the kitchen with something more than a beer, put two holes in me, dump me in a mine shaft in the desert. My worry over Pamela shot up, too. I kept my breathing steady, prepared to unholster the gat and thumb back the hammer quick enough to drop him.

Good detectives have a sixth sense about these things. Good private eyes, too. The ability to see through walls.

I pulled the gun from the shoulder holster, cocked it, and put it between my legs just as he stepped into the room with a revolver aimed at me and fired. My right side erupted with fire and pain. I aimed and fired one round, hitting him in the chest. He flew backward into a china cabinet shattering it and falling to the floor. One round was enough. He stared at me with dead eyes.

"Goddamn it!" I shouted through my ringing ears to a room swirling with gunsmoke, taking the Lord's name in vain. Or maybe it was me that was swirling.

I heard a banging on the door.

"You alright in there?"

It was a brave soul to be at the door after hearing a gunfight. It was a postman, my guardian angel.

"I'm a Phoenix Police detective," I tried to shout. "Let yourself in." He did.

"Call the police. We need an ambulance now!" My coat and shirt were wet with blood. I applied direct pressure, trying to stop the bleeding. My side was searing with pain as the postman spoke urgently on the telephone.

Then my world went black.

Twenty-Six

When I came to, Pamela was holding my hand. Captain McGrath was asleep, slumped in a chair on the other side of the bed. Don was standing at the foot of the hospital bed, watching me.

"He's awake," he said, and McGrath stirred himself.

"You're lucky," Don said. "The bullet went in and out your left side, but you were bleeding badly. Lucky twice that the mailman was there to find you."

"How long was I out?" I said, feeling groggy. A glass bottle was hanging from a pole above my bed, with a tube leading into a bandaged area of my hand.

"It's the next morning," Pamela said, leaning in to kiss me. I stroked her hair. "I was so wrong in having us split up. I should have been there with you."

"You couldn't know," I said.

"Henry Taft is dead," McGrath said. "One shot from that hand cannon you carry was enough, straight through the heart. We executed a search warrant of his house and found a box of live grenades, a knife with blood matching Sherman's, and a piece of scalp matching his. We arrested his son as an accessory to murder. Good job, Gene."

"Good job, Gene," my brother said with an edge in his voice. "It's too bad the Chief of D's didn't have confidence in his real detectives to solve this case. And try not to get addicted to the morphine they gave you for the pain."

"That's enough, Hammons," McGrath said.

Don pivoted and strutted angrily out of the room.

I raised myself in the bed causing my side to explode in pain. After it eased, I filled McGrath in on the visit to the boss at Mobest Yard, which led me to Henry Taft. I also told him about the railroad man mentioning the gold courier. He took it in, said he would await my report, and I should take my time until I was feeling well enough to get back to the office. I wasn't on the force, but I still had the work that all detectives hated: writing reports, and ones detailed and accurate to stand up in court—or at an inquest.

"Thank goodness you're okay," I said to Pamela.

"I was only worried sick about you," she said.

"How about Carl Taft?"

"It went off without trouble," she said. "He was very shattered by his sister's death, alternating between tears and anger. He didn't understand why the police hadn't made a single arrest." She avoided looking at McGrath. "He's a big guy, certainly capable of having killed Bill Sherman, especially along with his father. When I brought up Sherman, he grew really enraged. He knew Sherman had hurt and threatened his sister. To say he had no use for him would be an understatement."

McGrath finished the thought. "Carl doesn't have an alibi. Our theory is that he helped his father assault Sherman and nail him to the wall with railroad spikes."

I said it still didn't explain why they had targeted me, forcing Bill Sherman to call me and lure me into an ambush at his apartment.

"Bill had your business card," Pamela said. "Maybe they thought you were his accomplice in murdering Caroline? Maybe Sherman even said that, hoping he could talk his way out of it, or buy time for you to get there and rescue him."

"Makes sense," McGrath said.

Made only a grotesque sense to me.

McGrath stood and gently touched my shoulder. "When you feel better, you still need to find Caroline's scalper. I wish I could count on your brother and the other detectives, but I can't. I'm behind the eight ball."

"Too bad I'm only a civilian playing cop."

"Gene," he said, "I need you on this. What if the killer strikes again? You're the only one who has what it takes to find him."

That made me want to drag out my convalescence for years.

But, of course, I wouldn't.

———

It took me a week to get back to the Heard Building. Pamela was back at the courthouse, looking into Walter Humphrey. I was halfway through typing my report to Captain McGrath on the Henry Taft incident when Lewis, the reporter, let himself in.

"How about a story about you killing the murderer of Bill Sherman?" he said, notebook and pencil out before he even sat down.

"No," I said.

"Well, why did you kill Henry Taft? C'mon, Hammons. You're a hero. But the story's got to be more than that. The grieving father of the slain nurse attacks a private eye and ends up shot dead. Tell me off the record. What caused you to burn powder on him?"

I pushed the typewriter away and faced him. "Because he annoyed me."

His eyes widened.

"I'm only doing my job. See how the police lie? They said Sherman died in a gas leak explosion. Turned out he was killed by the father and brother of Caroline Taft, the murdered nurse. They were after revenge! I knew it was connected!"

"You're a smart guy, then."

"But you knew, and you're just a gumshoe. No offense."

"Now you know, and you're just a hack. No offense."

It took him a few moments for the cogs to turn and realize the insult.

"So, you won't tell me why the grieving father shot you, nearly killed you, and you shot him. A gunfight in a peaceful neighborhood." He seemed to talk mostly in newspaper jargon. "Police are baffled!" I was waiting for that one. "My readers still want to know why there hasn't been an arrest in the nurse's murder. People are afraid the killer will strike again. Unless it was Sherman that did it."

"He didn't," I said. "He had an airtight alibi."

"Can I quote you?"

"No." I thought about it. Maybe publicly clearing Sherman's name would smoke out the real killer. It was a risk, but I was out of options. "Off the record. Say it was a source close to the investigation."

He scribbled quickly, pulled out a cigar and lit it.

"What happened to your wife not liking cigars?"

"I'll chew some gum. Hope for the best. This is good stuff, Hammons. Go on."

I shook my head. "Give and take, remember? What can you give me?"

He leaned forward. "I looked into that lawyer you told me about, Humphrey. He's an investor in the Camelback Inn."

"Tell me something I don't know."

He took a puff on the cigar. "The nurse was scalped. And she was having an affair with Kemper Marley. My editors won't let me put it in the paper. You know the power Marley has."

"How do you know any of this?"

"Reporting," he said. "Reporters dig for the facts. The people's right to know."

I lit a Lucky and concealed my reaction. My side started throbbing. Without any morphine, I could sympathize with my brother's addiction to opium because of his war wounds. I was determined not to follow his twisted path. But Lewis was moving to the top of my prime suspects list.

———

Pamela came back an hour later, excited. First, she wanted to know how I was feeling, and I told her the truth about my pain. Indeed, when I turned to the side to reach the return arm of the typewriter, I let out a yelp. Her kisses helped immensely.

"I never made it to the courthouse," she said. "Helen Lincoln was coming in the building. They have a new demand from the blackmailers."

"Big surprise."

"She showed me an envelope they received in the mail, a letter and photos," Pamela said. "The letter demanded another fifty grand, or they would release the photographs to the newspapers, and not only ones in Phoenix."

She handed me the envelope and I slid out the black-and-white pictures. They showed John C. Lincoln holding ingots. Looked convincing. But Victoria had shown me how photos could be doctored, and these were obviously fake. A famous example was how Ulysses S. Grant's head was attached to the body of another general on horseback. I explained the process to Pamela.

"She's the one who broke your heart," she said. "Victoria."

"I'm very over that."

She gently hugged me. "I'll never break your heart."

I promised her the same. After a few seconds, I told her what Lewis had said about Caroline being scalped.

"How could he know?"

"Maybe Navarre told him," I speculated. "Frenchy can't keep his trap shut. He loves to see his name in the newspaper. Or Lewis is our killer. We don't have time for this distraction."

"We need the money," she said.

"I just got my six-hundred-dollar bonus check for being a veteran," I said.

"And we owe these clients our help."

That seemed to settle it. I scanned the letter. It was as Pamela had laid it out. But the crooks said they would be in touch for the time and place for the handoff.

I sighed. "Okay. But this time we'll do it my way, and not hypothetically."

She laughed. "I won't stop you. But promise me you won't get shot again."

I promised.

Twenty-Seven

We waited until sundown to drive to shady Pickwick Gables motel on Van Buren Street. The Depression had eased enough that people were traveling again, not merely Okies heading to the Promised Land. Those who could afford it took the train. But more and more loved the freedom of the car, the open road. East Van Buren was U.S. 60 and contained rows of motor hotels—"motels"—with elaborate neon signs. The same was true on Grand Avenue where U.S. 60 continued to Los Angeles, and Seventeenth Street turning south to Buckeye Road, U.S. 80 to Yuma and the Coast.

Pickwick was a few blocks west of the highways. The lights were on in the same room where we followed the blackmailers from Union Station and two cars were parked in back. No one came or went. We parked on the street.

I handed her the sawed-off shotgun.

"Use this if things go south," I said. "This will give you more firepower up close."

I showed her the two triggers, one for each barrel. "Here are four backup shells. Break the shotgun open like this." I demonstrated. "Let the empty shell fall out and reload." I snapped the weapon back together, showed her how to cock it. "It's twelve-gauge buckshot, so be prepared for a kick. Only use it if you have to."

She reluctantly took it. I told her to wait in the car while I went to the office. I showed the desk clerk my badge, getting far more use of it than McGrath intended, and asked to see the register. The owlish man in Coke-bottle glasses opened it for me. Room One was registered to Walter Humphrey. I asked the clerk for a spare key and instructed him not to tell them I was here.

"We run a respectable place here," he said. "We don't want trouble."

"Good. Then do as I ask."

Finally, I asked him if there was a back door. The answer was a pleasing no, only one way in and out, the front door.

"What's going on?" he asked.

"Routine."

Outside, I walked across the lawn, a good twenty feet from the curtained window of Room One and waved to Pamela. She crossed the street, carrying the sawed-off. I pulled out my M1911 but only thumbed back the hammer and slipped on the safety, "cocked and locked." I was hoping things didn't go south.

I motioned for her to pause beside the building near their front door, which was closest to Van Buren but facing east, into the shady courtyard. There I met her and showed her the key. I didn't want them to see shadows in front of the window.

Next, I stood before the door and gently slid in the key. It went in slick, turned smooth as silk. But when I tried to open the door, it caught on a chain. Subtlety was over. I thumbed off the safety on my gun and kicked in the door.

"Nobody move," I said. "You move, you die. Police."

I stepped far enough in for Pamela to come behind me

and aim the shotgun, then she kicked the door closed behind her. Surveying the room, I saw three men, one of whom was Humphrey. He indeed looked like Wimpy, hair standing on end, a messy troll with small black eyes, but I didn't have a hamburger to give.

The next was the handsome one who snatched the hatbox, and finally the hood who came at me with the pipe in the express room. He was younger than the other two men, lying on a bed, and slowly moved his hand toward the pillow.

"Ah, ah, ah," I said, leveling the M1911 at him. His hand stopped.

"Reaching for some reading material?" I continued. "Well, let's see it. Very slowly."

I really didn't want to kill two men in as many weeks.

He slowly produced a revolver. I ordered him to hand it to me holding the barrel, then I slid it in my belt.

Humphrey started to speak but stopped, mouth open, when Pamela leveled the sawed-off at him. "We know who you are," she said. "So don't think you're talking your way out of this. We're here for the blackmail money, the photographs, and the negatives."

He closed his mouth. One by one, I searched them, then a cursory pat-down of the room. The revolver was the only weapon I found. The hatbox was in the closet but it was empty.

"Blackmail is a dangerous business," I said. "Blackmailers get killed."

"We're not…" Humphrey said.

"Yes, you are and, like the lady said, don't think you're talking your way out of this."

Suddenly, the young tough on the bed lunged at me. I swung the gat at his temple, dropping him to the floor. Thankfully for him, it was his other temple from the one that met my blackjack at Union Station, and I didn't knock out more of his teeth.

Now my blood was up. I holstered my gun and grabbed the handsome courier from his chair. "Who's next? You?"

I slammed my fist into his solar plexus and kicked him in the balls. He fell to the thin carpet, writhing in pain.

Humphrey came up by the lapels. I backhanded him.

"That's for your rotten defense of Jack Sullivan."

Again. Blood streamed from his nose.

"That's for blackmailing the Lincolns."

Again. He'd have a shiner from this one.

"And that's for being in my town."

I briefly turned away and smiled at Pamela.

"Where's the money, Walter?"

"Gambling debts," he blubbered. "Greenbaum would have killed me if I hadn't paid."

"And the bullion you doctored into the photos?"

"There's no gold, I swear." He raised his hand. I looked skeptical.

"Swear to God! Got it from another picture and spliced the negatives."

"Where are they?" I demanded.

He pointed to a briefcase. I nodded to Pamela, who retrieved them.

"This looks like all of them, photos and negatives," she said.

I pushed Humphrey back into the chair. Then I collected their driver's licenses and other identification—a phone bill from the man on the floor, a letter to the thug on the bed.

"Here's the deal," I said. "I want you all gone. If I find you in Phoenix or blackmailing again, it's prison." I nodded toward Humphrey. "Plus, disbarment for you, Walter. You're an officer of the court involved in a blackmail scheme."

He started to protest but I went on. "You ever wonder why Phoenix has so few box jobs? It's because when the police find the safe crackers, they beat them nearly to death with billy clubs or blackjacks. Smash their hands. Word gets around. Now the same is true for blackmailers. Now blackmailers are going to face much worse. Beaten to death and dumped in another county. Got it?"

Mr. Ball-Kicked nodded from the carpet. Humphrey protested about his law practice.

"Go to Tucson," I said. "Anywhere. But not here. Never again. And I'll make sure Greenbaum knows all about you. Messing with the Chicago Outfit is deadly."

We backed out the way we came.

When we crossed the railroad tracks at Nineteenth Avenue, Pamela asked, "Were you serious back there?"

I sighed. "I've seen so much violence in my life. The Great War. The police. A private investigator. Sometimes I wish I'd never done any of it. I'm not a violent man."

"I know you're not that man, Gene," she said, taking my hand. "Your violence is to protect people. And if you'd never done any of it, you never would have met me."

"Then I wouldn't change a thing," I said. "Sometimes we deal with violent criminals and downright evil in this city of dark corners. Who speaks for the victims, for the innocent? We do. Everybody counts or nobody counts." I shrugged. "End of speech."

"It's a good speech," Pamela said.

"So, with those guys back there, they need to believe I'm capable of carrying through my threats. Now, you can deliver the photos and negatives to the Lincolns, and we have a murderer to run down."

———

That night the phone woke us. My watch said it was two a.m. It was beside the bed. I answered and was met by silence. Then the call ended.

"Wrong number?" Pamela said, raising herself on an elbow. Her breasts showed pleasantly in the ambient light.

"I hope so." But I got out of bed and walked to the window, which was open against the heat. The parkway held a dozen or more parked cars, but none appeared to be occupied or running. I heard a locomotive whistle in the distance, but otherwise the city slept. I couldn't see any lights on, only the streetlamps on the parkway and the neon of downtown in the distance. I climbed back into bed but lay on my back, unable to sleep.

Then the phone rang again. It was three a.m.

This time I simply picked up the receiver and listened. A man was breathing.

"I know you're there, Hammons." It was a man's voice, but unfamiliar and scratchy as if he was speaking through a handkerchief or dish cloth.

"I'm here. I'd ask who you are, but you're not going to tell me."

"Of course not. That might give you an advantage you don't deserve." By this time, Pamela was leaning against me, listening in as best she could.

I listened to him breathe. Then I said, "Why do I need an advantage?"

"Because you're good at what you do," he said. "The famous detective who nabbed the University Park Strangler. The 'lust killer' expert. Your reward was to be laid off from the police department. You must be bitter."

"I'm fine," I said.

"I know you better than you think. I've been following you, watching you. I was waiting in your office and hit you from behind. I could have killed you, but that wouldn't be sporting. I was disappointed that you didn't have anything about me in your files."

"I might have information on you if you tell me your name."

"Liar," he came back and laughed. Five beats and then: "I killed the nurse."

Now it was my turn to laugh. "Why would I believe you?"

"Because I scalped her," he said. "Pulled that pretty red hair right off. Took the necklace, too. Put them in a shack. You found them there."

"Go on."

He did. "I watched her for days before I killed her. So cute. Left her apartment windows and drapes open. Bad taste in two of her boyfriends. I followed her home from the hospital, night after night. I love to watch, have for years. You really cramped my style during the Strangler's reign of terror. He went for redheads, too. I had to stay inside."

"Sorry about that. What made you change from a Peeping Tom?"

"I hate that term," he said. "Voyeurism is very arousing. Don't tell me you haven't heard your neighbors having sex and couldn't stop yourself from listening. Maybe they even wanted to be heard and seen; it added to their pleasure. Maybe you felt that way with Victoria Vasquez in your apartment or your new love, Pamela. Pretty name, pretty girl. Who was listening in or watching as this happened?"

I said he still hadn't answered my question.

"Something about the redhead changed me," he said. "I wanted more. She had a neighbor, another one with red hair, even more beautiful. But you know that..."

I suppressed an answer. Pamela wrapped an arm around me.

"That night I got inside and pulled her down. I loved seeing the fear in her eyes. I told her if she kept quiet, I'd let her live. So, I had her. Took her from behind, too, facedown in the bed, ass in the air, submissive. Extra points if she'd been a virgin. She cried anyway as I raped her. Then, when I was done, I said, 'I lied.' Pulled out the knife. She screamed and I kept stabbing. Then I scalped her and left. The scalp came off very easily. That last part was a sudden inspiration."

It sounded like our guy, but I made one more test.

"It's a good thing none of the neighbors called the police."

A scratchy laugh. "They couldn't. I cut the phone lines outside the building. You know that."

"It's time to turn yourself in," I said.

"Turn myself in to whom? You? You're a shamus. Oh, I forgot, the chief of detectives hired you to find me. Must chap your ass, considering you'll never get back to being a real policeman again, at least in this town. He mustn't have much confidence in his real detectives, including your opium-addicted brother."

"They'll all be happy to slap the cuffs on you."

"As if they were capable, which they're not. I'll do things that will make them run like a scalded dog."

I forced myself to take in a breath. "I guess you'd know. People like you start off by torturing animals."

"You think you know me!" he screamed. "You don't know anything but what I allow you to know." That laugh again. "I like gardening. Does that surprise you?"

"It bores me," I said. In fact, it did surprise. I made a mental note. "I'm only getting started and only you can catch me," he said. "You and me. Who will win? So far, it's one to nothing, my favor. This is the last time we'll have such a long chat, Hammons. I know you'll get your line tapped to trace the call, if poor Phoenix PD has the technology and can get Ma Bell to go along."

"I'm sure you could call from a pay phone and disappear before the call was traced."

"Smart guy. Oh, I forgot. The girl, Ginger, another nurse. Natural redhead. 'Carpet matches the drapes,' as they say."

I felt cold, wanted him off the telephone. "What about her?"

"Go find out. She's a virgin. Or was. Catch me and this will be your greatest case. But you won't ever catch me. And make sure the newspapers give me a good nom de guerre. Better than the University Park Strangler. We'll talk again."

Twenty-Eight

I immediately called police headquarters and said a woman was being assaulted in her home. The crime was in progress—*in progress* always got the attention of the police. I gave Ginger Davis's address and hung up. I'd make explanations later. In the quiet outside the window, I heard the siren atop headquarters alerting all on-duty foot patrol officers to check in at call boxes, then the wailing of the westside patrol car going, I hoped, to Ginger's apartment.

Pamela was already dressed. I pulled on some clothes, and we ran down the stairs to my Ford.

I tossed her the keys. "Would you drive? I want to write down the particulars of that phone call before I forget."

There was no time to worry about being watched or followed. She raced over to Fifth Avenue, then south to Washington and west toward the copper dome of the capitol building. Not a car was on the streets until we got close to Ginger's apartment. As we approached, I could see three marked police cars, an ambulance, and two unmarked. Maybe McGrath was already here.

We stepped out on the curb and walked down the same sidewalk where we'd followed Ginger home safely all those nights.

Now it was different, and not just because of the cool breeze blowing out of the west, mocking us.

A big, uniformed cop stopped us. "Nobody passes."

"Let 'em through." It was Captain McGrath, in a suit and tie in the middle of the night. His face was frozen in an angry grimace. He led us inside, past other uniforms, two newer detectives I didn't know, and the ambulance crew whose attention wasn't needed.

"You called the police, right?" he demanded.

"I did."

He wanted to know why.

"Because the killer phoned me tonight."

McGrath's eyes widened. A whisper: "Damn it to hell, Gene."

Beyond all the living being allowed to walk around, contaminating the crime scene, was the dead. Ginger Davis was face up on the floor. Her body was completely nude, her legs spread wide, knees raised, with semen and blood trickling from her vagina. Pamela touched my back, any human contact to hold off this horror.

Ginger's beautiful hair was gone. Multiple stab wounds penetrated her chest, two of which mutilated her small, firm breasts. Blood spread across the hardwood floor. Her eyes were wide with terror. I felt like a voyeur in hell.

"She fought him," I said. I knelt and raised her hands, examining the fingernail broken off her right index finger and skin under her other nails. The detectives looked on, bystanders.

"Will somebody bag her hands, damn it!" I said. Maybe we could at least get his blood type, maybe match his skin color. McGrath ordered it done.

I continued, "He's got to have a nasty gash on his face from this." At least I hoped so.

Rising up, I looked around the bedroom. The bed was

turned down and pillows knocked sideways. A lamp on the bedside table was ready to topple off. The University Park Strangler would never have been so messy.

"She got off work hours before," I told McGrath. "She was asleep when he came in, if he picked the lock. Or he followed her in before she could close and lock the door."

"Or he was waiting for her," McGrath said. "That would have allowed him to take his time with her. He probably called you from here. After he…" a shudder, "…arranged her." This reaction from a cop who had seen some horrific crimes.

I picked up the phone, using a handkerchief to avoid leaving my fingerprints. "The line's dead. So he must have called from elsewhere. Do we have prowl cars canvassing the neighborhood, officers going door to door?" These seemed insulting things to say, but the department wasn't at its best right now. Orders were shouted and half the apartment cleared out. Good.

I thought further. "We need to make sure she actually worked at the hospital tonight."

"Think he's good for it?" one of the detectives said. He looked as if he were capable of drooling on himself.

"I know he's not," I said. "But he might be dead."

Echoes sounded in my head. Grace Chambers and Ben Chapman, both students, boyfriend and girlfriend, killed by the Strangler. It was as if this killer was following his footsteps, at least a few, but with a knife instead of strong hands around their throats.

McGrath put a hand on my shoulder. "You were right about her," he said. "I'm sorry I backed you off."

"None of us could be sure, Jack," I said, for some reason feeling empowered to use his nickname.

"And yet he called you tonight."

I pulled out my notebook and reconstructed the telephone call as best I could.

McGrath asked for my impressions.

"He's smart and sophisticated and cocky. Asking for a 'nom de guerre,' properly using 'whom' in a sentence instead of 'who,' and showing intimate knowledge about tracing phone calls. He knew I solved the Strangler case. Looking back, I realized he'd called before during the past several weeks, always around two a.m., but those times he only hung up."

"You're sure he's our man?"

"Absolutely," I said. "He laid out all the details of the Taft murder, things only the killer would know, including cutting the phone lines. He wanted to tell his story, how he'd been a Peeping Tom all the way back to the Strangler days, wanted me to understand what brought him to murder." I took a deep breath, "He knows about Pamela."

People rustled around us, a photographer taking shots— Victoria's old assignment—detectives finally making notes and a sketch of the apartment layout. Then officers covering Ginger's body with a blanket and loading it onto a stretcher. They carried her out.

I continued. "He wants to show he can best me. It's personal, whether I'm on the force anymore or not. Definitely a lust murder, based on everything he's said and done. He talked about enjoying the look of fear in their eyes. And he's homegrown. This isn't the killer from El Paso or Little Rock. He's so proud of himself, he would have mentioned those if he'd done them..."

McGrath finished my thought. "And he's not done here. Not by a long shot." He thought for a moment. "You said he sounded as if he was concealing his voice, maybe speaking through a handkerchief or a cloth. Any chance it could be Marley?"

I nodded. "Possibly. Or someone else whose voice I'd know."

"Oh, my God!" one of the uniforms shouted. We moved into

the kitchen, a neat, welcoming place, except for the pantry door that sat open. The officer regained his composure, adjusted his Sam Browne belt, and pointed.

Inside a young man was stuffed. His hands were cuffed from behind. A gag was tied in his mouth. No pulse.

We dragged him out, seeing his face was hideously burned. Scalded. And a Bowie knife was sticking out of his chest.

I pulled out his wallet, got a name. My guess was he was Ginger's boyfriend. My other guess was that he'd been attacked, restrained, and forced to watch Ginger's rape and murder, powerless to help her. Looking around, I saw a large pot in the sink and a burner still going on the range. After seeing all this, he was forced in here to be scalded in the face and murdered with the knife. I knew we wouldn't find any fingerprints.

Yet another figure contaminated the crime scene. I looked behind me and saw the chief of police, his face set in anger. He looked me over, then motioned his head to McGrath: outside.

"My slacks will fit better," he said to me, "after the ass chewing I'm about to get."

Laying all this out for McGrath, I was reminded how ordinary people weren't like psychopaths. They could be surprised on encountering a psychopath, too surprised to fight back. And the killer was becoming bolder. J. Edgar Hoover told me 150,000 murderers were roaming the United States. One of them was enough to wreck our summer.

Afterward, Pamela and I walked back to the car, arms around each other, propping each other up.

"When will the feeling pass," she said, "that we let her down? Both of them?"

I suppressed a sigh. "Never."

———

The next morning, I was in the records room at police head-quarters. Back in the Strangler days, I kept a file with every Peeping Tom or burglar who had been arrested in the previous year. Juliet Dehler was still there, happy to see me, and dug out the file, still intact. We caught up over the police swill called coffee—she married last year—then I sat at a table and dug through each arrest report, each suspect that we sweated as the citizens of Phoenix locked their doors, bought guns, and the Hat Squad was under unrelenting pressure to get results. Back then, of course, our murderer wasn't among them. He was a respectable employee of a building and loan company. This time might be different.

I separated out those who had been repeat offenders and did time in the county jail, up on the fifth floor of the building, or burglars who were sent to prison. In another pile were the ones who were put on probation and released. O.M. Haggerty caught my attention. He was nabbed looking into windows of a house in the University Park neighborhood. No priors. But he went to trial, represented by Walter Humphrey. The jury let him off.

I asked Juliet if any records of the trial existed. The last thing I wanted to do was interact with Humphrey again. None were there, but she promised to check with the county, look through other arrests that might match the man I was seeking, and call me.

Back at the office, I saw Pamela was reading the *Phoenix Gazette*, the afternoon paper, "hot off the presses," as the reporter Lewis would say.

"Safe so far," she said. "They don't have anything on it. The temperature is supposed to be one hundred one."

July arrived and it was getting to be sleeping porch time. I brooded over how we'd make the apartment safe: chair against the front door, maybe a wire strung at ankle level and screwed into the wall a few feet in to trip an intruder and give us time to arm ourselves. But being on the screened porch, even on the second floor, was an invitation to being watched.

That night we slept uneasily.

The next day, we went out for breakfast and took the *Republic* to share. Prescott's big July Fourth rodeo was in full swing. Back in Phoenix, the grape harvest began. Railroad refrigerated box-cars would take the grapes as far as the Midwest and Buffalo, New York. Peaches and cantaloupes were being boxed up in the produce sheds down by the railroad tracks on Jackson and Madison streets. An advertisement invited veterans to use their bonus checks to begin building a house. Hitler and the Nazis were making moves to take Danzig, further shredding the Versailles treaty.

Meanwhile, another man was set to die in the Arizona gas chamber for a murder in the desert near Beardsley Road, north of Phoenix. Thankfully, it was one I had nothing to do with. Like Jack Sullivan, he protested his innocence, saying his father did the killing and fled to Mexico. A few days later, I read that his widow was allowed to view the man's body in his wooden coffin on the way to the prison graveyard. She kissed him and acciden-tally inhaled the deadly cyanide fumes. They nearly killed her, but a doctor saved her in time.

As to the rest of the news, as I'd hoped, the papers ignored the murders. They were much less aggressive than even a few years before. Most of it was national and international stories by the Associated Press, United Press, and other wire services. David Lawrence and "Hi!" Philips wrote editorial columns that ran on the front page, along with staff artist Reg Manning's drawings. They were uniformly anti-Roosevelt in a pro-Roosevelt state. Neither paper carried the news of my shooting of Henry Taft or the arrest of Carl Taft for the murder of Bill Sherman.

Interesting news was hidden in the "Little Stories of Phoenix Daily Life." It was heavy on mundane comings and goings but also carried crime news. Today one paragraph said twenty-seven-year-old Bernice Burnett paid a fifty-dollar fine for running "a house of ill fame." She was one of my informants. I hoped Marley, the real owner, reimbursed her. Another paragraph, more promising, "The trial of Lionel Ramirez, on a rape charge, scheduled for Monday in Maricopa County Superior Court, was postponed until September 17th." I'd check him out and the details of the rape, although the caller didn't have a Hispanic accent. Which meant nothing. Victoria didn't have an accent.

I filled in Pamela on my time reviewing the records of arrests of nearly ten years ago. She told me that McGrath had tapped our phone in the apartment and office, and was working with Mountain States Telephone on setting up tracing. As the killer told me, our technology was primitive.

But our luck ran out the following morning when I picked up a *Republic* at the corner newsstand. The main headline was boldface capital letters:

NURSE MURDERS BAFFLE POLICE

Feeling the blood pump through my temples, I scanned the story. It read:

> The killings and rapes of two nurses over the past six weeks in Phoenix are the work of the same individual, dubbed 'The Angel of Death' by detectives, according to police sources.
> Both nurses were also scalped after they were assaulted and stabbed to death, according to Detective Leonce Navarre.

I cursed Frenchy aloud and read on. The story went on to

name the nurses and add that the killer had also handcuffed and stabbed to death Ginger Davis's boyfriend. Then:

> *Police sources say Gene Hammons is now leading the investigation that has left detectives stymied for weeks. Hammons caught Emil Gorman, the infamous University Park Strangler who terrorized Phoenix in 1929. Gorman was hanged at the State Penitentiary in Florence in 1930.*
>
> *Hammons is an expert on "lust killers" and homicidal psychopaths. He left the Phoenix Police Department in 1933 and has been working as a private detective, most recently partners with Pamela Bradbury. Hammons declined to comment.*

I stalked into the newspaper offices, past the front counter, and into the half-deserted newsroom, trying to cool my rage. I found Lewis, who looked up just in time for me to pull him up by the necktie.

"We need to talk," I said, roughly dragging him by the arm upstairs to our office. Gagging by my necktie lift, he didn't have the opportunity to protest.

Pamela was already there with her own copy of the newspaper. I dumped Lewis into one of the straight-backed wooden chairs, and we stood on either side of him.

She said, "You write too many run-on sentences."

I pushed the chair backward, and Lewis yelped. It didn't fall all the way to the floor, but stopped against the wall, held precariously by the two back legs.

"Don't move," I said. "I'd hate for the chair to fall and you break your head."

"I can explain!" His forehead was wet with sweat.

"Oh, I bet you can," I said. "You named Pamela, putting her

in danger." Further danger, I thought, because the killer already knew her name and more. "The 'Angel of Death' was a nice touch. Guaranteed to panic the city."

"That wasn't me!" he said. "That only came in the second edition, after the AP put it on the wires and the *LA Examiner* added it!" That was the Hearst newspaper that called the Strangler the "Fiend of Phoenix."

"You didn't have to copy them, much less attribute it to the police," Pamela said. "It looks like you made up most of this."

"Except the parts you didn't," I leaned in. "Only the killer would know the nurses were scalped, raped, and stabbed to death. I'm liking you more every day as the killer."

"No, no!" he pleaded. "It was Detective Navarre who told me about it. He's a really good source, likes to see his name in the paper."

That, unfortunately, was true. But I demanded he tell us where he was on the nights when Caroline Taft and Ginger Davis were murdered.

"I can't remember far enough back…"

I kicked the chair out from under him. It slammed to the floor, bouncing his head.

"Then you're going to jail."

"Wait!" He was watching us from the floor like a small, caged animal. "On the night Ginger Davis was killed, I was in the city room until one a.m. You can check with my editor!"

I said, "I will. Why didn't you go out for the story when the siren at headquarters sounded? I was there, didn't see you."

"It was after deadline!" he said, still not sure what we'd do with him.

"Do you like to watch?" Pamela said.

"Watch what?" Lewis rubbed the back of his head.

"Peeping Tom," she said. "I bet if we checked, we'd find you have a criminal record."

"No," he shook his head. "I'm no Peeping Tom. I've never even had a traffic ticket."

I pulled him up by the necktie again, him doing a crab walk so he didn't choke to death. Then I pulled him to his feet and pushed him against the wall. I pulled out my sap, ready to swing it. His eyes widened.

"Don't think we won't check," I said, tapping the heavy leather instrument against his temple. "Not that we'll be persuaded by your story, either. The University Park Strangler never had so much as a parking ticket, either."

He brushed himself off and scurried out the door without looking back.

Twenty-Nine

The next morning, the phone rang at two a.m. We were both waiting but let it ring six times before picking up.

"Busy?" The same scratchy voice.

"Never too busy for you." I said.

"You've tapped the line."

"Not yet. We're not as quick as big-city police departments."

I listened to the silence, hoping no clicks or tapping sounds came. So far, so good.

He spoke again. "Did you enjoy my handiwork with Ginger?"

"You're a common murderer," I kept my voice calm as Pamela came close to hear, and I held the earpiece out a bit.

"Oh, don't be a sore loser, Hammons. She tried to fight me, for all the good it did her. I made her beau watch as I took her. It was a bonus that I caught him there with her. Did her twice, including in the ass. She screamed in pain. Did I tell you I'm well-endowed? By the time I was through with her, she was crying uncontrollably, too exhausted to resist. All the kid could do was look on, be a voyeur himself, me doing things he only dreamed of doing. Then…well, it's not like I could let him live. He'd seen my face."

"Where'd you get the handcuffs?"

"Maybe you think I'm a cop," he said. "May be. Wouldn't that be sweet, that I'd been under your and McGrath's noses all these years? But I might have gotten them at a pawn shop. Look, you should be grateful for our conversations." He gave an unsettling laugh. "You never had them with Emil Gorman when he was at large and at work."

"Why do you like hurting women?" I asked. "Do you have mommy issues?"

"You don't know me!" he screamed. A nerve struck and how.

"Oh, I know you pretty well," I said, "and I'm learning more every day." I forced myself to laugh. "You're the well-dressed man who left Caroline Taft's scalp and necklace in a shanty, then drove off in a Buick Roadmaster. You're the one who followed Ginger Davis from the hospital all those nights."

I thought: *Just keep talking, asshole.*

He did. "You know less and less. I do like the Angel of Death name. Fits perfectly."

"Glad you like it."

"It'll ensure fear, thank you. And the shit will come rolling down on you and McGrath like an avalanche from the chief of police, city commissioners. The chamber of commerce, too. Who wants to visit a city where the Angel of Death prowls?"

"If you're a cop, that avalanche will hit you, too."

"Maybe. That's for you to find out," he said. "If I'm a policeman or not, don't think you're safe. That badge won't mean a thing if I come after you."

"But you like knives," I said. "Why is that? If you were a cop, you'd use a blackjack or a gun."

"What do you think I used on you in your office? You dropped like a ton of bricks. But I like to cut, slash, and stab. It instills more fear."

"I see."

For a moment, I thought he was gone. Then his scratchy voice came back. "Get to work, Hammons, because another one's coming. I'm a horny one, you know. And nothing makes me more aroused than when they're afraid and try to resist. Far better than watching, although being watched in the act added to my thrill, especially when it's the girl's boyfriend or lover. Maybe I'll do that to you someday with the beautiful Pam."

He hung up before I could promise I'd kill him.

Pamela held me tight to calm me down. "We need President Roosevelt to give us a personal fireside chat," she said and it made me laugh.

Ten minutes later the phone rang again.

"Hammons."

"We traced him, Gene." It was my brother, sounding sober and focused. "The call came from a pay phone at the Salt River Hotel in the Deuce. Frenchy's on the way with some uniforms. I'll meet them there."

"Be subtle," I said. "No sirens or lots of cops converging, especially this time of morning. I don't want him to know we can trace his calls."

Surprisingly, Don agreed.

"Good hunting," I said, and he rang off. I resisted the temptation to go down there myself.

In fact, the killer had chosen a good location. The Deuce, centered along Second Street, was dense with bars, pool halls, pawn shops, low-end retailers, and cheap single-room occupancy hotels. The down-and-out clustered there even with the economy improving.

The Deuce bled into the central business district, a stone's throw from the Fox Theater, Korricks, Goldwater's, and other respectable businesses. And Chinatown, with its many storefronts, legal and illegal. The Deuce was an easy place to move in and out of unseen—especially if the beat cops who walked the streets didn't know who they were looking for. It might have people on the streets even at this time of night.

Pamela could see I was stewing so I talked.

"I don't like it that he threatened you," I said.

"It'll never come to that," she said. "You protect me, and I'm well-armed." She smiled. "I'll kill him because I'm not Pam."

I laughed but prayed to God I could protect her.

"And the handcuffs," I said. "He talked about maybe being a policeman. What if he was or is? That would explain so much. He could be one step ahead of us because he's on the inside." I took a quick inventory of officers I knew, but it was far from complete, and I didn't want my suspicions to run away with me.

I lit a nail and exhaled. The smoke looked blue in the darkness. "Cops aren't perfect. They're open to bribes and other corruption. What if one of ours is worse than on the take? What if he's a murderer?"

"Is there any way to identify those cuffs used on Ginger's poor boyfriend?" she asked.

"Unfortunately, not," I said. "We don't have 'PPD' engraved on ours. Like he said, you can buy a pair at a hock shop."

Pamela said, "If what he's told you rings true, he's been at work since late 1929..."

"You were graduating high school."

She smiled. "Naughty boy, but yes. My point is, where was he between the time of the Strangler, when he claimed to be a Peeping Tom, voyeur, whatever, and a month ago when Caroline Taft was murdered?"

It was a key question.

"He might have been in prison."

"Do 'lust killers' just stop and then start again?"

I said I'd never run across that before. It was possible. "But more likely he was in stir or moved somewhere, such as California, where he could continue his crimes, before returning here."

We had many avenues to follow. The killing of George Parris and the gold. The blackmailing of the Lincolns. Those seemed like a lifetime ago.

———

Cyrus Cleveland called a few hours later when we were in the office.

"Hammons," he said. "You're a man in the news, not in a good way."

"Tell me something I don't know."

His voice rumbled. "Don't talk to me like I'm one of your informants! I deserve respect."

That was a dubious assertion, but I apologized.

"I appreciate that," he said. I heard him puffing on a cigarillo. "Thought you'd want to know a strange white man's been taking in the attractions of Darktown." I waited for him to let out a long plume of smoke. "I'm told he got in an argument with the madam, wanting a particular girl who was occupied at the time, then he whipped out a badge, said he was police."

"When was this?"

"Last night," Cleveland said. "We know the cops who work the colored neighborhoods, and he's either new or impersonating a police officer. I ran it past Frenchy. He said he didn't know the man."

I asked for a description, and he gave it. Tall, good-looking, well dressed, a fresh scar on his left cheek. That would fit with a man who Ginger fought and scratched. "Of course, all you white folks look alike to me."

"Ha ha. Did he end up paying for the girl when she wasn't occupied, as you put it?"

"That's one thing that surprised me," Cleveland said. "He whipped out a wad of twenties and started flipping them off, so I'm told. Gave a hundred to the madam and a hundred to the lady. You see, the girl he was looking for also works at Good Samaritan in the laundry. If they paid her enough, she wouldn't have to sell herself like this. He wanted information on a nurse there."

"Why ask her?"

"She has the run of the hospital," he said. "So, she knows the staff. But being colored, she's invisible to most white folks. If I was this killer, I'd ask someone like her for information rather than asking around the hospital."

I sucked in a breath, let my side hurt, and stuck a nail in my mouth and lit it.

"Do you know the name of this nurse?"

"Name of Rebecca Howard," he said. "Twenty-five years old, red hair, single, lives alone. Sounds like the Angel of Death, hunting. He was very specific in describing her, and my girl didn't know better than to tell him. Fortunately, she also told me. I'm doing your work for you, Hammons."

Thirty

I stood next to McGrath at in the ornate commissioners' chambers at City Hall, on the west side of the City-County Building. Ornate phoenix birds were carved into each side of the entrance. McGrath and I had chosen it as the best place to be away from headquarters and prying ears, especially if the killer really was a policeman. Six members of the Hat Squad and some select uniformed officers gathered around.

"Gene is acting as a consultant on the Taft and Davis murders. Some of you youngsters don't know he…"

Don interrupted: "Solved the University Park Strangler case, is an expert in lust killings, star of the newspaper story, stalker of the Angel of Death, a gentleman and a scholar."

But none of them chuckled. All, without exception, looked scared. It was something I'd never seen from the Hat Squad. I could even see it behind Don's smirk.

McGrath's voice was struggling to hold back anger. "Shut up, Don. If all of you had been doing your goddamned jobs, none of these killings would have happened. Now, the city commissioners, the ones who sit in this room, are demanding fast action. They think we're incompetent." He turned to me. "Walk us through it, please."

I explained lust killers, the ones who received sexual gratification from murdering their victims. Sometimes during the act. Others got it after the victim was dead. The term was coined in the late 19th century and held abundant examples. The University Park Strangler was one. I also told them about Fritz Haarmann, the Butcher of Hanover, who did some scalping of victims. I wrapped up our little map of hell: "Another is the work of the Torso Killer, which began a couple of years ago in Cleveland, Ohio. The victims were beheaded, had their hands and genitals cut off. Eliot Ness, whose squad of Untouchables got Capone, is in charge of the investigation. The killer sends him postcards. He still hasn't caught him." I looked them over. "We have to do better."

I felt as if I needed to give an "eve of battle" speech as inspirational as our colonel spoke to the troops before Belleau Wood. But I didn't have it in me.

Behind me was a blackboard where I'd written a timeline of events and taped the photos of Caroline Taft and Ginger Davis, including shots of them after being raped, stabbed, and scalped. In addition, I placed the photo of Davis's boyfriend, run through with a Bowie knife.

"You can read how we got here," I said. "He claims to being a Peeping Tom all the way back to the Strangler days. But we don't have any crimes since 1929 that fit his description. One of the mysteries is where has he been. Prison? Another state..."

"Looney bin with your girlfriend Ruth Judd," Don whispered.

I continued, "He's not afraid of us. We should consider him armed and dangerous. He uses knives on his victims. But he knows they're defenseless. He might also carry a gun and he's capable of killing a police officer. He's said as much. It gets worse. He used handcuffs to restrain Ginger's boyfriend and made him watch him rape and kill her. He told me he might be one of us."

A murmur ran through the room.

"I'm interested in how we can stop him before he kills again. A few of you know he calls me, brags about his murders, talks about his methods. No question he's our man. He had information about three killings that only the murderer would know. We have my line tapped and so far, he doesn't know it. He likes to hear the sound of his voice, almost can't help himself. I hope that's a vulnerability we can exploit. The other night, two a.m., we traced a call to a flop house in the Deuce. But no luck in catching him, even though the streets were empty that night except for a few rummies lying on the sidewalk. He probably got in a car and drove off."

Lefty Mofford said, "He took a hell of a chance, that time of night."

"He likes to take chances," I said. "That's part of the thrill for him."

"Did the hotel manager have a description?" Lefty asked.

Frenchy shook his head. "Ordinarily, he'd have a clear view of the pay phone in the lobby. But when the call was made, he was dealing with a fight upstairs between two drunks over a dame."

I said we did have some inkling of what he looked like. I relayed what the Okies in the shanty had told us, along with the information from Cyrus Cleveland.

McGrath interrupted. "This is confidential information." He glared at Navarre.

"Now we have a good idea of his next target," I said, attaching a photo to the blackboard beside the three other victims.

"Rebecca Howard," I said. "She fits his MO: twenties, red hair, attractive. Works the night shift at Good Sam, gets off at eleven p.m. Lives alone. He hasn't called me to hint at her yet, but my information is solid."

"You've got to tell her," Don said. "She might want to leave town."

"I've thought about that," I said, "but if she does, we lose our best chance to catch him."

McGrath crossed his arms, and for some reason everybody else took that as a cue to light up cigarettes. I did the same.

He asked me how I wanted to play it. I laid out my plan.

———

Later that day, Pamela contacted Rebecca and asked to meet with her during a break on her shift at the hospital. They agreed to meet in the cafeteria and Pamela described herself and what she'd be wearing. I thought it was better that she go alone. My hope was that speaking with a woman her age might ease the dangerous information she was going to receive. Rebecca actually knew Caroline Taft, had worked with her. Now, Rebecca— who preferred Becky—had a choice to make.

———

Becky worked "the floors," meaning the floors containing the patient rooms, as opposed to operating rooms or the emergency room. Starting that evening, she always had a new colleague nearby. Although he was dressed in a white coat like a doctor, he was a detective, one I had vetted to make sure he wasn't our killer who might have been a cop, too. He carried a gun in an ankle holster.

After her shift ended, she walked as usual the three blocks north to an apartment on Eleventh Street and Coronado Road. It was a mile or so from the house where Ruth Judd and an accomplice killed her two roommates and dismembered them in 1931. Oddly, I had to keep pushing that out of my mind, a silly distraction. Other detectives kept watch of Becky at a careful distance. Still more staked out the apartment itself.

Becky was level-headed and determined to help us. I was surprised. Pamela was persuasive. We had the advantage, so far. Only the information from Cyrus Cleveland pointed us to Becky as the killer's next victim. But the Angel of Death didn't realize that we knew, and we would be ready. The city commissioners would not complain about the mounting overtime. Pamela and I kept our distance from the operation. He knew us, after all.

Yet it had been several days since he'd called. This worried me.

Two nights later, I closed up the office late. Pamela had already left for the apartment, promising to pick up Chinese takeout from Sing High. I went out the alley-side door of the Heard Building, toward the two-story Western Business College to the north. The downtown streetlamps, elegant five-globe arrangements atop poles, didn't reach their illumination here. As a result, I didn't see the man waiting for me. I never saw his face, only felt the gun against the back of my head, pushing me face-first against the brick wall.

"You're up to something, Hammons."

It was the same voice as on the phone, without the cloth to conceal it. Definitely not Marley. One of his henchmen? Maybe. I ran through the list of cops I knew by their voices. Nothing sounded familiar.

He braced me against the wall like a pro, tossing my gun and sap onto the pavement.

"I could kill you so easily," he said. "Would you ask the Lord to forgive me, choirboy? Forgive my trespasses as he forgives yours, such as failing to save Caroline and Ginger?"

I did what you'd do when a gun barrel is tickling the nape of your neck. Nothing.

"But if I killed you," he said, "I wouldn't get the satisfaction of watching you helpless as I kill again and again. I'm on the hunt. Maybe your Pam."

"Pamela."

"What?"

"Her name is Pamela, and if you hurt her, I'll kill you."

He chuckled and pushed the gun barrel harder against me. "You're not in a position to make threats or promises. You need to remember that."

I needed a lot of things. I needed a drink. I needed my gun in my hand. I needed Pamela in my arms and a long vacation together, some place cool.

Suddenly, I heard a voice from the street.

"Put the gun down, bud, and do it slow."

From my peripheral vision I saw a uniformed policeman twenty feet away on the sidewalk. His gun was drawn.

He reiterated: "Put the gun down!"

But my antagonist didn't hesitate. The gun left my neck and fired two shots, dropping the cop in a heap. Someone on Central screamed. When I turned around, he was running to the alley to Monroe Street, dark hair under a straw fedora and wearing a pale summer suit. I could have pursued him, but a higher duty called. I gathered my weapons and ran to the sidewalk.

I cradled the officer's head in my lap as a crowd gathered.

"Someone call the police!" I commanded. "Tell them that an officer is down and has been shot! We need an ambulance."

But it was too late. I set my hand on the side of his neck and the carotid pulse was absent. His eyes were open, surprised, then they involuntarily fluttered and closed. The two shots had hit him in the middle of the chest, one in his badge and the second into his heart. His standard-issue .38 revolver lay uselessly in his right hand.

Thirty-One

Then we were right back to protecting Becky as if nothing had happened. Which was dead wrong, of course. A police officer was buried with full honors. The front pages of the *Republic* and *Gazette* were plastered with lurid stories of the shooting, half true. Lewis, the reporter, avoided me.

The monsoon came early. Thunderheads rose above the mountains and brought spectacular lightning and rain into the city. Occasionally a dust storm rolled through, too. It cooled down the temperatures enough for us to move back in from the sleeping porch, feeling safer inside the apartment.

Our man was a cop killer. If he was a cop who killed cops, it was the worst of the worst. One thing was clear: This chase had only one inescapable conclusion and that was him dead on the business end of my gun.

In the meantime, we needed a break in the case. He'd stopped calling, and the officers protecting Becky hadn't noticed anything unusual. The *Republic* editorialized about the lack of progress on solving the murders.

I took Pamela down to headquarters and introduced her to Juliet Dehler.

She had examined the case against Lionel Ramirez for rape and found no similarities with the Angel of Death. Ramirez might well be innocent.

"Anything on the case of the guy Walter Humphrey represented?" I asked.

"Orville M. Haggerty," she said. "He was arrested for allegedly trespassing on a property in University Park, in 1929, the height of the Strangler panic. He was twenty-eight then and admitted to peeping in windows. But Humphrey got him off, not least because we caught the real killer at the time of the trial."

We. I was happy to share the credit because without Juliet's help Emil Gorman might have gone on killing.

"Haggerty's still in town," she said. "Works for a medical supply company." She handed us a slip of paper with his home address. "He's never been in trouble since. That we know of."

"We're missing something about the murderer," I said. "The Angel of Death. He was a cool character when he got the drop on me in the alley outside our building. Same when he shot the policeman who had him in his gunsights. Yet he got away despite a downtown dragnet, maybe because he looked exactly like a man who sold medical supplies and had easy access to hospitals and nurses. Ordinary." *Looks deceived.*

Pamela's expression turned from concern to thoughtful. "Why does he stalk and kill nurses with red hair?" She unconsciously fluffed her hair over her shoulders.

I asked her to continue.

"It's possible he was spurned by a nurse," she filled in the blanks. "Or he was married to one who cheated on him, filled him with rage."

"Or she caught him cheating," Juliet said. "And divorced him."

Pamela nodded. "Maybe all his talk about going from a

Peeping Tom in 1929 to a lust killer now is so much bunk. He's definitely a lust killer. But maybe he's acting out revenge for something that happened recently."

Juliet said, "That could mean another nurse might have been killed before Caroline Taft. The first one, the one who set him off. Then the scalping came later."

She agreed to look through the open-unsolved homicide and missing persons reports for someone who fit the profile.

"And could you look at domestic violence calls over the past two years?" I asked. "I don't mean to saddle you with work, but the killer might have given his nurse wife a black eye and the cops were called. If one looks promising, maybe it led to a bitter divorce instead of murder, at least that time." I thought about my brother doing the same in one of his heated fights with Dottie. They each knew how to push each other's buttons.

"I'll help," Pamela said. "If Juliet doesn't mind showing me the ropes."

It was settled. And I was relieved to have Pamela working in the safest place in the city. As long as the Angel of Death wasn't a policeman.

Outside, I looked at the front page of the *Republic*. A headline said, "THIRTEEN MURDERERS EXECUTED IN 24 HOURS." It was across nine states, by hanging, electric chair, gas chamber, and firing squad. I wished it could have been the Angel of Death.

That night we made love with a rumor of thunder over the mountains. Then the storm rolled in with white stabs of lightning. Afterward we lay side by side, her leg across mine, as it began to rain, a heavy tapping on the roof.

Thirty-Two

After the storm rolled through, the phone rang. The clock said one a.m. I picked it up without saying anything.

After a few seconds: "Are you there, Geno?"

"Frenchy?"

"He attacked Becky an hour ago."

I held my breath.

"She's alive," Navarre said. "But you'd better get over to her apartment."

I leapt out of bed and started dressing, putting on my shoulder holster, and telling Pamela what had happened.

"I'm coming, too," she said, quickly putting on some clothes and a green beret.

I'd rather have her with me than alone here. We ran to the Ford, the top luckily raised, and sped east.

At Becky's apartment, she was sitting on the bed shivering, a blanket over her shoulders even though she was fully dressed. Pamela sat beside her and draped one arm over her back and held her hand with the other. I couldn't see any sign of injury, although on closer examination I saw her uniform was torn.

Navarre started to fill us in. As Becky walked home from

Good Sam, someone started following her. Fortunately, a plain-clothes policeman picked him out and matched him step for step, about a half block behind on the dark street in the rain.

Suddenly, from the living room, I heard Captain McGrath shout, "Where the hell is Hammons?"

I didn't know which one he meant. Don was technically the primary, but I hadn't seen him. I walked into the room.

He came in and glared at me. "Where the hell is your brother?"

I was not my brother's keeper. Lord knows I tried. I simply shrugged.

Frenchy joined us and continued where he left off. Becky was a block from home when the plainclothesman lost the man following her. He yelled for her to run, which she did, keys in hand. Another detective was inside her apartment.

Reaching the door, she sensed a man behind her. Turning, she saw a shadow and a flash of knife. But she gouged the shadow with her house key. She might have gotten him in the eye, but wherever it was, he screamed in surprise, pain, and rage.

"Don't think I won't come back for you, little bitch!" he shouted, running off.

The detective opened the door, by which time the plain-clothesman was there, too. One stayed with Becky, while the other set off in the rain and lightning in search of the Angel of Death. The apartment's telephone line had been cut from the outside, same MO as the other murders. So, the detective took Becky with him to a neighbor's and called headquarters, before bringing her back here.

Fifteen minutes later, a perimeter was set up in a ten-block radius while prowl cars prowled. Yet he escaped into the night and storm. Somewhere I heard barking in the distance, a large bad-tempered dog.

"Find out what's making that dog bark," I said. "Check the emergency rooms. He might have gone to one if Becky's key slashed him badly enough."

"Use the radio," McGrath said.

"Go to the neighbors and use their phone," I countermanded. When McGrath looked at me, I said the killer might be monitoring the police radio.

He nodded and lit a nail. I did so, too, but stepped outside. This was the closest we'd gotten to nabbing him. We also foiled his plan to attack and kill Rebecca Howard. Maybe that put her out of danger. But given his ego, he might come back after her again. He said he would. Or he might pick another victim, another nurse or someone else who attracted his evil mind. After I smoked down the cigarette, I walked to the curb and tossed it into the street.

"Geno!"

It was Navarre.

"Just got a call from Good Sam emergency room. They're treating a man who lost an eye to a sharp object. He's there now."

McGrath was with us. He nodded to me. "Both of you go. Now."

———

I jumped in the passenger side of Frenchy's unmarked car. He gunned it south on streets still wet from the monsoon storm. We crossed McDowell Road, which was empty of traffic, and parked on the street outside the emergency entrance. He went to the trunk and pulled out a pump shotgun, racking in a round. I slid my .45 from its shoulder holster, clicked off the safety, and thumbed back the hammer.

"Let's get this bastard, Geno," he said, and then walked quickly toward the lighted entrance with the word EMERGENCY in neon. I was two steps behind.

I heard other units pulling up behind us, then the captain in charge of patrol directing his officers to establish a perimeter around the hospital. None of us knew which of the many doors were locked at this time of night or could be pushed open to escape the building.

At the ER we opened one of the two doors and stepped in, ready for action. For Frenchy, who for all his flaws was no fool in situations like this, it meant holding the pump-action shotgun at an angle to the floor. My barrel was facing the ceiling, both hands holding the gun with my arms bent at the elbows. A woman at the front counter stared at us in fear.

"We're police," Frenchy said.

This didn't lessen her fear. She cocked her head, aiming it to double doors and mouthing the word "Help!"

We came close and she whispered, "A man came in with his hand over his eye. He said he'd been attacked and gouged. We took him right back. Then you called and asked if anyone matching his injuries had come in, so of course I said yes. Then I heard a scream in the ER."

"When?" I asked.

"Maybe five minutes ago." She checked her watch.

I told her to tell the policemen who followed us the same thing and that two detectives were already back there.

Then I pulled Frenchy close. "I'm going in first, low. Follow me and be careful with that scattergun."

He nodded.

I got on my haunches and pushed slowly through one of the two wooden doors, which had a window at the top of each. I didn't want him to see us coming. The door opened soundlessly.

It opened into a long hallway with a desk and several

curtained-off exam rooms. I rose and walked quietly ahead with Frenchy behind me. The door whooshed shut.

Suddenly I saw two figures, a terrified nurse and a man holding a menacing piece of stainless steel at her neck. I could barely make him out before he started talking.

"Don't take another step, Hammons," he rasped, obviously in pain. "You either, Navarre."

I sighted my semiautomatic at his head. He was ten feet away, and I knew I could drop him with one shot. The trouble was his nerve-endings still might run the scalpel across her throat.

I took him in: He was tall and broad-shouldered, mussed dark hair, and a gauze patch taped over his eye. High cheekbones and square jaw. In different circumstances some might have considered him handsome. But he was ordinary handsome, someone from an insurance office who blended in with the movie crowds on Washington Street or riding a streetcar, or visiting a hospital. Looks deceived.

One relief: He wasn't a Phoenix cop. I'd never seen him before since I didn't have eyes in the back of my head when he held a gun on me in the alley beside the Heard Building.

"It's all over," I said in a conversational voice. "The place is surrounded. Put down the scalpel and let her go. Then walk toward us with your hands on your head."

His voice was stronger. "In your dreams, Hammons. Little bitch Becky put out my right eye, but I can see fine with my other one. Now I've got another nurse, had to settle for a blond. I swear I'll kill her if you don't put down your guns."

One of the axioms of law enforcement was that you never gave up your gun. Never.

"I'm putting down my shotgun," Frenchy said. "So I can get my handgun. Now do as you're told."

"Don't be ordering me around, Navarre!" He pulled the

nurse closer, one arm around her breasts and the other holding the scalpel closer to her throat. It gleamed in the overhead lights. I said, "Let's play this out, genius. You kill the nurse and we kill you. There's a good chance she'll live because she's right here in the emergency room. I don't think they'll be of a mind to treat you, especially with two bullets in your head. There's only one way this ends well and that's when you let her go and give up."

I whispered to Frenchy: "Can you find a way to turn out the lights? Just one bank might confuse him long enough for me to shoot the bastard."

He whispered back: "I'm right beside some light switches but it's risky."

I realized that. Sudden darkness might panic him and cause him to kill her. We didn't have flashlights, so darkness didn't give us a tactical advantage. I was grasping at solutions.

"This is no game, Hammons," he said. "She'll be dead before she hits the floor. But all your training and foolish compassion will make you run to her, see if she's alive, try to help her, and I'll be gone."

It was the strangest Mexican standoff. The smart thing was to wait him out. I whispered it to Frenchy and his silence concurred.

But he read our minds. "Don't think you Keystone Cops are going to stall your way out of this," he said. "I'm not some amateur like the University Park Strangler. I want to see your guns on the floor and hands on your heads."

"Not going to happen," I said. "How's it working out for you, genius? You let a ninety-eight-pound nurse stick a key in your eye and now the police have you surrounded. Very amateurish, if you ask me. Your spree ends here."

Frenchy whispered, "Easy, Geno."

He was probably right. The Angel was cornered and unpredictable. I'd never been in this kind of hostage situation before. We didn't know how many people were huddled in the treatment bays: doctors, nurses, and patients. The scalpel was close enough to draw a tiny trickle of blood from the blond nurse's neck. Her cheeks were streaked with tears and her hands clenched.

"What's your name, ma'am?" I asked.

"Daisy," she squeaked.

"We're going to get you out of this, Daisy. Try not to be afraid."

"You all should be afraid!" he yelled. Then, in a lower voice, "Are you praying to forgive my trespasses, choirboy?"

I was onto *deliver us from the evil one.*

In the next second, I saw a shape behind him: my brother. He'd come in quietly from behind. Don pulled the killer's elbow down, then his hand away from her throat.

Several things happened almost instantaneously. The nurse ran toward us. Frenchy grabbed her and shoved her into one of the treatment bays. We both advanced on the killer, our weapons drawn. Don struggled with him, but he was strong and difficult to subdue. At one point, Don had him from behind, but he slammed his shoe onto the top of my brother's foot, an expert move. Don dropped to one knee, blood spattering from cuts inflicted by the scalpel, including one on his right hand that caused him to drop his snub-nosed revolver. It hit the floor with a crash magnified by the silence elsewhere, thankfully not discharging.

Then the killer disappeared the way Don had entered. I scanned the floor: He had Don's gun.

"Take care of him," I ordered a doctor who peeked out from behind one of the curtains. Don was on his knees, bleeding. But

I forced myself forward. Frenchy was right behind me, having doubled back to get the pump shotgun.

Through the double doors was a long hallway heading into the hospital. The killer leapt up and smashed one light fixture, then another. The hallway was going dark.

"Get down, Geno!"

I hit the floor as Navarre fired the shotgun, sending double-ought buckshot past me. The killer screamed and fell sideways. But it was too far for the shotgun's "choke" to hit him with more than a few pellets. He came up on a knee and fired two shots. I flung myself behind a wheeled laundry basket.

"I'm hit, Geno," Frenchy gasped, his Cajun accent thickening. "Oh, damn, *mon ami*."

"Bad?"

"Bad enough," he said. I looked behind me to see a dark red ruin of a wound on Navarre's left shoulder. "Go after him!"

I did.

The half-lit hallway was empty. How the hell could that be?

"Come get me, choirboy!" Then a maniacal laugh. It came from a distance. I kept quiet and crept forward in an infantryman's crouch. He'd killed one police officer, wounded two others. I pushed the distraction of Pamela out of my head. *She's safe. Get him.*

Moving slowly, I passed locked doors, then open ones. I had to check each room. Nothing. Next a stairwell and an exit. What would I do? I flung open the exit door and moved out low and fast. He fired, twice again, and the bullets ricocheted off the wall. I only saw a flash in the darkness and didn't shoot back. He was down to two bullets in the revolver.

I got my bearings. This was the southeast side of the hospital and where were the other policemen? I moved as quickly as I could, guessing his direction. Residential neighborhoods were to the south, places to hide and heal up, take hostages if need be. Then I heard the clang of a streetcar. The Brill line car running south. What was it even doing operating at this time of night? Now I was full-on running. A flash and boom came from the trolley, and I felt a tug at my coat. A figure was in the doorway. I aimed and fired, but too fast for a decent aim. J. Edgar Hoover's boyhood axiom rang in my head: *Work hard, run fast!* But I was out of gas.

By this time, Woodward and Littlefield were beside me.

"We've got to stop that streetcar," I said, panting. "He's there."

But by the time officers caught up with the streetcar and stopped it, he was gone.

I walked around to McDowell Road, where the front doors of the hospital stood between columns and the building was set off by palm trees, low hedges, and lawns. Above the doors a sign said GOOD SAMARITAN HOSPITAL. Eight years before it had been Deaconess Hospital, established by the Methodist Church. Now it was surrounded by police uniforms, chatting in little clusters. I wondered where they had been when I needed them.

A few yards away, I saw an animated conversation between McGrath and the patrol captain. It was not a happy conversation. I dragged myself back into the ER, where Don, Daisy, and Frenchy were all being treated. I took time with each one.

"That was a brave thing you did," I said to Don, taking his hand. Several dressings were on one arm, hand, and his shoulder.

He jerked it away. "He got my fucking gun! Where is he? Dead?"

"He got away."

"Goddamn you, Gene," he growled. "Why am I not surprised?"

Frenchy was winged, sleepy with morphine, and more generous to me. But the result was the same. The killer escaped.

Thirty-Three

By the time I got to police headquarters at eleven the next morning, Pamela was back in records working with Juliet. I set aside the newspaper, which had a story about Howard Hughes, the millionaire aviator and oil mogul, being arrested in Los Angeles for running down a pedestrian. He was released on his own recognizance. It would take at least the afternoon *Phoenix Gazette* to report on our overnight fiasco.

"We have something promising," Pamela said.

Juliet held up a file. "O.M. Haggerty."

"The one represented by Walter Humphrey," I said. "Peeping Tom in 1929 and the jury found him not guilty of trespassing." That was the strongest charge the county attorney could bring, but it wasn't much. By the time he went to trial, we'd already arrested Emil Gorman.

Pamela said, "In 1931, Haggerty was arrested for domestic violence after he attacked his wife with a knife."

"She was a nurse, a redhead," Juliet said.

Pamela pointed to the report. "Then he used the same knife on the policemen who arrived. He was described as 'crazed.' It took three cops to take him down."

I said they'd told me he didn't have any priors.

"That was before 1929," Juliet said. "We didn't look beyond that. I'm kicking myself."

I opened the file, and the face from the booking photo stared at me. It was him. The Angel of Death.

"You've got him!" I celebrated. "Great work!"

"Be right back," Pamela said and ran from the room.

"Her stomach is upset," Juliet said.

I'm sure it didn't help, me filling her in on the violence and chase last night and getting so little sleep.

Scanning the file explained a lot. He was examined by a psychiatrist, who said he was a sociopath, maybe worse. A judge gave him a choice between prison or voluntary commitment to the state insane asylum. He was there until he was examined and released this past March. By this time, his wife had divorced him and left for San Francisco.

"That's where he was all this time," I said. "Make copies of these photos for McGrath."

I rushed toward the Chief of D's office, pausing with Pamela. I took her hands.

"Are you alright?"

She nodded.

"Great work," I said. "I'm so glad you didn't decide to teach English to seventh graders!"

Pamela's smile was radiant.

By early afternoon, his photograph was distributed to every patrolman and detective, as well as to police departments as far as Texas and California.

At two, detectives armed with shotguns and Thompsons executed a search warrant on Haggerty's last known address, a bungalow west of the state capitol building. They found a woman living with him, a dyed henna redhead of course, who claimed to know nothing of his crimes. Of course, she would. Gorman's wife had done the same. She had no explanation for the scalp of red hair in the desk drawer, probably from Ginger. They ran her in and sweated her for hours while placing the house under surveillance.

———

Late that night, after another storm blessed us with rain, Pamela woke me and told me she was pregnant. I wasn't surprised.

"I thought we were being so careful, Gene!" The words poured out of her as fast as her tears. "But I missed my periods..."

"And you've been having morning sickness." I took her hands.

"I was afraid if you found out, you wouldn't want me."

I pulled her close and showered her with kisses.

"It makes me want you more," I said, feeling my own tears in the warm night.

"Really?"

"How could you doubt it?" I climbed out of bed, went to her side, knelt, and proposed properly. "It was something I was planning for weeks," I said. "Now you're carrying our child. We'll never be orphans again and neither will he. Or she."

"Our child. I love those words," she said. "I also love the name Pamela Hammons."

"Pamela, will you marry me? Will you have me?"

She said yes.

———

An hour later, the phone rang. I was sure it was news of an arrest. But it was not.

"Did you think you could stop me so easily?"

It was Haggerty, now making no effort to conceal his voice.

"So, you've got your eye on me, literally."

"A comedian," he said, his voice eerily calm. "Little bitch Becky's on my list. She'll pay, believe me. But my list is expanding. Didn't I say you couldn't stop me?"

"You already took some buckshot," I said. "The next time you'll go down hard."

"Big talk."

"We know who you are, Orville," I said. "Have you looked at a newspaper? We're being deluged with tips. Time to turn yourself in."

"I'll never turn myself in," he said. "I'm going to leave a pile of bodies, and you're to blame, Hammons. The cops are spread too thin. Did you hear the explosion tonight? An ammonia tank in the warehouse district. I did that, just to see how many cops would come. The ammonia killed two men. Too bad, so sad. That shows how I can create a distraction next time I kill."

That laugh again.

I said, "They never should have let you out of the looney bin."

I was trying to get a rise out of him, but it didn't work.

"Well, choirboy, tell me why they did."

"You could have walked out any time, like Winnie Ruth," I improvised. "But you decided to let them think they could shrink your head. Better than being an escapee. You were still becoming the Angel of Death. It wasn't really *you*, yet, right? But they allowed you newspapers, so you read about the Strangler, and you were inspired. You read about me. Your IQ was high, and they allowed you to use the library. You became an autodidact."

"Big word," he said. "You must have learned it from your college-educated lady, Pam. Keep going."

"The electro-shock therapy was tough," I continued.

"You should try it sometime."

"The endless sessions with the shrinks. But you didn't really change into what they wanted. Only they didn't know it. You faked remorse. You faked the behavior they wanted. They even made you a nurse's aide."

"True. Is that ironic?" he said. "So, they finally let me out."

It was classic sociopathic behavior. But they didn't realize they were dealing with a homicidal psychopath.

Keep talking, asshole.

He said, "My main psychologist didn't have a great deal of experience, even though he was forty years old. Only two years. Before that, he was a gym teacher. He concealed his lack of knowledge behind pronouncements that seemed cocksure, so people deferred to him. He was a vain little man and easy to fool. He signed off on me being sane and cured."

"But why start killing?"

"You bore me, Eugene," he said. "We've been all through this."

The phone went dead.

The call was traced to a house two blocks away. With the owners on vacation, Haggerty had broken in and used the telephone. By the time officers arrived, he was gone.

It chilled me to think how many Phoenicians were out of town, their houses inviting places for the Angel of Death to hide. I let Pamela sleep while I propped one chair against the door and sat in another with the sawed-off in my lap. If he came through that door, he'd get both barrels.

Thirty-Four

The next night I brought Pamela to the poker game at Barry Goldwater's house on Garfield Street. They welcomed her and set her a place at the table.

"Five-card draw?" Del Webb said. "Ever play?"

She smiled. "I'm a fast learner."

Harry Rosenzweig cut the deck, and Webb dealt out the cards.

Barry's wife, Peggy—they were barely past their honeymoon phase—was content to watch, serve cookies, and toss in the occasional observation. One started a debate over the civil war in Spain, the consensus being that the communists that had gained control over the Spanish Republic were as bad as the fascists.

I laid out a full house and pulled across my chips. Del quickly flipped out cards across the table.

Next, we talked about the drought that had seized much of the country, killing thousands. They lacked Phoenix's dams and reservoirs, which captured the winter snowpack as it melted and kept the Salt River Valley well-watered throughout the year. Plus, we'd gotten plenty of rain in this year's monsoon.

"I hear John Udall is going to run for governor," Barry gossiped. "I don't know if being mayor of Phoenix helps or hurts him."

"And as a Republican," Del said. "Never happen."

"Don't be so sure," Harry said. "He's got the Mormon vote."

I wanted to move the game along, but the talk inevitably turned to me. "No offense, Gene, but how is the killer still at large?" Peggy asked.

Harry said, "I propose we suspend the 'no work at the poker game' rule."

"I second the motion," Goldwater said.

"You ought to go into politics, Barry," I said.

He laughed. "That's what Harry keeps telling me. I'd be too outspoken, and I've got a department store to run. But get back to Peggy's question."

I sighed and asked for two cards.

"First, nothing we talk about leaves the room," I said. Everyone nodded. "He's crafty, and we've been a step behind him for too long. He was willing to take a hostage at Good Sam when we thought we had him cornered, another nurse, held a scalpel at her throat. Then he attacked my brother and shot Frenchy Navarre. Shot at me. I came close to nailing him, but he caught a lucky break when the Brill streetcar was running late that night, testing the tracks. So many things worked against us."

"But you saved two nurses that night," Del said.

"That was the good part. But he's still out there."

"And he calls you?" Barry said.

"He does."

Peggy said that would scare the daylights out of her.

"It's creepy, no question," I said. "But it allows me to learn more about him. He lies, of course. My job is to sort truth from manipulation, where he's trying to play me and get under my skin. Or, on the other hand, gain some insight into his next move. Plus, we've tapped the phones in the apartment and the office. It let us trace him, but he gets away. He's getting bolder."

"Don't worry tonight," Barry said. "He won't get away. I've got a loaded thirty-ought-six rifle."

"I brought a piece," Del said.

"The city is armed up more than any time since the University Park Strangler," I said. "But this maniac won't hesitate. So, you shouldn't, either. Just make sure it's him."

"His picture's been on the front page of the newspapers every other day," Peggy said. "I hope that helps."

Because of my experience with Lewis, I had a sour disposition toward the press, but maybe she was right.

I barely looked at my hand as the betting began and Del called.

Pamela laid down a royal flush.

She laughed and gathered her winnings.

Harry grumbled, "Fast learner."

"Don't be a sore loser," Goldwater said. "See that engagement ring on her finger? She's going to make an honest man out of Gene, no easy feat."

"A lovely ring, if I do say so myself," Rosenzweig chimed in.

Suddenly there was a knock at the door. Barry stood up to answer it.

"Don't," I said, rising to go to the curtains. "Are you expecting anyone?"

Barry and Peggy froze and shook their heads. The poker game stopped.

I carefully slid aside an inch of curtain. "Your porch light is out."

Barry sidled beside me. "It was working when you got here."

That was true. It might have burned out. Or someone

unscrewed the bulb to conceal himself. All I saw was a dark shape standing in front of the door.

"I'm going out the back," I said, producing my M1911 and clicking off the safety.

"I'll come, too," Webb said, drawing a .30 caliber Luger.

Barry said he'd get his rifle.

"No," I said. "Everybody stay here. Call the police. Tell them I'm here, and the Angel of Death is at the front door. Protect Pamela at all costs."

For a change she didn't protest. She told me to be careful.

The knock came again. Four loud raps.

Peggy walked with me into the kitchen, where I peered out in the backyard. I kept her from turning on the back-porch light. For a moment, I thought about my Army unit's unofficial motto in the Great War: "We own the night." Sometimes we did, but we contested it with the German stormtroopers, specially trained to infiltrate our lines. They carried Lugers and MP-18 submachine guns.

I quietly thumbed back the hammer, unlatched the door, pushed open the screen, and stepped into the darkness. The yard was surrounded by a wooden fence, eight feet high. Peggy quietly locked up behind me, as I asked her to do. I walked in a crouch, making sure I was alone, until I reached the west side. I lifted a metal latch with care, slowly opening the gate. It swung silently and I came through with purposeful strides.

I own the night.

Crouching behind a hedge, I came within sight of the porch. A streetlight showed Haggerty standing at the door with something in his hand. I didn't hesitate. I fired two rounds and at least one hit home, going through his left arm and beyond. He screamed in pain and flipped sideways.

"Oh," I said in a friendly voice. "Halt. Police."

But he slithered in the lawn like a deadly snake and returned fire. I hit the dirt and fired again.

Now sirens were converging from two directions. I moved toward him, and he only groaned. He was face up on the grass, the gauze patch still over his eye, gasping for breath. I kicked the pistol out of his hand, holstered my weapon.

Another gasp and something shiny came at me. A knife. I wrestled it out of his hand, then flipped him over, burying his face in the lawn.

"You like suffocating those men in the warehouse district," I snarled, my blood up. "How's it feel? You're not making any more lists. You're not scalping any more nurses. You're going to the gas chamber."

I heard cars screech to a halt and doors open. Suddenly I was surrounded by uniformed officers. They handcuffed him and pulled him up, roughly. My poker companions watched from the porch as Barry screwed in the light bulb.

Then a hand on my shoulder.

McGrath said, "You got him, Gene."

Thirty-Five

Orville Haggerty was handcuffed and taken to St. Joseph's Hospital by ambulance. I rode in the jump seat. My gunshot had shattered his upper left arm, the humerus, then splintered into his side, collapsing his lung. He was treated while handcuffed to the bed and guarded by policemen.

A month later, with his arm in a cast and a sling, he was arraigned on multiple counts of first-degree murder, assault, kidnapping, and rape. He and his court-appointed lawyer stood and pleaded not guilty. The echo of Emil Gorman sat beside me in the courtroom. My testimony was superfluous, given the weight of evidence against him. Haggerty was denied bail and bound over for trial.

The courtroom was packed. Pamela sat beside me and, beside her, brave Becky. Pamela held her hand. Lewis from the *Republic* was there, along with his competitor from the afternoon *Gazette*, and a reporter from the Hearst newspapers. Photographers were banned, but *Republic* artist Reg Manning sat in front of me, sketching important moments in the hearing.

One row behind the defense table sat the henna redhead who had been living with Haggerty, wearing a black dress and gray pillbox hat. She was nervously chain-smoking, dropping the butts on the floor and crushing them out with the toe of her shoe.

When the bailiff and deputy stood him up, she tried to hug him.

"No touching!" the deputy said.

"Just a kiss, please," she pleaded, looking at the judge.

"Go on," he said. "Make it quick."

And she did, an open-mouth kiss, passionate for a one-eyed monster. It never ceased to amaze me how certain kinds of women were attracted to killers. It was the same with Gorman. Between the night he was arrested to the day he was hanged, he received a dozen letters from women professing their love for him. Now, I felt a sudden jolt.

"Wait," I stood up and looked at the deputy. "Check his mouth. Check hers, too."

The entire courtroom stared at me. The deputy asked why.

"Just do it," the judge said. The deputy made Haggerty, then the woman open their mouths.

"Nothing," he said.

Haggerty smiled at me.

Then they marched him out of the courtroom, handcuffed in front.

———

I walked down the steps of the Maricopa County Courthouse with Pamela and Becky. We offered to buy her lunch and Pamela's mandatory slice of pie, but she wanted to get home. She was obviously shaken by being so close to the man who wanted to rape, kill, and scalp her. We watched her board the streetcar and wave goodbye.

"Does he stand a chance of getting off?" Pamela asked.

I shrugged. "I can't see how."

We ate lunch at the Saratoga and walked back to the Heard Building, where Paul greeted us from his tiny, fold-down seat in the elevator and whisked us up to the sixth floor.

An hour later, Pamela was filing the carbon copies and photostats of the Haggerty case. She slipped them in a folder, and Don burst through the door.

"He's gone."

"What are you talking about?" I asked.

"Gone!" Don said, looking more rattled than I'd ever seen him.

"Haggerty is gone?" Pamela stood up.

"A deputy took him to the elevator to go up to the jail," Don said. "At some point the elevator stopped midway. Best we can figure it, Haggerty got out of his handcuffs, knocked out the deputy, changed into his uniform, then rode the elevator back down and walked out of the building. It was forty-five minutes before anyone discovered what went wrong."

This wasn't the first time someone had escaped from the county jail on the top floor of the courthouse. Three years before, five inmates made a break at the busiest time of the day and disappeared into the crowd. A few days later, they made the mistake of coming toward the parked car where Don and I were sitting, armed and hoping to jack it. We shot three dead and the other two surrendered. I remember the headline, which included HERO HAMMONS BROTHERS.

Much water had gone under the bridge since then, and the bridge had been burned.

"It was the damned kiss!" Pamela said.

Don cocked his head. "What?"

"Remember when the woman kissed Haggerty? I bet she passed a handcuff key into his mouth."

"But I had the deputy check them," I protested, fighting feelings of anger and fear.

Pamela looked at Don. "Give me your handcuff key."

He slid the small piece of metal off his key chain and she put it in her mouth. "Now, check my mouth the way the deputy did."

And I did, making her open wide. No sign of the key.

Then it hit me. "Hell!"

She raised her tongue and the key was beneath it. She let it drop in her hand and returned it to my brother.

She said, "The deputy never made him raise his tongue. At some point, he spat it into his hand and unshackled himself. We've got to get to Becky's apartment, now!"

Thirty-Six

Pamela wasn't showing yet by late-August, but she said she felt our baby kicking. All her clothes still fit her slender figure. We picked out a crib and diaper pail and paid for them on layaway. The "blessed event" was to be March. In the meantime, the killer was still at large, and she went with me each day to our office in the Heard Building. I trailed her to the restroom in the hall to make sure it was safe.

Out in the world, Hitler opened the Berlin Olympics. The Nazis were helping Franco win the Spanish Civil War, while Stalin and the Russians backed the losing side. The presidential campaign heated up. The paper showed a photo of the battleship USS *Arizona*, "the pride of the U.S. Navy." And not a sign of Haggerty or his accomplice. If they were smart, they would have hopped a freight train out of town.

The bank account was still doing fine thanks to the Lincolns, who never received another blackmail threat. So, when we opened up shop Monday, the last day of the month, the lack of clients wasn't a worry. This wasn't even the case with the diamond engagement ring she wore and our wedding bands. Harry Rosenzweig gave them to us at a wholesale price. My finger got used to the ring. I loved its feel and symbolism.

Our wedding was at Central Methodist Church, with Don as my best man, and Juliet Dehler was Pamela's maid of honor. Don and Dottie set aside their quarreling for the moment, and he seemed happy for me. All the Hat Squad, Captain McGrath, and a good part of the force turned out. My poker pals were there, along with Gus Greenbaum and Cyrus Cleveland. It was an eclectic group, to say the least. Pamela's photo appeared in the Sunday paper's bridal news. She looked ravishing. We spent a week's honeymoon in Santa Monica, missing a plane crash that killed four in a field near Thirty-Fourth Street and Washington. Back home, with the August highs around one hundred eight, the search for Haggerty continued.

Another change was made to our door. Etched in the glass was:

HAMMONS AND HAMMONS
PRIVATE DETECTIVES

It seemed happily appropriate. Still, we kept the door closed and locked.

The office clock showed eleven forty-five, and I was about to suggest going for lunch. Pamela was caught between morning sickness and ravenous hunger.

"You pick the restaurant," she said. "But afterward I want pie."

I laughed at the very moment a knock came at the door. I asked who it was.

"Lewis," came the voice. "Let me in. I have some important information."

I was tempted to tell him to come back after lunch but sighed and undid the lock.

Lewis was standing there, shivering in fear, his slacks wet from being peed on. And for good reason. The Angel of Death was right behind him, pushing him forward into me. Haggerty had covered his dead eye with a black patch held by a band around his head.

Lewis's body shoved into me put me off balance as I reached for my gun. Haggerty didn't have that problem. He advanced on me with a revolver aimed at my head. Lewis ran out the open door.

Suddenly two shots exploded in the room. Pamela had her .38 Detective Special out and hit Haggerty with both rounds. I saw blood bloom on his right shoulder and his chest. He started to speak but was falling, firing wildly. Just enough life remaining to pull that trigger.

I kicked his revolver away, flipped him over, and handcuffed him. A check of the carotid pulse showed none.

"Gene…"

I turned toward Pamela, and she was slumped forward over the desk. I yelled her name, asked if she was hurt. But, of course, she was.

Pulling her back, I saw a wound in her middle. It had missed her heart, but she was bleeding badly.

"Pamela, Pamela," I was gently saying her name as I lowered her to the floor. I called louder for help.

She looked at me. "Did I get him, Gene?"

"You got him."

She coughed and blood came up. "But I'm afraid he got me," she whispered.

"Be easy, baby, be easy. You're going to be all right." I tried to keep the hysteria out of my voice. But I yelled again for help.

"I can't afford to lose you, Gene," she whispered, her eyes closing. "Can't afford…"

And those were her last words. My whole world collapsed around me. I kept her cradled in my arms as I cried for what seemed like hours. In fact, it would be a lifetime.

———

A month later, a month after the funeral with everyone who came to our wedding in attendance, I placed fresh flowers on her grave at lovely Greenwood Cemetery on Van Buren Street. The police chief issued a special commendation to Pamela, posthumously, for stopping the Angel of Death. It sat framed in the apartment, beside photos of us together and her alone, that radiant smile.

I was still barely able to put one foot in front of the other. Just as I had barely made it through the eulogy I spoke, weeping as I tried to convey all that she was, her great heart, the most courageous person I'd ever known, how she saved me and, except for the end in the office, how I saved her back. *Earth to earth, ashes to ashes, dust to dust, looking for the resurrection and the life everlasting...*

The tombstone was freshly placed.

PAMELA BRADBURY HAMMONS
1910–1936
BELOVED WIFE OF GENE HAMMONS

And beside it on the same stone:

EUGENE SHERWOOD HAMMONS
1900–
AND THEIR UNBORN CHILD

———

Later, when I could bear to do it, I gathered up Pamela's things at the office. Among them were several mystery novels that merely amused her once she came to know that not every real mystery ended up neatly solved at the end, with a bow tied around it.

Nevertheless, the mailman dropped off a single letter that morning. It had no return address but was postmarked Washington, D.C.

I slit it open with a letter-opener and began to read:

Dear Mr. Hammons:

Enclosed find a check for your services in recovering the gold carried by George Parris. While I can't go into all the details or disclose investigative methods, I can tell you that Parris was in reality an undercover Secret Service agent. He was assigned to exchange gold for counterfeit money, in order for the Secret Service to track and arrest the counterfeiters.

As you know, things didn't go as planned. I wish the Bureau had been brought into this from the beginning, fully informed, and not sent on a wild goose chase about so-called organized crime, which is a myth. Rest assured I will punish the pinheads that allowed that to happen.

I do appreciate your assistance in this matter. Please accept my condolences on the loss of your wife, Pamela.

Sincerely,
Edgar

It was not a bow tied around it, but I knew a bit more about the strange man who showed up at my office with a suspicious proposition.

"All that glistens is not gold." That's Shakespeare. Pamela taught it to me, and she taught me so many other things. Love most of all.

Now, with high summer past us and the subtle change to autumn, Captain McGrath wants me back on the force as a member of the Hat Squad, my pension reinstated. The Los Angeles Police Department and the Denver Police have sent me job offers. Or I can stay on at the Heard Building as a private eye, although the ghosts would overwhelm me. The stones around my heart would pull me under.

Whatever happened, I knew one thing.

I'd walk alone.

AUTHOR'S NOTE

Barry Goldwater became a Phoenix City Councilman in 1949 at the urging of Harry Rosenzweig, running as a reform candidate. In 1952, he was the surprise winner of a seat in the U.S. Senate. Goldwater's Department Stores were sold in 1963. Barry Goldwater is widely credited with being a pivotal figure in the rise of modern American conservatism. He was the Republican nominee for president in 1964, losing to Lyndon Johnson. Although never officially connected to organized crime, Goldwater enjoyed the company of a fast crowd. When he died in 1998, Barry Goldwater was the most beloved figure in Arizona. He maintained a long friendship with Gus Greenbaum and attended his funeral.

Gus Greenbaum enjoyed a long career in organized crime, becoming legendary as a turnaround artist for Las Vegas casinos. He was dependable and professional, "master of the skim"— where the mob stole money from casino winnings before it could be recorded and taxed. Greenbaum didn't want to leave Phoenix and repeatedly asked to retire so he and his wife could enjoy their home there. But the Outfit kept calling him back to fix problems at casinos. He was torn between a desire to live

full-time in Phoenix and his love of the Las Vegas excitement—
and being a big man in the town. Greenbaum became an alco-
holic and a heroin addict. The Outfit began to question his
reliability. This proved true when they found the master of
the skim was skimming himself, and too much to be tolerated.
In 1958, he and his wife were assassinated in their Encanto-
Palmcroft home in Phoenix. The crime was never solved.

Joe Island was hired by the Phoenix Police in 1938, becoming the first African American officer in the city of the modern
era. He mentored other Black officers and retired as a detective
in 1961 after a distinguished career.

John C. Lincoln was one of Phoenix's leading philanthropists, along with helping build the Camelback Inn and becoming president of the Bagdad Copper Co. in Yavapai County,
Arizona. Lincoln Drive, a major thoroughfare from Phoenix
through Paradise Valley to Scottsdale is named after him. So
is John C. Lincoln Medical Center in Sunnyslope and John C.
Lincoln Deer Valley Hospital. He died in 1959, aged 92.

Louise Lincoln Kerr became one of the most influential
leaders and philanthropists of the arts in Phoenix. "The Grand
Lady of Music," Kerr helped found the Phoenix Symphony,
Phoenix Chamber Music Society, Scottsdale Center for the Arts,
and the Phoenix Chorale. She was instrumental in helping establish the Herberger School of Music at Arizona State University.
As a musician, she studied violin, viola, and piano with renowned
mentors. She composed more than one hundred works, from
symphonies to chamber music. Kerr died in 1977.

Reg Manning spent decades at the *Arizona Republic*, set-
tling in as its editorial cartoonist. Generations of Phoenicians
grew up with his cartoons. He became syndicated and his work
appeared in 170 newspapers from 1948 until he retired in 1971.
He won the Pulitzer Prize for Editorial Cartooning in 1951.

His *Republic* cartoons often featured a small anthropomorphic cactus in the bottom of the panel. Manning died in 1986.

Kemper Marley remained the richest man in Arizona thanks to his liquor business and extensive land holdings, which became very valuable as Phoenix emerged into a major city and spread out. Marley eventually got a part of the Outfit's gambling-wire business when Greenbaum was called away to Las Vegas. Marley was suspected of orchestrating the bombing death of *Arizona Republic* investigative reporter Don Bolles in 1976, but it was never proved. Most Arizonans today know of him from the Kemper and Ethel Marley Foundation, which has placed his name on institutions around the state. He died in 1990.

Lefty Mofford joined the Phoenix Police in 1929 after his Major League Baseball career with the Washington Senators. He retired as a captain in 1949. In 1957, he married Rose Perica of Globe, Arizona. At Globe High School, she was an All-American softball player. She kept his name after they divorced a decade later and went on to become Arizona Secretary of State and the first woman governor of Arizona. A beloved figure, Rose died in 2016, aged 94. She and Lefty remained friends until his death in 1982.

Frenchy Navarre continued as a detective until he shot and killed Phoenix Police Officer David "Star" Johnson in 1944. Johnson was a popular Black patrolman walking a downtown beat. Although Navarre was acquitted, Johnson's partner arrived at police headquarters and confronted Navarre. After a wild gunfight, Frenchy was killed. In life, he was friends with Gus Greenbaum and other mobsters.

Earl O'Clair went on to become the chief of detectives and, in 1948, Phoenix Police chief. He successfully fought for improved pensions and overtime while officers were testifying in court. He attended the FBI's national academy.

Harry Rosenzweig became the founder of the modern Republican Party in Arizona, leading it to dominate a state long run by the Democrats. For decades, he was the political boss of Phoenix. In addition to his jewelry business, Harry and his brother, Newton, developed the high-rise Rosenzweig Center office-hotel complex in Midtown Phoenix. Harry's connections to organized crime were suspected but never proved. He died in 1993.

Adolfo Torrez started a family and became a businessman. He and his descendants established the Azteca café and bar, Azteca flower shop, Azteca furniture, and ultimately Azteca bridal shop and tuxedo rentals. The latter was still in business as of 2023. Torrez died in 2002.

Del Webb became the most successful contractor in the Southwest and a very wealthy man. Webb's projects ranged from the Poston Relocation Center, where Japanese Americans were interned during World War II, to Sun City. He was also a co-owner of the New York Yankees. In 1946, mob boss Bugsy Siegel hired Webb to oversee construction of the Flamingo Hotel and Casino in Las Vegas. He died in 1974.

One

JANUARY 1933, PHOENIX, ARIZONA

Night folded in early during the winter.

It was only half past six, the neon of the auto courts and curio shops on Van Buren Street giving way to the emptiness of the Tempe Road, indigo pushing against my headlights as I drove east. Only a few other cars were about.

Cars were fewer in general than they had been only a few years ago and seemed to fit the new times: fewer jobs, fewer businesses, fewer people getting by.

Just after crossing the bridge over the Grand Canal, I parked, shut off the Ford's purring V8, and stepped out. I pulled down my fedora close to my eyes, a habit I kept from my police days on the Hat Squad, stuck a Chesterfield in my mouth, and lit it with the Dunhill lighter brought back from London years ago. I buttoned my suit coat against the desert chill and walked toward the cottonwoods to the south, which loomed like storm clouds on a moonless night.

After walking beyond the trees, I was suddenly inside the camp. It held perhaps fifty denizens. Okies. Workers laid off from the closed copper mines. A miscellany of hoboes. It was outside the city limits and away from the attention of the cops. One of several Hoovervilles that had sprung up during the past three years. Hoover himself seemed ever more isolated and powerless, even though he'd be in office until March. Calvin Coolidge just died. Hoover, the "Great Engineer" who was so popular when he won in '28, might have wished it were him instead. Now he was reviled and rejected.

In the camp, people kept to their clans. The Okies drawn and clad in tattered clothing, the miners with beaten-down faces and muscular bodies in canvas pants, they clustered around campfires and next to cars on their last miles.

Charity wasn't to be much found in Phoenix now; everyone from the county to the churches, Kiwanis and Rotary clubs was tapped out. The Municipal Woodyard to provide help to the "worthy local unemployed" was struggling. Businesses continued to close and lay people off. The lettuce harvest and shipping were complete. Only pink grapefruits were being picked, boxed, and shipped now through March. Any new work in the fields and groves was months away. Maybe some of the travelers would make it to California, the promised land, by road or freight train.

Even with the nighttime cold, the weather was better now than back east. It would be different come summer, and the population of the hobo jungles would plummet.

The campfires glared at gaunt faces. Beyond the next stand of trees, a Southern Pacific freight train trundled past eastbound, shaking the ground, the smoke of its locomotive rising into the night sky. I saw a young man watch it as if it was the fanciest passenger train, only awaiting his presence in the parlor car.

And me? I had a photograph and a hunch and a pocket of dimes. It was my job.

"Hey, buddy, you look too well dressed to be here."

He came out of the shadows and had friends. He was almost my height and had a face that looked like a dry desert river: brown, pocked, and creased by lines that shifted as he spoke.

"Well, here I am," I said, handing him a dime and showing him the photo. He kept staring at me, and I noticed what looked like silver rings on every finger of his right hand. But I knew better and unbuttoned my coat.

"Who dares not stir by day must walk by night."

This came from a rail of a man at his right. He held out his arms as if to fly, then bowed. A thespian.

I ignored him and focused on the big man. His eyes were as barren as an abandoned house. I nodded toward the photograph. "Have you seen this fellow here?"

"We don't truck with cops or cinder dicks." His lips barely moved as the words came out. "You're in the wrong place. Wrong time."

His right hand came up fast. Brass knuckles wrapped around a fist headed my way. But I was faster, slashing my sap against his left temple. Training and experience had taught me how to swing the leather-covered piece of lead just enough to stop a man without killing him. It was all in the wrist.

I was in no mood to have my jaw rearranged or my brains scrambled. Experience had also made me especially wary of brass knucks; some of my former colleagues would have shot him for merely possessing them. His eyes rolled back, and he dropped straight down as if a trapdoor had suddenly opened beneath him. The others backed up.

I assessed them for a few seconds, the black come-along still dangling from my hand. "I'm not a cop or a railroad bull. This face. You seen him?" I showed the pic again and this time the men studied it.

"No need to get sore," the thespian offered. "He's about fifty yards that way, beyond the Okie truck with the piano in the bed. Give him a bottle, and he'll tell you his life story. Claims he was a businessman, if you can believe that."

I slid the sap back inside my belt, gave him a dime, and walked. I took a drag on the cigarette, which had survived the altercation, letting the tobacco settle my nerves. Sure enough, a Model T truck with wooden slats and an antique upright piano was parked beside a campfire. A raggedy family huddled next to it eating beans out of cans. Ten feet beyond, a man sat on his haunches, watching me.

I knelt down. He looked about my age with oily dark hair and a tattered muslin shirt, an army surplus blanket around his shoulders. His eyes took a moment to focus on me.

"Samuel Dorsey?"

"Sam. Who wants to know? I ain't done nothing."

"This is your lucky day, Sam," I said. "Your family paid me to find you."

"You a cop?"

"Private detective."

"Well, gumshoe, I've got nothing for you or for them." He used both hands to rub his face hard, as if he could rearrange his features into a different man. He was several days past a shave. "Lost my job when the plant closed and took to the rails. No greater shame than when a man can't provide for his family."

"Things change. Your wife wired me and said she's come into an inheritance. She wants you to come home."

He eyed me suspiciously, processing my words. Finally: "Her Uncle Chester. He was pushing ninety, and he was a rich man. Never did a thing for us."

"Now he has." I held out a wad of cash.

He reached for the bills, but I pulled them away.

"No, it doesn't work that way. I'll take you to Union Station and put you on the late train to Chicago. Back home."

I'd be damned if he was going to use it on booze, whores, and gambling, ending up back here. Or being robbed by Mister Knuckleduster, once he got over the headache I'd given him.

He looked at me and started sobbing. "How can they want me now? After I walked out?"

"Maybe they love you." I handed him a nail and lit it. He took a deep drag.

He didn't think long. "Okay," he shrugged. "I want to go home. You got a drink?" I shook my head. He hesitated, then stood, leaving the blanket on the ground.

Many people went missing in the Great Depression. Hardly any of it was as grotesque or glamorous as the Lindbergh kidnapping. Men lost their jobs and left their families. Sons and daughters disappeared. Bonus marchers were scattered and lost.

Looking for them was a big part of my business. It often started with a wire from Chicago or Cincinnati or Buffalo, then, if I thought I could help, a photo in the mail. I charged $25 to begin an investigation, another $25 if I found some usable information, and an even hundred if I found the person and could get them home. Money was tight all over, and happy endings were rare.

I walked him out of the camp and back up to the road.

"That's a sweet flivver," he said, indicating my red Ford Deluxe Coupe ragtop.

Opening the passenger door, I let him slide inside to admire it.

Then headlights caught me from behind, and a pickup slid in ahead of me to stop, throwing gravel like a hailstorm. "Stay here." I closed the door.

Half a dozen tough mugs piled out of the truck bed. They were carrying baseball bats and cans of gasoline.

"Gene Hammons." My name came from the driver walking

toward me. I could have enjoyed an evening or a lifetime without seeing Kemper Marley.

"It's dark for a ballgame, Kemper," I said. "In fact, I don't even see a baseball."

"You always make me laugh, Hammons," he said, unsmiling. Kemper Marley was only twenty-six, but he looked older, with thin straight lips and a challenging glare in his eyes. In this light, one could see the old man he would turn into, if he lived that long. He had the posture and personality of a ball-peen hammer but decked out in a new Vic Hanny suit, bolo tie, and a gleaming Stetson, giving the lie to movie Westerns in which good guys wore white hats.

I folded my arms. "What are you going to do when Prohibition is repealed?"

"What Prohibition?" It was the answer I expected. Marley was the leading bootlegger in Phoenix.

His posse shifted restlessly behind him.

I said, "So what's this?"

"We're going to clear out this bunch," he said. "Communists aren't welcome in Phoenix. This country is on the brink."

"And you're going to roll back Bolshevism by burning out a bunch of poor Okies doing the best they can? There's no Reds down there."

He patted me on the shoulder, about as affectionately as a swipe from a mountain lion. "You were always naive, Hammons. Always. Sentimental."

"Sentimental enough to know your thugs should leave those people alone. They've lost their farms and jobs. Mines have closed or are mothballed all over the state. Even the railroads have cut employees."

He spat in the dirt. "I'm not a political man, Hammons, but this country's in big trouble."

"True, but maybe Roosevelt can turn things around."

"Maybe," he said. "But he doesn't take office until March. If it even happens, I'm not sure I trust the man. You know, he's a cripple. I saw him when he campaigned here in '31 with Carl Hayden and Governor Hunt."

"He had polio."

Marley shook his head. "He's a damned cripple, Hammons. People see that handsome head in the newspapers. They hear his voice on the radio. But they don't see how he has the braces on his legs and needs to lean on someone or the podium to stand. I don't trust a man like that."

I stared at him.

He said, "Did you know that only about 20,000 Bolsheviks took over Russia, a country of more than a hundred million people?" His eyes blazed like a blast furnace of paranoia. "It can happen here. Look at Germany. Brownshirts and Reds fighting in the streets. This Hitler will put a stop to that if Hindenburg names him chancellor this month. Mussolini got it right in Italy."

"I don't care for dictators." I lit another cigarette.

"Those are very bad for your health." For a bootlegger, Marley could be quite a prig. He waved the smoke away. "Maybe we need a dictator. I'll tell you this: No Reds are going to take away my property. No Huey Long, either."

"Nobody in the camp down there wants your property," I said.

"Well, I'm not taking chances, and we need that rabble gone. Sends a message. We have to stop these people from bumming their way from town to town. Gas moochers. Our help should only go to local taxpaying citizens."

"It's hard to pay taxes when you've lost your job," I said.

"Look, there's the worthy unemployed and the others."

I couldn't resist blowing smoke in his face. "And you're the one to make that determination?"

He made a face and waved it away. "I agree with President Hoover, no federal relief for individuals. It will sap the American spirit. There's plenty of work for a man who wants to show some gumption. This Depression, they call it, is only a passing incident. That's what President Hoover says, and he's right." He tried to push me aside, but I didn't move. "You want to stop me? Oh, I forgot, you're not a policeman any longer." His thin lips turned up.

I briefly considered shooting the SOB but thought better of it. I'd killed tougher men than him during the war. But I didn't need the distraction tonight.

Reading my thoughts, he said, "I would have fought over there if I'd been old enough. Don't think I wouldn't have."

Marley would have lasted about a day against the Huns. He's the kind of idiot who would have stuck his head above the trench and had it turned to pudding. Or be badly wounded and end up a cripple himself, without Roosevelt's leonine head, fine voice, and first-rate temperament. I let that pleasing thought go and stepped aside.

"Who's that in your car?"

I spoke over my shoulder. "A lost soul I'm putting on the train back to Chicago."

Marley shook his head. "I'll never figure you out, boy. Come by and see me tomorrow. I have some work for you."

I felt bile coming up my throat and walked back to the Ford. By the time I had made the U-turn to head for town, Marley and his gang had disappeared toward the tree line. Me, letting it happen.

PAYING MY DEBTS

I owe my editor, Diane DiBiase, for her skill, patience, thoughtful suggestions, and good cheer in bringing the second Gene Hammons novel home. We both cried about Pamela's death. Beth Deveny and the staff at Poisoned Pen Press/Sourcebooks were also most supportive.

The Phoenix Police Museum—located in the old police headquarters downtown—provided essential research about the department of this era.

The Arizona Room at the Burton Barr Central Phoenix Library is a treasure for every researcher.

Marshall Trimble taught me Arizona history at Coronado High School before becoming the beloved state historian. Likewise, my friend, the late Jack August, plumbed many depths of Arizona history—we lost him too soon, the embodiment of a gentleman and a scholar.

As always, blame me for any errors, inconsistencies, or deliberate alterations.

ABOUT THE AUTHOR

 Jon Talton is a fourth-generation Arizonan and author of fourteen award-winning novels, including the David Mapstone Mysteries, as well as one work of history. He studied history at Arizona State University and Miami University of Ohio.

A veteran journalist, he worked for newspapers in San Diego, Denver, Dayton, Cincinnati, and Charlotte. A former columnist for the *Arizona Republic*, he is now the business columnist for the *Seattle Times*. In a younger life, he served five years as an EMT-paramedic, much of that time in downtown Phoenix. Now, he divides his time between Seattle and Phoenix.